FOOL ME ONCE

COURT OF PAIN
BOOK ONE

ARIANA NASH

Fool Me Once, Court of Pain #1

Ariana Nash - *Dark Fantasy Author*

Subscribe to Ariana's mailing list & get the exclusive story 'Sealed with a Kiss' free.

Join the Ariana Nash Facebook group for all the news, as it happens.

Fool Me Once is a dual point of view, dark MM fantasy brimming with courtly spice, morally ambiguous characters, and the fool who plays them all. This is a dark world with adult content. For content warnings, please see the author's website.

COURT OF PAIN #1

FOOL ME ONCE

ARIANA NASH

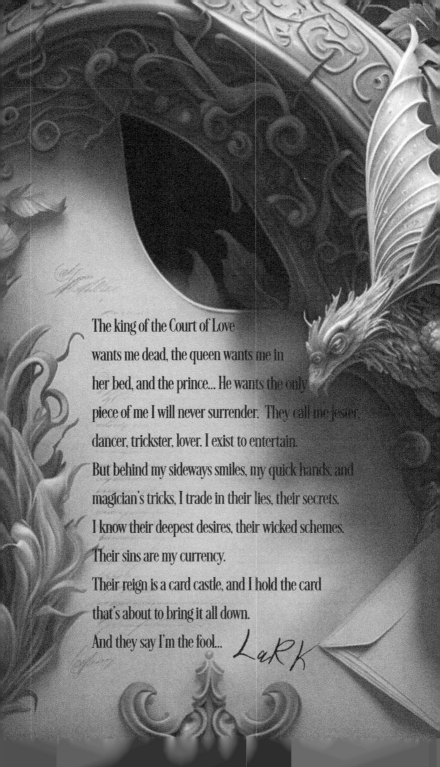

The king of the Court of Love
wants me dead, the queen wants me in
her bed, and the prince... He wants the only
piece of me I will never surrender. They call me jester,
dancer, trickster, lover. I exist to entertain.
But behind my sideways smiles, my quick hands, and
magician's tricks, I trade in their lies, their secrets.
I know their deepest desires, their wicked schemes.
Their sins are my currency.
Their reign is a card castle, and I hold the card
that's about to bring it all down.
And they say I'm the fool... *LaRK*

COURT OF JUSTICE

COURT OF LOVE

COURT OF PAIN

COURT OF WAR

CHAPTER 1

For a thousand years, the people of the shatterlands raged war. Until Dallin, God of Order, grew tired of their endless bickering. He forged four crowns for four courts:
Love. Justice. Pain. War.
Each court was responsible for protecting and safeguarding the balance of the shatterlands, and only by working together would they prosper.
Under Dallin's watchful gaze, the courts of Love, Justice, Pain, and War nurtured peace and harmony, and the people of the shatterlands thrived.
But when Dallin vanished, the shatterlands and its courts once more fell into chaos.

❧

"Dance for us, Lark." The Queen of Love laughed and fluttered a hand in my direction. Her flushed cheeks glowed, not from rouge, but from the potent wine I'd filled her cup with all evening.

I flashed her an agreeable smile, hopped off the table

where I'd been on display long enough to numb a few muscles, and bowed deeply. "Anything for you, my queen." Taking her hand may have been a little much, but I wasn't here to be subtle, and when I brushed my lips across the back of her fingers, her blush reddened. Queen Katina was easier to please than her husband, Albus, seated beside her.

It was always best not to meet his eye. The King of Love suffered from a dire absence of humor.

I let the queen's hand fall and sashayed toward the pirou- etting dancers in their brightly colored gowns, peacock feath- ers, and sparkling jewels. Like the villain of the ball, my black tailed jacket and trousers stood out for their lack of embell- ishment. I didn't need lace and feathers to pretty myself up when everyone knew I was the most desired among them. Princes, lords, ladies, and even the queen herself—they all wanted me in their beds.

Before the night was over, I'd have multiple offers. I'd deny most, especially the women. There was no easier way to snare a man than fall into bed one night, only to have your lover return a year later with a mistake clinging to their petti- coats, a familiar pair of eyes pleading. Men were the far easier prospect, and there were plenty to choose from among the dancers this night. My true pleasure, however, came from another game I played at their expense. The game of lies.

I inserted myself among the guests, took hands, and danced as though the music lived within me. Most people I knew, but some were fresh faces visiting from deep within the shatterlands, curious about the whispers surrounding the Court of Love's infamous jester. Most rumors were mine, sent into the world to take on a life of their own. Some less desir- able teases had sprung up like weeds in my carefully managed garden—*he's a whore, he'll pick your pocket as soon as kiss your lips*. Those nasty little rumors I nipped in the bud before they grew unwieldy. Gossip was another weapon in my arsenal, just so long as it danced to my tune.

There goes Lark, the court jester, a fool. They say he fucks the queen, and the kitchen maids, and the squires. If all the rumors were true, I'd have little time for anything outside of bedding the entire Court of Love. Of course, much of it was fantasy. Tales spun to keep me alive. A fool is nothing without his reputation.

Music flowed, smiles flashed, fans fluttered secret codes to meet behind the drapes later, and scandalous glances flew back and forth. The Court of Love was an intricate tapestry of lies and desire, of the forbidden and the denied. A tapestry with many a loose thread.

The music reached its crescendo, the band ceased, and the dancers stopped, breathless, plumage sagging. Some of their makeup had smudged, lipstick had smeared, and eyes were darkened by brushed kohl. We bowed and clapped, all playing our parts in the ludicrous game of courtly life.

The queen's trill sounded again. "Won't our jester entertain us?"

The queen was one such loose thread.

All eyes turned to me. Whispers simmered of how the queen and I were engaged in an affair. Such rumors were undesirable, and like the most determined of weeds, they refused to die despite my best efforts to kill them.

I broke from the throng and donned a frivolous grin. "A poem, or a tale more befitting this joyous celebration? The Tale of a Queen's bird, escaping her cage?" The queen—a woman of some forty years to my twenty-three, was not as dimwitted as she allowed others to assume—tilted her head, hearing something in my tone I hadn't meant to reveal. Weariness, perhaps. I must have been off my game for her, in her pickled state, to sense a fracture in my polished exterior.

3

Better to distract her than have her concerns multiply into paranoia. Suspicion now would make her far less pliable later.

The royals' table was elevated on a dais, raising it above every other table and the guests, both in situation and status. I took to its stage as though I had every right to be there. The audience eyed me with a curious mix of envy, trepidation, fascination, and even hatred. How dare I, a common fool, stand above them, lords and ladies all.

My heart fluttered at the thought. I didn't wear a crown, and I wasn't a king, although I'd make a fabulous one—a better king than the man who watched me now, his glare like daggers in my back.

Perhaps, had these people fucked and lied their way to the top as I had, then they too could have the Court of Love eating out of their silk-wrapped hands. But alas, they were all too weak, too small-minded, too blinkered to step outside their gilded cages, into my dirt.

"A poem, then," I announced, drawing the crowd's lagging attention back to where it belonged. On me.

"An orphan boy, his world all void of color. He lived in a land so cold and dreary, where no one cared and few were merry." I gestured at my crowd. Their faces bloomed with delight now they featured in this evening's entertainment. "One grey day, he saw a boy prince, so fair and fleet, wearing a crown of shining gold, and a cloak that billowed in the cold." I flung a hand at the empty chair beside the king, and quickly moved on, once more avoiding Albus's glare. His face might have turned a darker shade of purple than the inside of my coat, but I wasn't paying attention to that. "The prince took the boy by the hand and said, *Come with me, my friend.* Filled with glee, the orphan boy agreed. The prince took him in, gave him a home. And the orphan boy was no longer alone.

4

He learned to read and write and dance." I spun, and curt-seyed, pausing for affect, then lifted my head. Yes, everyone was watching. The thrill of it unleashed butterflies inside. "And his life was filled with joy and chance." I marched back across the dais. "The orphan grew into a man, never forgetting the prince who took him in. He lived a life full of love and light. Thanks to the prince, his future was bright." From my pocket, I scooped a fistful of glitter and flung it over their heads.

The crowd erupted in applause and wonderment.

Arms spread, I absorbed the adoring praise, soaking it into my veins. Was there any greater thrill than the adoration of an audience? Of course, the poem was all lies, much like the court we all danced in. Orphan boys didn't get happy endings. Not in this court. Jesters did not marry princes, and fools could never be heroes. But I dealt in the currency of dreams. And here, in this moment, I had more power than any king.

Riding high, I mingled among the crowd, pulling cards from my sleeves and dazzling the nobility with sleight of hand. I skimmed my fingers along powdered cheeks, pulled cards from elaborate swirls of hair. I teased kisses while standing scandalously close to a husband or wife, producing flowers from behind their backs. More than a few hands roamed where they had no right to go. Never mine—my hands were always in plain sight, lest I lose another finger to some jilted lord. Still, what was a finger? I had nine more. Nine more lives. And I planned to live every one of them to their fullest before fate caught up with me.

Four years a fool, and I'd loved every second of it. The scandal, the rule breaking, the freedom that came from saying that which should never be said. The king? A buffoon. The queen? A drunken whore. Court of Love? Truly the

Court of Broken Hearts. And the prince? Well, he was so hideously ugly and unloved he feared leaving his chamber.

Jester's privilege rendered me immune to punishment... at least, in this court I could do and say as I pleased. Others courts were far less forgiving. But among the weakest court, the Court of Love, I was untouchable.

Out of the corner of my eye, I caught sight of the queen stumbling her way through the guests toward me. She tripped on her skirts and fought with their many layers, muttering under her breath. Her golden hair had fallen free of its pinned swirls and spilled unchecked about her flushed face. Around her, a few of the guests arched eyebrows and curled their lips. I loved a spectacle as much as the rest of them, but if the queen unraveled here on the dance floor, Albus would place the blame at my feet and I didn't have time for his bluster.

I swooped in and tucked her against my side. "Your Majesty, some fresh air, no?"

"Lark, so thoughtful! Where would I be without my favorite fool?" She leaned against my side and patted my chest, lips pouting.

"Facedown on the floor, my queen."

"Ha, yes." She giggled and hiccupped. Her behavior was partially my doing, considering I'd been topping up her cup all night. But I had my reasons, which would soon become apparent.

We passed through double doors onto a terraced hallway, open along one side toward the ocean. The cool, salt-laced breeze touched my face and lips. A glance over my shoulder revealed several guests watching our departure moments before the doors slammed closed. The disgraced queen, saved by her pet jester. Whispers would swirl, reinforcing untruths. I'd need to return quickly, so those whispers died on painted lips before they grew too loud to ignore. If Katina had a husband who cared, I wouldn't have needed to be her crutch, saving us both from this merry dance. Where was the king? Probably too engrossed in eyeing whatever new serving girl had caught his eye.

"Take me to bed, Lark." Katina giggled and grabbed my cheek in an attempt to turn my face toward her, and from there it would descend into far too much touching. She'd begun her seduction early tonight. We had witnesses. A couple sauntered by, laughing and pretending not to notice us.

I brushed off Katina's wandering touch, sweeping her eager hands back into mine to keep control. "Now then, you know the king will have my cock if he sees you so enamored."

"Well then," she scoffed, then plucked her hand free and poked at her ragged hair, trying to fix herself up. "He'd have more of you than I've ever had."

We passed by the prince's gilded doors, always locked, and then the king's. No light flickered from beneath his door. Back in the feasting hall, he was probably aware both I and his wife were missing from the celebration.

The queen's chamber lay ahead. Once inside, her waiting aides would see to it she was cared for. I opened the doors, expecting the fires to be ablaze and the room warm and lit by candles. But the aides weren't here, and the fires were too low. They hadn't been tended in hours. Worse, Katina and I were alone.

Katina frowned at the gloom and sighed.

I abandoned her side and lit the standing candelabra, keeping the woman in the corner of my eye at all times. "I'm sure your aides will be along."

"More like they've found themselves some fun."

With the candles all lit, I moved on to stoking the fires

and tossed on a few more logs. "The room will be bright and warm again soon."

Katina still hadn't moved from the door. "Court of Love?" she snarled, marching toward the four-poster bed. "More like the Court of Wrongs." She tore off her shoes and flung them across the room with impressive force. "My husband ignores me, I haven't seen my son in months. I don't know—" Her voice trembled. "I try..." She sniffed.

"Oh yes, you're very trying. Now, forgive me, I must return to the gathering—"

"Lark." Her tone caught me at the door, fingers already wrapped around the handles, freedom so close.

"Stay."

I bowed my head. "My Queen of Hearts, you know I cannot."

"You fuck everyone else."

I turned and all I could see was a woman wrapped in the trappings of royalty. Her colorful dress hung askew from her slim shoulders, while her expression somehow portrayed fury and desperation in equal measure. She could be fierce, but her fire had faded years ago.

"They think we fuck, so what does it matter?" She dropped onto the end of the four-poster bed and stroked the drapes as though they were the lover she so pined for.

"It matters."

"I suppose you're right." When she swept her bangs from her forehead, her fingers trembled. She noticed, and curled them into a small fist. I almost went to her, but I'd made it as far as the door, and any step toward her would be a mistake. She wanted—needed—company.

She grinned suddenly and tucked her hand against her heart. "Fine then, go be with your many lovers. What's another night alone in this prison?"

"That's the spirit. Good evening, my queen." I opened the door behind my back and retreated through it. "Sleep well."

She snorted and flopped back.

Good, she'd be asleep in moments and her aides could wrangle her moods while I did what I was good at and slithered among the crowd, gathering courtly gossip while spinning some of my own tales.

I hurried along the hall, passing the king's chamber—still dark— and might have hurried on by the prince's chamber too if I hadn't spotted a shadow glide under the door. I slowed. The hallway was empty. No staff, no guests. No witnesses.

I pressed a hand to the prince's closed door and listened. The crackle of a fire, perhaps the sweep of fabric—someone moving. Well, that someone could only be the Prince of Love. Color me intrigued. It had been so long since I'd seen him, I'd assumed he'd died behind these doors and nobody had noticed.

I plucked a pencil from my jacket's inner pocket and a slip of paper from its opposite pocket—I never roamed the palace without my tools—and scribbled a note:

Why could the prince not see his crown?

I flipped over the note and wrote the answer: *Because he was always loo-king in the wrong direction.*

Not my best work, but it's far harder to think of jests when I'd exhausted my repertoire months ago. I'd probably left him over a hundred notes. I posted this newest one beneath his door and watched for his shadow again.

The minutes ticked on. Had he kept my past notes? Did he collect them in a bureau? I didn't have the time to waste waiting on the prince. Yet I remained standing at his door, apparently unable to leave. Call it morbid curiosity or perhaps some kind of desperation on my part, because he alone was the only person in the entire Court of Love who hadn't noticed me. Four years, and we'd shared just as many words. It wasn't normal. *He* wasn't normal. Prince Arin vexed me. Few in this world had that honor.

It was time to leave. I'd been absent from the feasting hall far too long—long enough to fuck a queen.

I abandoned the riddle of the Prince Behind the Door and swept back into the ballroom's brilliant lights and shrill laughter. I took a breath, filled my lungs and blood and body with the rush of knowing this was my world, and got to work.

The red- and black-clad guests from the Court of War and the blue-clad guests from Justice spoke of illness and affliction among their people, droughts, delayed supplies, and general unrest. I distracted them with card tricks, made them gasp in disbelief and laugh in wonder. For a little while, I had them forgetting their woes. A magic all of its own, making me their magician.

After inserting myself into everyone's evening, all that remained was for me to secure an alibi for my brief exit later. A fool for the fool, as it were. And I had someone in mind. I'd spotted the young warlord earlier in the evening, a delight of a man in loose black clothes and a slash of red silk around his waist. Draven appeared to be enjoying his debut in the Court of Love, out to prove a representative from the Court of War could behave in public. His dance card was full; everyone loved fresh blood. He was handsome, muscular, with cropped dark hair, an intriguing side plait, an axe-sharp jaw, and arresting eyes. And if my instincts were correct, he wasn't interested in the ladies, at least not while I was nearby. I sympathized. Sometimes, a man needed to fuck another man against a wall. This was the Court of Love after all. If he wanted to get it out of his system, tonight was his opportunity. The Court of War had little time for love. Who better to sample carnal desires with, than the infamous Court of Love's promiscuous fool?

I'd made sure to cast him a few lascivious glances, enough to get his blood flowing south. Several guests had already paired off, some in groups of three or four. On another night, I'd have been among them. There were few better ways to end a social event than some well-managed, slightly intoxicated, free of inhibitions group sex. But not tonight. Tonight, Draven would be the sole object of my affections.

All gatherings had a heartbeat. Most began slow, building through the night to a crescendo of dancing and delight after which they'd wind down. For all but me, the entertainment was over.

After skirting the ballroom's fringes, I positioned myself behind an arch within eavesdropping distance of Draven and the young man accompanying him, probably a squire.

After a few moments, he sent his squire away to retire for the night and leaned against my archway, his back to me, just the pillar between us.

"You're somehow loud and quiet, aren't you," he mused aloud, keeping his back to the pillar, and me. "How long have you been lurking behind this arch?" Draven's voice held a delicious rumbling note and a hint of the exotic, the kind of voice that could summon a throaty growl from the depths of all that physical prowess he carried around with him. The men and women of War all had substantial presence, but Draven wasn't as substantial as most of his kin. Strong enough to crush me though, should I find myself on his bad side. That was not the plan tonight.

"Long enough to know your squire is so upright he should be an honorary member of Justice, and you're as bored as I am."

His deep, smooth chuckle traveled through my bones.

Seducing this one would be no hardship. "Jude is my cousin," he said.

"There's no accounting for family."

"And who says I'm bored?"

He couldn't see my shrug, but he'd hear it in my voice. "Not enough bloodshed. Far too few murders. No bloody knuckles."

"Is that all you think my court is, bloodshed and violence?" He stepped into my peripheral vision and braced an arm on the arch above my head, displaying a finely honed arm of corded muscle that his shirt sleeves barely contained. His smirk produced a cheek dimple that was unwarlike and adorable.

"I know it is."

"Hm, you do, huh? And how does the Court of Love's jester know so much about my home? Do they even let you out of this pretty little birdcage?"

I lifted my chin. Draven shifted close enough to make it clear he either wished to threaten or fuck. Perhaps both. My heart raced, blood warming. My cock warmed too. Yes, he'd be no hardship at all. "You'd be surprised what this bird knows."

He leaned in, blue eyes sparkling, "I like surprises."

I laughed and rolled my eyes, tipping myself out from under his less than subtle advances. After a few steps, putting some distance between us, I flung a look over my shoulder. He remained by the arch, expression puzzled, unsure if I'd brushed him off and if he'd misread our silent glances. Warlords weren't bright, much preferring axes to end an argument than debate. Skipping on the balls of my feet, I turned, walking backward. "You'll like this one." I swept both hands down myself so he didn't miss the point. "Are you coming?"

His smile kicked into his cheek again and he shoved his

muscular body into motion, steps quickening. I faced ahead and hurried outside, onto the terrace and down a flight of steps into the gardens. Moonlight iced the manicured lawns, turning greens silver. A few squeals erupted from deeper in the gardens, others frolicking nearby. Most came out here not to be seen, but I rather needed the opposite. I needed to find somewhere private enough to keep him comfortable, but also public enough to provide witnesses.

Draven was keeping up, his smile a clear indication he enjoyed the chase. I wove among high hedges, tossing a few smirks behind me, leading him along like a fish on a hook.

"By the endless winds, you're a tease..." There was his growl.

Time to reel him in.

I dropped onto a bench, propped up a boot, and sprawled like a feast waiting to be devoured. Draven loomed, breathing hard, eyes glittering in the moonlight. A bulge upset the lines in his trouser crotch. He'd liked the chase. I'd read him well.

"You caught me." I gestured at my oh so vulnerable self. "Now what are you going to do?"

"Why me?" he asked, trapped in a moment of indecision. If he was new to this, I'd have to help him along with the logistics of it all. Men of War were taught how to fuck their women counterparts, but not their men. That desire, if they had it, they were left to discover on their own.

"Why you what?" I asked.

"You could have anyone in that ballroom. Why choose me?"

Hm, interesting. Few even cared to wonder. Most just wanted to fuck without knowing why. I dropped my boot to the ground, propped my elbows on my knees, angling myself at the perfect height to suck the dick that was very interested, and peered up the man's broad chest.

13

"Must there be a reason? You want me. I want you." I wasn't about to tell him the truth, that I needed his tongue to wag about how he'd bedded the infamous court jester.

His large hands came around his front and his fingers began to unbutton the lower fastenings on his doublet, then pried at his belt, fumbling in his haste. He wanted this more than I'd realized.

No, this wasn't a mere want, it was a *need*. The poor man was desperate.

I caught his hand, steadying its shaking. "Allow me?" Our gazes met, and an understanding passed between us. He was in safe hands. I didn't know the Court of War like I did the others, but I'd heard enough rumors and whispers to suspect Draven had little say in any romantic pairings. Love, romance, fucking—it was all a needless distraction from soldiering. But that didn't mean it didn't happen. The War nobles likely took what they wanted. A young, handsome lord such as Draven could have experimented. There wouldn't have been any love in it, just a rushed, frantic release.

It was a wonder he hadn't already demanded I bend over for him. Perhaps he liked it slow.

I plucked at his fastenings and tried to ignore how, when his hands carefully cupped my face, my breath stuttered in my chest. I'd expected roughness from a man of War. Not... whatever this was.

"Your hand..." he said.

I smiled, as I always did whenever anyone noticed my right hand was missing its smallest digit. "It's nothing." His trouser fastenings finally gave, freeing his thick dick, hidden only by a slip of red silk. My own cock pulsed, trapped in my figure-hugging pants.

Rough fingers skimmed my chin, tilting my face up. "You're him, aren't you? I wasn't sure... until now."

I was so eager to suck the cock of the man who'd somehow surprised me when I was supposed to be the one doing the surprising, his words didn't reach the guarded part of me. That part that would have recognized my mistake and shut this down before it went too far.

I just needed to get this done, enjoy myself while at it, and leave Draven with a story to tell so everyone would know where I'd been during the early hours of the morning.

"You're the traitor's son."

His words landed like a punch to the gut. I jolted, abandoning the man's cock. "What did you say?" No, he couldn't know. Nobody knew. If he knew, a lowly lord from the Court of War, then who else knew? "Never mind." I brushed his words aside, hoping to ignore them while I considered their meaning. "Do you want me to suck your dick or shall we talk more nonsense that neither of us cares for?"

Giving him no chance to reply, I wrapped my fingers around his heated length, through the silk, but it wasn't enough to distract him. Questions glittered in his eyes, theories running through his mind, truths he thought he knew, stories he'd heard. Fuck. I yanked his silk undergarments down and slid his cock between my lips. Whatever words that had been about to tumble from his mouth, he choked on them instead. His hands plunged into my hair, his hips rocked, and his cock stroked the back of my throat, thick, hot, salty, and everything I needed to chase away the alarming rush of fear his accusation had unleashed.

Draven moaned. I took that to mean whatever he thought he knew, he still wanted this, and licked him from balls to tip, then used the tip of my tongue to lap his slit and gently suck his tender head. He made some kind of grumbling demand, and his fingers knotted in my hair and the big man thrust, sinking himself so far down my throat I struggled to fight the gag reflex.

He looked down, perhaps alarmed at his own actions. I grinned around his cock. I could take it. And more. His expression shifted from concern back to wide-eyed demand and I wrapped my hand around him, sucking and stroking, listening and feeling for his shudders and moans and how his body signaled its wants. Seduction was an art, like any other. His body told me what his words could not, and I gave him what he needed, but not too much. Just enough to keep him teetering on the edge of pleasure.

"Oh by the endless winds, yes—" He moaned, head back, cock buried in my hand and mouth.

I had him slick and sensitive, primed like a bow's string, ready to break.

A scream shattered the night. It was no ordinary scream, its sound tragic and broken. Draven yanked himself free and stumbled away, tucking his dick out of sight. "What was that?"

I reeled, light-headed, and wiped my mouth dry. He wasn't the only one in need, and my own cock demanded to be sated.

Another scream erupted.

My night had begun to unravel, through no fault of my own. And rather than enjoying sucking cock, I was beginning to lose my patience. I wiped a thumb across my lips. Whatever the scream meant, it had nothing to do with us. Not all was lost. All I needed was to focus Draven on the delicious prospect I was offering him.

I met Draven's gaze, which was no longer full of hunger. His body was still hungry though. He'd sampled what my tongue could do and wanted more.

"It was probably nothing," I said, then made sure he

watched as I adjusted my trousers, trying to alleviate some pressure. He might not want to suck me in return, but I'd settle for getting off in one of his large, rough hands, if that was all he'd be willing to give.

"Let's go somewhere else," he growled.

That wasn't going to work for me. I needed witnesses. I reclined on the bench again and spread my arms along the back rails, displaying everything he could have—almost had—countless lovers, talents at the tip of my tongue that would ruin him for anyone else, and a body that didn't quit. All he needed to do was step forward, forget the screams, and get on his knees. He wanted to fucking ride me like there was no tomorrow, and there was no use him denying it. The Court of War didn't hide their expressions, they wore their them like badges on their shields.

I dropped my hand again and rubbed my pinched erection, then swept my tongue across my top lip. Draven tracked every gesture as though he was a starved man presented with a feast. His cock would be demanding it find its place between my firm lips again, and maybe my ass too, but we'd get to that later. If he did as he was told.

Light flooded from the palace, igniting the gardens. Torches blazed along the terraces, shouts barreled into the night.

Clearly, my chosen location was no longer appropriate for everything I'd had in mind.

I prowled to my feet. There was another hidden part of the garden we could explore, just a few moments' walk away. Except, when I reached for Draven, I motioned with my right hand—forgetting my missing finger.

He stared at my hand, and the gap where its missing digit used to be. Then looked up, into my eyes. And he knew who I was, knew too much.

17

Such a shame I had to kill him. Maybe I could kill him while we fucked. I hadn't experienced that pleasure in a long time, and never alone. Although, the thought of such an act didn't sizzle through my veins like it once had. If anything, I'd hoped all of that was behind me, at least for a little while longer.

"The fool?" someone shouted from the terrace. "Where's the court fool?!"

I sighed. What had the queen done now? Stumbled naked from her chambers, returned to the ballroom as pickled as a gherkin? Could I not get a few hours of peace?

"Here!" Draven bellowed. "He's here." He stepped back, the knowledge of who I was written all over his face, turning him fearful. What did he think he knew about the traitor's son, about me?

I clicked my tongue, tut-tutting, and approached him in a slow dance all of our own. "That's your sexual awakening ruined."

Draven's eyes widened. Indecision, doubt, fear—he was too easy to read. The guards had seen us. My chance to lure him away had passed, but I'd have a second chance later. If he knew what *traitor's son* meant, then he couldn't ever leave the Court of Love alive.

When I stepped closer this time, he didn't back down. "If you want to know that pleasure you're so desperate for, warlord, come find me after this is dealt with." I tested his lips, to see if he'd move; when he didn't, I brushed a ghost of a kiss over his mouth. He tasted of desert spices and hot, exotic nights. I knew he was hard without touching him, could see the thirst in his kohl-lined eyes.

The moment his lips parted, I sauntered from his side, leaving us both frustrated in more ways than one.

Four palace guards spilled down the terrace steps. There

was a moment between one step and the next, where the fear that had earlier skittered through my veins returned, and tripped my stride. I should have known the ambiance was wrong, should have felt the tension in the air, seen it in the way the guards clasped their swords and how the guests hung back, not in awe, but in fear. But Draven's revelation left my mind reeling.

The guards rushed in. The one to my left kicked my legs out, and before I could bark a protest, I fell to my knees, hands locked behind my back. "Wait—what is this?" I writhed, instincts kicking in too late to fight.

"The queen," the guard to my right panted, his face in mine.

Had King Albus snapped under the weight of all the rumors? Did he believe I'd bedded her, hence the rough handling? "Easy, she's in her chamber. I haven't touched her—"

"'Touched her'?" The guard's lip curled. "You filthy whore, you murdered her!"

For the second time in a matter of moments, a man's words knocked the air from my lungs. I blinked at the guard, like the fool I apparently was, and tried to untangle the foreign-sounding words he'd just spoken to me. "Katina's dead?"

"You can't slither your way out of this one, Fool." His iron-fisted punch struck my jaw. The blow tore me from his companion's hold and flung me facedown, where thick darkness greeted me, and the wave of fear pulled me under.

CHAPTER 2

A dull, heated ache radiated through my jaw. I'd regained consciousness in worse places than this cold stone floor, but not by much. At least there was a bench in the palace dungeon, and torchlight, flickering from a sconce on the other side of my bars, and a pot to piss in. Such luxury. I probed my jaw with my tongue. Nothing felt broken, only bruised.

I dragged myself off the floor, staggered to the bench, and sprawled on my back. Water dripped from the stained ceiling, *plinking* into puddles.

I couldn't have been out for long. It was likely still the same night, or early morning.

Somewhere in the palace above me, Albus would have gathered his advisors, doctors would have arrived, the queen's body may already have been discreetly moved and placed in the nearby house of rest. Once the shock wore off, accusations would fly, and clearly, I was the favored guilty party. Someone had accused me, perhaps some jealous scrote who I'd snubbed at some point.

I had a day or two to plead my innocence before the king shipped me off to the Court of Justice.

And Katina was dead? It didn't seem possible. Had some accident befallen her after I'd left her chamber? She'd been intoxicated but otherwise well enough, hadn't she? But if it was an accident, why had the guards come for me?

It would work out. It always did. I just had to play the right cards.

The iron doors clanged, keys clattered. I expected to see the king standing at my cell bars, or at least Claude, his advisor. I did not expect to turn my head and see Prince Arin.

I blinked at him. Had I dreamed him up? He *looked* like a dream in the flickering torchlight. He had his mother's fair complexion, with a spray of near-invisible freckles. He'd tied his hair up in a brutal tail. If set free it would tumble about his shoulders like spun gold. Eyes so pale a blue, they were almost silver. And right now, Arin wore the nonchalant gaze perfected by all royals. Unreadable. Untouchable. So high above me, he barely acknowledged my existence. But while his expression was guarded, the rest of him radiated hate, perhaps a hint of disgust too.

The feeling was mutual.

Mostly.

Well no, that wasn't true. I didn't know him, he'd made sure of that. I knew only what I'd been told. *He was weak,* although he didn't look it, physically. In fact, he appeared to be sturdier than I. In the four years since we'd met, he'd grown into his body, filled out, become more of a man and less of his mother's pretty boy. Color me intrigued.

I laced my hands behind my head and lifted my gaze back toward the ceiling. Most people would have knelt and sniveled and begged for their freedom. I'd never begged and wasn't about to start now. This unfortunate situation wouldn't last. I didn't need him, or his lofty sneering. I had the king in my pocket. When Albus came to the dungeon, this would all be dealt with and I'd walk free.

"I know what you are," Arin said, in a clipped voice. Arin did not growl; he didn't need to. His voice had changed too. Deepened, as was natural. Four years had rarely felt so long. The prince was a stranger to me, and to his own court.

Odd, that he should emerge now. His mother's death must have rattled him from his chamber.

"What I am? Devilishly handsome? Blisteringly intelligent?" I examined my nails. "The subject of your dreams?"

"If I were to dream of you, Fool, those dreams would not end well."

"My name is Lark. I hope you don't mind my reminding you, as you appear to have forgotten."

"You're nothing."

So dramatic. I rolled my eyes and fixed the prince in my gaze again. Gold buckles punctuated his pristine white attire. He looked like a cake, accented with delicate gold icing. Pretty icing often hid a multitude of sins.

As he was here, and speaking with me, a minor miracle all of its own, I'd play his game. "How am I 'nothing,' fair prince?"

"It's your greatest fear, isn't it?" He wrapped white-gloved fingers around the rusted bars. "That we'll all discover how truly mediocre you are. You cannot bear to be ignored."

My lips twitched into a smile. "Interesting. I'd assumed I'd barely featured in your existence." I swung my legs off the bench and sat up, fixing him in my sights. "Yet how would you know my greatest fear unless you've been watching me? And not just watching me. You've been paying attention."

He turned his face away, exposing the flickering in his cheek, betraying his clenched jaw. What would his skin feel

23

like beneath my fingers? As soft as rose petals, like those sneering lips would be soft? Until he had my hand cut off for daring to touch him.

I'd heard rumors he was a kind prince, full of laughter, his mother's joy.

Hm, he wasn't kind now. But he wouldn't sever hands. That wasn't the Court of Love's way. I'd probably earn myself a vicious slap, and it might be worth it. I'd forgotten how blisteringly beautiful Prince Arin was. Four years had hardened him, and hardened parts of me too.

"You despise us," he said, still banging the same drum.

Despise was a strong word. Although, he was likely right, but did he know he was right, or was it a guess? I kept my smile on my lips even as my heart galloped faster. "What makes you believe that?"

"You belittle and ridicule my family, my court. Our lives are a joke to you."

Goodness, for a man I'd met once, the vicious hate was strong within him. So strong in fact, I could almost taste it. Hate like that, it was rare, and special, and did not stem from a single meeting. He couldn't know who I *really* was, could he?

"Never mistake my jesting for truth. I merely—" I waved a hand. "—entertain."

"But it's true, that's why you're so good at spinning tales, you believe them. My father's an idiot, my mother a whore, and me—"

"The prince so hideously ugly he's afraid to leave his chamber?" I stood and approached him. He unwrapped his fingers from the bars and lifted his chin, defiant and proud. He didn't retreat. We'd never been so close. And he was far from ugly. Or hideous. In fact, he might be the most beautiful creature in the Court of Love, besides me. "Where's the truth

24

in that tale, when you're the second most handsome man in this dungeon?" I asked.

"Ugly cannot always be seen behind a mask," he said, softening a little. Golden lashes fluttered. There was truth in those words. They may have been the first whole truth he'd spoken since entering the dungeon. Interesting. "You don't know me."

No, but I wished I did, even now, as he sneered as though I was something he should scrape from his boot. I wanted him to see me, to know me. He was right. I thrived on attention, on love and hate and all the emotions in between, so long as I was its focus. And when he left here, when he walked away, I'd crave his company, crave him, despite the disgust, or perhaps because of it. Four years he'd been the Prince Behind the Door, and now he was here. I almost reached through the bars to touch him, to see if he was real. "You'd think the Court of Love would have an abundance of love, yet it is the most bleak and empty court of all. You're the proof of that. Unloved, forgotten, exiled to his room. Why do you hide?"

He didn't look away this time, because we both knew I was right. I saw that which he could not, and he somehow saw the truth of me beneath my endless efforts to hide it. The prince and the fool, with bars between us. His lashes fluttered closed, his tongue stroked his top lip, and he stepped back. The bars were a good thing; without them, I might have inappropriately kissed him to spark a fire in him.

"You'll be executed for what you've done," he said stiffly.

"Perhaps." I smiled and grasped the bars, plastering myself to them, trying to get closer. "But you know I'm innocent."

"'Innocent'?" He laughed, and the sound echoed around us, bringing light to the darkest of places. "You are far from that." He turned away with a sweep of his white-fur-lined cloak and headed toward the steps.

"You claim to know me," I said, raising my voice, "so you know I wouldn't hurt Katina."

He stopped, one boot on the stair's first riser. "Oh, I know."

"Then tell the king, tell him I didn't do this."

"And why would I do that?" He peered over his shoulder, silver eyes shining. "When I was the one who told him you did."

He climbed the steps and the dungeon door slammed like the tolling of the execution bell. I stared after the prince, stunned in both heart and mind.

My lies could withstand much, but not the word of a prince.

The hangman's noose had gotten much closer.

CHAPTER 3

$\mathcal{I}$'d been fucked without all the fun of foreplay. And by a prince, no less. Hate was not a new emotion for me. I had so much hate in my heart it likely pumped black blood through my veins, but the hatred I felt for Arin in those moments after he'd left was a bright and vicious thing, and matched only by the desire to wrap my hands around his neck and tell him *everything*. See what he thought of me then. Oh, he'd still hate me, but at least the lofty prick would know I was the *least* of his enemies.

I paced my cell.

The queen's death, like the queen herself, was most inconvenient.

And then there was the problem of Draven, the lord from the Court of War, and the things he'd said moments before I'd had his delicious cock in my mouth. Things that could not be left to fester. Niggly little truths like that had a knack for escaping and growing into larger problems.

Four years I'd been weaving my lies. Four years, day and night. The death of the queen and the wagging tongue of one sexually frustrated warlord would not be what brought me down.

I had to get out of this cell.

"Hey!" I banged on the bars and rattled my cell door. "Guards!"

Someone would be nearby. They wouldn't risk leaving me here alone, forgotten... "Hey!" There would be a way to escape, there was always a way. Whatever the cost, I'd pay it. And I had multiple debts owed to me. Multiple angles to play.

But I could do nothing behind bars. I *was* nothing behind bars.

The dungeon door groaned open and a guard stomped down the steps, armor clattering. The same guard who'd punched me on the terrace. "Quiet, yah hear!" He was tall, slim, with a flash of short red hair and sharp green eyes.

"The king. I want to speak with King Albus. Bring him here."

He narrowed his eyes and studied me as though he hadn't heard a word I'd said. "Not so high and mighty now, are you?" He sauntered over and he raked his glare from head to toe, then recoiled, as though he'd tasted something foul. He clearly did not like me and was full of swagger and masculine bravado that seemed a little heavy-handed, unless...

"Have we met?" I asked, squinting a little. He did seem familiar. I was sure we hadn't been intimate, though. His eyes narrowed. "Before you struck me on the terrace, that is?"

"Yeah, we've met, fool. You sullied my sister."

"Ah." The red hair, the freckles, yes... I remembered his sister. A fun little thing. She'd told me her brother was a guard and that was how she'd gotten inside the palace walls. She'd demanded I pleasure her, and I'd been bored at the time. I'd had to cover her mouth to keep her from screaming as I'd tongued her to climax. "She rather sullied herself behind the parrot topiary—"

He spat. Sticky, warm spittle landed on my cheek. "I hope they cut off your dick when you're swinging from the noose."

I wiped my cheek. "Well, at least I have one."

"What did you say?" He squared up to the bars.

The poor man. "Deaf too, and so tiny a... package." I glanced at this crotch. "How unfortunate. Fate can be cruel. And you don't even have the intelligence to make up for such a cruel hand you've been dealt."

"You piece of shit." He groped for the keys at his belt, threw the key in the lock, and flung open the door. I danced back, avoiding his sloppy right hook, then I spun again, darting behind him, where I unhooked the keys from his belt, flew out of the door, and slammed it closed with a triumphant *clang*.

"What—" Heat blazed across his face. He grabbed the door and rattled it.

Hip cocked, I jangled the keys. "Next time, just ask me to dance. It's far easier."

"Give me those keys!" He thrust his arm through the bars and took a swipe in my direction.

"When you next see your sister—I forget her name—tell her Lark sends his regards, and she's welcome to *come* by anytime the desire takes her." I dashed up the steps and slammed the door on his roar.

Oil lamps spluttered along the wide corridors. Voices rattled somewhere far off, through walls, in other rooms. I hurried on, light-footed and fast.

The palace's layout was sprawled up a dramatic bluff with Dallin's Great Ocean to the north, and endless flower meadows and the local town to the south. The palace itself was all towers and terraces, gardens and courtyards, each

29

interconnected by marble pathways. I knew these paths and corridors like the back of my hand, especially the staff corridors, hidden behind false panels and tucked behind heavy velvet drapes.

The palace guards rarely ventured along them.

I eased one such panel open and slipped into the hidden, narrow walkway behind.

One problem dealt with. Perhaps the easiest: escaping the dungeons. Now I had several options, none of which included the easiest option of running away. I'd learned, long ago, I couldn't run fast or far enough to escape my fate. The alternative was to run headlong into trouble.

Find the king, have him declare me innocent, and then locate Draven before he could spread those nasty little rumors about me. With those fires extinguished, I'd turn my attention back where it belonged... destroying the Court of Love.

Although... My pace slowed, thoughts slowing with them, clinging to a new idea.

The queen's death could be an opportunity. It wasn't how I'd planned to do things, but I could use it. I *had* to use it.

The cards shuffled in my mind. Games I'd played for so long they were sometimes difficult to separate from reality. The queen was dead, the king would be distracted, the prince... was a problem, now that he'd made an appearance. But I'd deal with him, now he'd shown me who he was. Yes, this could all work out in my favor, if I played it right.

I veered toward the servants' quarters and spotted Ellyn kneading bread at the long working table. She wasn't alone, maids often weren't. I lingered in the shadows behind a cupboard and waited for a moment when nobody was looking. I grabbed a potato from the nearby bucket and tossed it toward her. It bounced once on the table. She snatched it up and shot me a warning glare.

"Ellyn, fetch the spices?" the housekeeper called.

I slunk back, hidden from view, and waited for her nod. Moments later, we met outside the kitchens.

Ellyn wiped her hands on her apron and swept her mousy hair from her damp face with the back of her hand. "What are you doing here?" she whispered. "I heard you were arrested, Lark."

"For a friend, you don't appear that concerned."

She rolled her eyes. Someone yelled *hot pan* inside the kitchen, followed by a loud clatter, drawing Ellyn's gaze. We stepped back some more, where the cacophony from the kitchens wasn't as loud.

"I hear so many rumors about you I never know what's true," she whispered.

I flashed her a charming smile and leaned against the wall. "Tell me some of these rumors."

Ellyn frowned. "You broke out of the dungeon, didn't you?"

"Not exactly, I had a key." I showed her the key. And then grabbed her hand and placed it in her palm. "Keep that safe. A very angry guard will be needing it soon."

She scowled but dropped the key into her apron pocket. "I'm not even going to ask. I can't be seen with you. They'll have my hide. I have to go—"

"I need a favor," I blurted, stopping her from turning away.

"Of course you do." She puffed her bangs from her forehead, leaned a shoulder against the wall, and glowered some more. "You always want something. What is it now?"

"I often drop in to see you, no ulterior motive. Just the other day, I brought you flowers."

"The palace is surrounded by flowers," she huffed. "Don't think I don't know how you steal fruit or saffron, or flowers to bribe the next poor sap who's caught your eye."

"I am wounded." I gasped and pressed a hand to my chest. "You wound me, dear Ellyn. And I thought we were special friends."

She snorted, but her smile was warming. "What do you want, Lark?"

"Oh, just a little thing... Nothing, really..."

"Spit it out."

"See to it the king's aides are delayed from tending his chambers?"

Ellyn narrowed her eyes. "The king? Why? What are you doing?"

A kitchenhand passed us by, carrying a tub of sloshing potatoes. I caught Ellyn's shoulder and tucked her behind the corner, out of sight. "Nothing insidious. You know me, this is all a misunderstanding. I just want to speak with him, alone. We're practically friends."

"If you're friends, just knock on his door." Her frown cracked the patch of flour on her cheek.

She'd likely heard what I'd been accused of. By now the whole palace probably knew. The longer this went on, the harder it would be to salvage the tattered remains of my reputation. "I need your help," I whispered, leaning closer. "You know I'd do the same for you."

"Would you?" Her eyebrows lifted.

Would I? "I'd certainly consider it." I grinned. She knew I *had* done the same for her.

She smacked me on the arm. "Why can't I say no to you?!"

Her frown softened when I tucked a lock of her unruly curly hair behind her ear. "Because you're a good friend, and I don't deserve you. And because you owe me?"

She sighed. "That's true. All right, fine. I'll delay his aides, but you may not have long."

"I don't need long." I turned, heading back down the corridor.

"Lark," Ellyn called. "Be careful. It feels different this time."

"I'm always careful," I called back, and slipped into the hidden side passage. The smile died on my lips. She was right. I'd been in difficult situations before, most I'd laughed off. It *was* different this time. I rubbed the stump of my missing finger and hurried on, steps silent. Only the spluttering oil lamps betrayed my passing.

THE KING'S chamber was a vast collection of private rooms, reception areas, and sleeping quarters. The panel I popped open delivered me to the second antechamber where the king stored his books. The opening panel knocked a bookcase, sending its contents tumbling.

I caught the small, dancing girl figurine in my right hand, and the bookcase with my leg. A few books tumbled to the floor with some alarming *thuds*. I waited, listening. Nobody came. The king wasn't here. Neither were his aides. Ellyn had delayed them a while. I reset the bookcase, then dashed through the chambers, toward Albus's bedroom.

The bed was always made, never disturbed. He rarely slept in it; instead he spent most nights slumped at his desk, lost in pennywort's embrace.

The main chamber door creaked open.

I spun, caught a glimpse of the king's fair locks and bulky stance, and flung myself at the daybed, sprawled and posed, as though I'd been waiting hours. He wouldn't know how my

33

heart raced, or how I measured my breathing, keeping him from seeing how I panted.

Albus froze in the doorway. Quite the opposite of his son, his muscular bulk would have been welcome in War's courts. He often used that substantial presence to bully others.

"Lark," he grumbled. "Do I need to call the guards?"

I dipped my chin, bowing my head. "My king, do as you please. I ask only that you hear me out."

He swept across the chamber toward the dresser and removed a decanter of potent wine, pouring himself a glass and raising it to his lips in a trembling hand. "My wife..."

"I did not kill her." Best to get the facts of the matter spoken. Now was not the time to dance around the truth.

He paused, cradling the glass in his hands. "I should have been there."

He'd get no argument from me. He should have been there for the entire four years I'd played their fool, and now he'd realized. When it was too late. He glanced away, towards the far wall, perhaps searching for the wife he'd lost. I was supposed to be the fool, yet I found myself surrounded by them.

"Tell Justice, when they come, I did not do this," I said.

He arched an eyebrow. "Check your tone."

"My tone?" I climbed from the daybed and crossed the floor to look the King of Love in his watery, unfocused eyes. He appeared formidable, but the king was just like the rest. He'd buckle under the right kind of pressure, like a wilted wildflower in his many meadows. "Katina was desperate for a love you denied her."

"She wasn't so chaste," he scoffed and side-eyed me, making sure to level accusations with his gaze. "You met her needs well enough."

I snorted and moved closer still. "No, I did not. What she

got from me was, at most, friendship. What she wanted was her husband. Last night, I didn't hurt her or fuck her. I put her to bed, intoxicated and forlorn, but very much alive."

Tears glistened unshed in his eyes, but they were so shallow that a blink banished them. "You're not a killer," he mumbled.

He was wrong there, but he'd only know that once it was too late. "Tell everyone, make an announcement, I'm innocent."

"My son, he said—"

"Arin is mistaken."

Albus tapped his fingers against his glass. "It is not so simple."

"You're the king, it is as simple as your word."

"I... If you did not kill her, who did?" he said with a whimper.

"That's an answer for Justice to find. And not my problem."

He shook his head. "People want answers *now*. Lark, until the killer is found, you must remain in the dungeons." He lifted his drink to his lips, the matter over with.

Clearly, he'd forgotten our past, forgotten what I'd done for him, forgotten everything I knew. I shifted closer still, so close the sweet smell of wine and his perspiration wafted around us both.

I looked into his eyes, and I saw the weakness there. Like a cancer, eating him up from the inside.

"Perhaps your precious people will also be interested to learn how the King of Love is addicted to pennywort and hasn't been able to satisfy his wife for years," I said calmly, and tucked a smile into my cheek. "In fact, the only thing he can get it up for is the serving girls, like the poor girl you had me deal with. I'm sure she'd be delighted to confirm how you fucked her into your bed, while she cried silent tears. Half your size, terrified, trapped. Now, tell me, is that how your court celebrates love?"

The glass slipped from his fingers and hit the floor, where it shattered, spilling jagged pieces of glass and wine around my boots.

"How dare you!" he growled and trembled, boiling in his pristine boots. "Get out!"

"How dare *you*. Lock me up, and I'll sing like a bird, Your Highness."

His mouth twitched into a snarl. "Be very careful who you threaten, Lark. This isn't one of your games. My beautiful wife is dead!"

"And finally free of you."

He reeled and stumbled backward into his dresser. "Guards!"

This man was a coward and a wretched excuse for a king. "You had better be calling them in here to declare my innocence, or Dallin help me, I will ruin your reign. The routine rape of your serving girls is just the beginning. I know how the royal coffers are all but empty, how you ignore War encroaching on your borders, how you turn away, too afraid to lift a finger. You are weak, and your kingdom is dying. But you can do this one right thing, one simple thing." I stepped close and adjusted his jacket, straightening it again. "Trust me when I say, you will much prefer I am your friend than your enemy."

His weeping eyes scanned my face, and sweat beaded on his brow. "This isn't you," he whispered.

Me? What did he know of me? Was he so naïve as to think my life revolved around his? He didn't know me. Nobody here *knew me*. Even I sometimes struggled to know the man in the mirror. "Oh, it is."

"Then you are not who I thought you to be, to use these... minor indiscretions against me."

Minor indiscretions? Rape was never minor, not even where I came from.

His chamber door flung open, and I recoiled from the king and the mess of the shattered glass on the floor. "Ah, perfect timing, the king has something of importance to reveal." I gestured for the three guards to listen to their liege, urged the king to speak, and waited.

The guards slowed. They looked from me to the king, confused. "Your Highness?"

"Yes, I..." Albus hesitated. "It's true. Lark is wholly innocent of my wife's terrible departure."

Departure? As though she'd taken some time away from the palace and her delusional husband.

The king smoothed his clothes and cleared his throat. "Please, let it be known how Lark is cleared of all suspicion."

"Of course, Your Highness. Do you want us to... search for another perpetrator? Or will that be all?"

"Yes, yes. I need my aides, where are my aides? And Claude? Bring Claude. Claude will know what to do." He waved them away. The trio bowed and left, and the king's stuttering, jittery movements stilled again, his shock passing. Behind the bluster, he could be dangerous. But so was I. "I will not forget this," he said, "nor will I forgive it."

I knelt, careful to avoid the broken glass, and took his left hand in my right. "Neither will the girls you raped."

He yanked his hand away. "Get out, Fool. Before I retract my generosity!"

Generosity, indeed. "My pleasure."

I left his chamber as free as I'd ever been in Love's Court, but now the cracks had begun to widen. And soon, the whole palace would shatter at my feet. Just like the king's glass.

CHAPTER 4

Free to roam, I walked the palace grounds. Dew from the manicured grass soaked my black boots, and the salty morning air dried my lips. Despite events, or perhaps because of them, the palace was quiet. Some days, I walked the meadows between the palace and the town and stayed there a while, sitting among flowers while the breeze whispered to swaying flowerheads. Not today, though. Today, exhaustion tugged at my body and mind.

Returning to my bunkroom—separate from the main residence chambers and the servants' quarters, a side chamber, like an afterthought—I swept inside, tore off my coat, and plucked at my shirt buttons, stripping off layers. Smells of salt air, dungeon dampness, and stale wine had followed me back. I could not abide uncleanliness.

I filled the washbasin with cold water, splashed my face, and blinked at the man in the patinaed mirror. A purple bruise had bloomed on my jaw, where the guard had struck me. Purple, the color of pain. I ran trembling fingers over it and winced.

It didn't matter.

It would heal.

Anything that didn't kill, healed eventually.

My reflection smiled, which meant I must have. I didn't feel it.

I plunged my hands into the water again, caught sight of the stump where my missing finger should be, and froze. Some things *didn't* heal.

But this court wasn't that one. For all the lies and hypocrisy, the Court of Love wasn't the worst of the worlds I'd been trapped in. The countless little white scars marring my chest were evidence of that, each cut accompanied by a memory of laughter.

I splashed water up the mirror, warping the man there, and snatched up a towel.

There was no use in dwelling in the past. There was nothing there for me but nightmares. I swept the towel across my chest, watching in the wet mirror how the tiny scars gleamed in the candlelight. A wax-sealed envelope lay on my pillow, behind me in the mirror.

I turned, and there it was, as plain as day. I'd missed it on my return. The door had been locked, hadn't it?

I approached, as though the note might bite, and eyed it cautiously. The seal was purple, of course. If I tossed it out of the window, would its words still find me? The symbol in the wax seal wasn't one I recognized. Perhaps the purple wax was just purple wax and didn't mean a damn thing.

I laughed. I must have been tired, for a purple seal to spook me.

Just a note. Nothing to fear. I snatched it up, broke the seal, and unfolded the thick cream paper, reading the words once, then again... Like the news of the queen's death, the words swept over me, through me, taking too long to sink in.

I know who you are.

Meet in my chamber.

D.

Warlord Draven. It had to be. The written words echoed those he'd spoken in the garden. Well then, it appeared the lord was determined to talk about truths that had nothing to do with him. I'd go to him, discover what he knew, who he'd told, and from there... we'd see. There was a chance he could be used. War weren't the brightest of foes. Which begged the question how he knew as much as he did. *Traitor's son.* He'd answer my questions, either by pleasure or pain.

News of my innocence was new; the note couldn't have been left for long, or it would have been delivered to the dungeon. I'd visit him now.

I threw on a plain grey suit, attire the court's jester would never wear, and shrugged my hooded coat over the top, then tucked the note inside a pocket—it wouldn't do for anyone else to see such things. One loose end was quite enough. After leaving my chamber, I hurried back inside the servants' corridors, keeping my chin down and hood up.

Ellyn took some finding. She wasn't among the organized chaos of the kitchens, nor was she in the steam-filled laundry rooms. There were others I could ask for help, but few I trusted more. I eventually found her in the communal sleeping area, folding clothes at one of the many beds laid out in rows. I stepped from the wall panel, emerging from the gloom, and snuck up behind her. The other maids chatted at the far end of the room, readying for bed now their shifts were over.

I poked Ellyn in the ribs.

She yelped and swung a right hook, forcing me to duck. "Lark!" she gasped, then shoved me in the chest and flicked my hood down. "Sneaking around the back walkways, you

41

fiend! Can't you just walk about the palace like a lord, now you're innocent?"

I grinned and dropped onto the edge of the bed. "News travels fast."

"Like wildfire, down here. Get off my clothes. Or make yourself useful and help fold them."

Back on my feet, I picked up her washing and began to fold alongside her. "If I walk the main halls, by the time I've juggled and spouted poems for the nobility in my way, a day and night would have passed."

Her brow crinkled but she kept her smile and picked up a shirt, quickly flipping it around—the motions so well-practiced she didn't need to think to perform them. "I forget you're *so desired* you get accosted wherever you go."

"It's truly a curse." I joked, but I also existed to please, and the demands of pleasure never ended. Most days, I loved it, but being accused of murder, thrown in a cell, and then blackmailing the king had rather ruined my mood. Ellyn saw some of that when she next side-eyed me.

To keep her from asking all those personal questions in her eyes, I picked up a blouse from her wrinkled pile and held it to my chest. "You'd look better in green," I told her.

She snatched it off me, but laughed. "What do you want?"

"I need another favor."

"By now you surely owe me a hundred."

"What's another favor between friends?" I folded some more, catching glimpse of a few of the staff watching me from across the room. Our banter had drawn attention. They'd be listening too. Being beautiful as well as an enigma truly was a curse, some days. "Where are the guests from War residing?" I whispered.

"What are you up to now?" she whispered back.

"Fighting fires."

She chuckled in disbelief. "I've never known anyone to find trouble like you do."

"I rather think it finds me."

"Hm, this is me, Lark. I know you." She scooted her pile of washing to the end of the bed and leveled her glare on me. "You thrive on chaos."

"No, I thrive on *controlling* chaos." Like keeping all the balls in the air at once. Chaos restrained. *That*, I loved. Not chaos unleashed and running amok.

When Ellyn met my gaze, like this, I was in for some stern advice or terrible news. "I'm glad you're free," she said, instead. "Thinking of you in the dungeons. It wasn't right."

"Well, imagine being there." I smiled, but she saw through the grin. She usually did. I let the flimsy smile go and sighed. "There is more happening here than the queen's death. I need to control it, before it turns into that chaos you believe I court."

"I know, and I'm sorry, for the queen. You and her were close—"

I laughed, startling Ellyn, and everyone listening in, including me. "That's one rumor which refuses to die."

"Laugh all you want, you liked her."

"Sweet Ellyn, I like a lot of people."

She planted a hand on her cocked hip. "You can admit it to me."

I rolled my eyes. "Where are War staying? Tell me that and I'll admit to liking the queen."

She smiled again, happy to have outmaneuvered me. "In the southern meadows rooms. Who are you looking for?"

"Draven, a lord—"

"Oh yes, *Warlord Draven*," she purred his name in a manner quite unbecoming of a lady, of which she wasn't, which was why I enjoyed her company above all others.

"You know of him?"

"No, not really, it's just..." With a wave, she tried to fight a bigger grin from her face.

"Are you implying something with that gesture?"

Flopping onto the edge of the bed, she leaned back and puffed her frizzy hair from her face. "I hear he's rather handsome, no?"

"Draven, 'handsome'?" I suspected Draven and I had been noticed in the gardens, and she'd heard all about it. That *had* been my plan, that we be witnessed. "I surely had not noticed."

Ellyn's left eyebrow arched. "You *propositioned* him, didn't you? Tell me, everyone says you did."

I perched my ass on the edge of the bed beside her. "Before or after I had his cock in my mouth?"

She squealed and landed a playful thump on my arm. "You're a fiend, Lark!" Heat warmed her face. Her chuckles faded and in a low voice, she asked, "Was it good?"

"It certainly would have been, had I not been arrested during the act."

She blinked, then snorted. "Your life is such a pantomime."

"You're more right than you know."

"I wish I was getting some."

"We both know it's not cock you want."

She turned pensive, and it was time to move this conversation on. "Draven's room?"

"The farthest from the entrance, the meadow side, right by the balcony overlooking the southern end of the gardens. Be nice to him, hm? I hear he lost a son a while back."

A son? He hadn't looked old enough to have much of a family, but they started them young in War. I pressed a chaste kiss to her forehead. "I'm always nice, and I'll pay you back."

"Lark, I want details!" she called.

"A fool never fucks and tells." I chuckled as I slipped back inside the servants' corridor, but my smile wilted as I left Ellyn and her friendship behind. For all my jests and flippancy, I couldn't shake the sense a net was tightening, choking off my air. My heart ticked like a clock, its hands close to midnight. If I didn't get control of the rumors, my time at the Court of Love would soon come to an end. Four years, *poof*. I'd become accustomed to Love's strange ways. Home was so far away, and so long ago, I could dismiss it as a dream. Or a nightmare.

I threw my hood over my head and navigated the corridors and twisting staircases, careful to keep my gaze away from anyone I passed. Unfortunately, being blessed with beauty and flare made navigating the palace anonymously almost impossible. *There goes Lark, what's he up to now? Lark, won't you tell us a tale? Lark, juggle these apples. Lark, dance for us. Lark, come to my room. Lark... I'll cut you where they won't see. Lark, kneel, lick my hand, my cock, drink me down...*

Memories twitched, unbound inside my head.

I stumbled, tripped over my own feet, and fell against the wall.

My heart galloped up my throat. I slammed my hands over my face. Brittle panic tried to drop me to my knees, rendering me helpless, but I couldn't let it get a hold of me. I pressed my back against the cool wall, then my hands, closed my eyes, and breathed. The panic would pass. Everything passed, eventually. Wasn't that the only truth survivors had? They'd survived. No trifling thing, yet as simple as continuing to breathe.

You exist to please me.

You are mine.

My traitor's son...

The ghost of my missing finger throbbed a second heart-beat. But its heated beat soon faded, and so did the memories.

Memories, dreams, they were all the same. They couldn't hurt me here.

I pushed on, tasting a scream. I held it back. I always did. If the screams escaped, they might never stop.

A chuckle slipped free instead, the sound slightly unhinged. But that was fine. One slip, no more. I controlled it, controlled myself. I was Lark, the dancer, the lover, the fool.

With my head clear, and my heart slow, I approached the meadow-side rooms.

The sweet smell of flowers drifted through open windows and the large public balcony at the end of the corridor.

I strode on, hood up, head down, careful not to be seen. It was still late—the night had dragged on for an eternity. The open windows revealed dawn's red ribbons creeping along the horizon. Was it too early to visit Draven? His note hadn't specified a time. He'd probably be asleep. And perhaps he wouldn't mind if I eased between the sheets alongside him, prying him with questions as I pried him in other ways too.

I approached the farthest room and the last door beside the balcony—Draven's, according to Ellyn. His body would be willing, and with him under me, he'd tell me anything. They always did.

Voices mumbled from behind the door. He had company, I'd have to wait. Or return later. Hurrying on, I ventured outside onto the balcony and leaned against the rail. Vast gardens spread below, dotted with lamplights. Just the rumble of the sea and fleeting early morning birdsong disturbed the quiet. There were no birds where I came from, no flowers either.

A new day broke over the horizon, so full of hope and potential. A dream yet unlived. I wasn't as free as people assumed, but in quiet moments like these, I sometimes had a fleeting taste of it.

A heavy *thump* shuddered through the floor.

The voices in Draven's room fell silent.

Instincts tingled at the back of my neck. The same instincts I'd been too distracted to notice last night, and paid the price.

Perhaps Draven had found himself another willing cock to suck, but if I walked away, and whatever was going on behind that door was something else, something insidious, then I'd have missed my opportunity to get the warlord under me.

I tried the handle and eased open the door. Hopefully, I'd find him in the throes of passion. Perhaps they'd like a third?

Light from the hallway spilled around me, through the opening doorway, into a room draped in black-and-red silks, the colors of War, and Draven lay on the floor, sprawled on his back. A slim, hooded figure straddled his twitching legs.

"Hey!"

The figure twisted, fixed me under their glare. A scarf covered the lower half of their face, like a mask. They bolted toward the window.

I lunged, but the hooded figure had too much of a head start. They threw open the window and leaped.

I skidded to Draven's side. He kicked uselessly and clasped a hand to his bleeding neck. Blood leaked between his fingers. He grabbed my arm, lips moving, but making no sound.

"Be still. Let me see." I pried his hand back. The wound

didn't spurt; it was just a thick dribble. Our fingers mingled, slippery with blood. He'd live... if he had help.

Or he might die here, if I did nothing.

He grabbed at my arm again, eyes pleading to save him.

He knew too much. I could walk away, let him bleed out while I chased after the attacker. Someone else had done the killing for me. But if I walked now, I might never know who had told him the truth about me, and that person was likely far more dangerous than a hapless warlord who'd wanted to dip his cock into a willing participant during his debut ball.

I gripped the man's face, smearing blood across his pale cheek. "You're going to survive, and you won't tell a soul I was here. Nor will you tell anyone what you believe you know about me. Do you understand, Draven?"

He blinked, gurgled, and nodded.

I patted his chest and stood. "There's a good lord —*Guards! Attack! Guards!*"

Doors slammed outside, voices rang. Someone would come soon. He'd be saved.

I dashed for the window. Draven's assailant couldn't have gotten far. The drop to the gardens below was doable. Movement caught my eye to my left, among the orchard trees. Someone running... And there he or she was, sprinting away. "Oh, no you don't." I vaulted the window, dropped, heart in my throat, and landed in a roll among trampled roses.

Run.

Running, I could do.

"There he is!" someone yelled from the balcony behind me, probably mistaking me for Draven's attacker.

I flung up my hood, tore across the lawns, dashed through an arch in the high hedges, and burst into the orchard, where the grass was taller—the assailant's trail obvious. I bolted after them and rounded an arbor. They were heading toward

48

the hedge maze. I slowed... The maze's arched mouth beckoned, eager to swallow any fool who happened to think they could outwit its many turns. I knew its turns, and also knew one wrong step would see me trapped inside with a potential killer, and the palace guards about to spill in behind us.

One night in a cell had been more than enough.

I veered away from the maze, and headed toward the palace and its terraces. Perhaps the maze would swallow the assailant. Although, considering how well he or she had darted through the gardens, they clearly knew what paths to take, and likely knew the secrets to the maze's interior.

Which suggested whoever had attacked Draven lived in the palace.

There was another killer in the Court of Love, muscling in on my territory. And that would not do.

THE SUN'S morning rays warmed my window when I returned. No guards waited for me, so I hadn't been identified as Draven's attacker. Hopefully, the warlord would do the sensible thing and keep quiet, if his voice returned.

I filled the basin and washed Draven's blood from my hands. I hadn't been the one to silence the lord, but the outcome had been desirable, nonetheless.

Draven wouldn't be telling any secrets, not for a while. And now I had room to breathe. The queen's death, Draven's attack, my arrest. These things, while unfortunate, were not my fault.

Collapsing on the bed, I let my eyes close, let my heart slow and my mind wander. The quiet settled over me like a quilt. Just a moment to stop, to breathe. A moment all my own.

"You seem so innocent like this, asleep."

I open my eyes and froze.

"Vulnerable." Prince Arin's face hovered an inch from mine. His cool fingers pinched my chin, holding me still while his silver-eyed gaze roamed over me, drinking in my unguarded expression.

I hadn't heard him enter.

The prince jerked my head to one side as he let go. He straightened, revealing two men behind him—not guards. Something else. Their faces stoic, eyes cold, and they carried enough muscle to rival Draven.

My morning was about to get painful.

"Welcome, gentlemen," I greeted, leaning back against the wall. "If you wanted to join me in bed, Prince, you merely had to ask."

Arin's eyes widened, and for the briefest of moments, shock stole his rage, but it didn't last. His lip curled, and his anger flooded back in. He raised a hand, flicked his fingers, and his brutes rushed in.

CHAPTER 5

*P*erhaps Arin expected me to fight, because when his men pulled me from the bed and flung me to the floor, he watched, as though waiting for *something*. But as soon as the first punch landed, I stopped watching his face and concentrated instead on protecting mine. The first punch was always the worst, the second, less so. And by the third, I'd withdrawn into my own mind.

The blows kept coming, and the prince watched it all, stoic and unflinching. Or so I thought, but at some point, he turned away and moved toward the window. A little blood stained his pearly-white cloak. My blood, I supposed.

Thick hands gripped my neck and pinned me to my bedside. Everything burned—my chest, my stomach.

My head lolled, vision blurring, then sharpened to Arin on one knee, peering into my eyes. Whatever he was searching for, his frown suggested he hadn't found it. "Why didn't you fight?" he asked, his voice soft now. I preferred this softer, less sneery version.

I smiled and licked blood from my lips. "If *you* hit me, we both might enjoy it."

His slap landed hard, splitting the inside of my cheek. I hadn't expected him to do it. But now he had, I might have won this little battle of ours. His face suggested I wasn't the only one surprised by the slap.

I tongued the cut in my cheek, spat blood to the side, and smirked up at the Prince of Love. "What use is there in fighting when I cannot win?"

His lips ticked, almost smiling. "You're not even sorry, are you?" He straightened, looming over me.

"And what am I supposed to be sorry for?" I dabbed at my lip, wiping more blood away. If he'd thought to hurt me, a beating was not the way to go about it.

"You have my father seduced, and the rest of my court under your spell, but not me. This is the least you deserve."

I dabbed at my tender cheek, struck by a guard and now a prince. I really must have been special to warrant such attention. "Nothing I say will convince you I'm innocent, will it?"

He turned away and swept toward the door. Something had snagged on his cloak's fluffy, white hem. A twig of some sort, with tiny green leaves. I'd seen its like before, but I couldn't remember where.

"Answer me one thing," I croaked. "Just one?"

He paused but didn't deign to look back.

"Did you keep my letters, the ones I slipped under your door?"

He didn't move, didn't breathe. He paused for so long, I may have earned a second beating. "Why did you leave them?" he asked.

"Why?" I shifted against the bed. Sharp heat poured down my right side, probably a broken rib or two. Dancing would be difficult for a few weeks. But the pain felt good, felt real, reminded me who I was and where I'd come from. "I don't know. Fleeting moments of insanity?" The real reason was far more complicated and considering the prince's punishment, I had no wish to reveal it.

"I burned them all." In three strides, he flung open the door and left with his brutal guards trailing behind him.

"But did you read them?!" I called.

No reply came. The door hung open for anyone to peer in and see the results of his visit.

A second wave of fire ignited my side. I gritted my teeth, tried to keep each breath shallow, and waited for the agony to pass.

At least, with the palace in mourning, and considering my apparent relationship with the queen, I might take the opportunity to withdraw to my room for a few days. Jubilant songs and sleight of hand were unlikely to be in high demand at Katina's passing ceremony.

I dragged my battered body off the floor, kicked the door closed, and collapsed back onto the bed. Bruises would heal, the pain would fade, the drama of the queen's death would pass. Everything would be controllable once more. Everything, except that prince.

In four years, he might have been the only real challenge I'd encountered. And I'd felt the sting of his sweet wrath. I smiled and licked blood from the cut again. Yes, Arin was going to be a problem, one I couldn't wait to sink my teeth into.

But first, I'd close my eyes and drift...

A BANGING on the door dragged me back to semiwakefulness, where everything ached. I stayed quiet, hoping whoever they were would assume I wasn't in my room and head off in search of me.

When I next opened my eyes, Ellyn was at my bedside, hands on her hips, face stern. "Lord Draven was attacked. Nobody had seen you. I thought—" Biting off her own words, she looked away.

"I'd been tossed in the dungeons again?" I croaked and tried to lever myself up. Arin's many gifted bruises sparked alive again, reminding me of his recent visit. I'd slept, but I wasn't sure for how long. All the days and nights had blurred together. Chills shivered through my body.

"No, I thought you'd been hurt too. And you have! Look at you!"

"Ah yes, well." I clutched my side and dropped back, against the wall. "I had nothing to do with Draven, and this is... tough love, I think..." Some dislodged part of my chest jabbed against a lung. I gasped, and winced, at the mercy of Ellyn's glare.

"You've been like this all day?" she demanded.

Day, night? What day even was it? "I have no idea."

"Remove your damn shirt." She caught the gleam of mischief in my eyes. "Do not jest, Lark, this is no laughing matter. Your breaths are rattling. I want to see how bad a state you're in." I struggled with my shirt while she clanged through my sparse cupboards. "Where are your basic supplies? Bandages, iodine? At least some henbane to numb the pain."

I winced, tugging on my shirt sleeve. "I rarely sleep here. Everything I need, I borrow from others."

She turned, about to plow into another round of chastising me, when her voice failed and her mouth fell open. I could pretend it was the bruises that had stolen her voice, or perhaps my handsome physique, but she'd seen the scars on my chest, hundreds of them. They weren't deep, but there were many. In soft candlelight, they disappeared. But cruel daylight was pouring through my window, making the scars shine. Ellyn saw it all.

"Who did that to you?" She knelt.

I huffed and brushed her reaching hand away. "They're old."

The bruises weren't though, and those caught fire again, wrenching the air from my lungs. She shouldn't have asked. We'd made a pact, not long after I'd arrived. I'd helped her out of a difficult situation. She'd owed me. And my only request was that she never ask about my past. As far as she was concerned, my life began four years ago, the day I'd walked into the Court of Love.

Nobody asked about the scars, ever.

Remembering her promise, she blinked away. "Some salts, and warm water, a little henbane for the pain. Hm... This will be easier at the bathing house. Can you make it there?"

"Leave me here, I'll be fine."

"No." She slammed a cold hand to my forehead. "You have a fever. Where's your coat?" She scooped it off the hook and made it clear she wasn't going to leave until I obeyed. Perhaps I did need some help.

"Lark, don't mess with me. This is serious."

"Fine." She helped me into my coat, then together we shuffled down the staff corridors, passing the second kitchens and laundry, toward the bathhouse.

As we approached the echoing baths, voices rang from inside, rolling toward us on warm, damp air. My stride faltered. "Ellyn, I can't be seen." The scars, the bruises... "Not in this light."

"Don't be silly. It will be fine." She laughed it off. "They won't mind. It's late in the morning, the palace guests are all occupied with lunch. It'll just be a few lords—"

Panic fluttered my heart, making my lungs ache. "No, you don't understand. I cannot be seen like this."

"Lark—"

I dug my heels into the polished tiled floor. "No."

How could I tell her that my power came from the fantasy, the act, the lies. If people saw me broken and battered, I'd lose my luster, my desire. They didn't want to see their fool limping, broken, in need of sympathy. If they saw that, they'd know I was just a man. And a weak one, at that. I didn't exist in that world. My world, and the world I spun for them, must always be a desirable dream.

Ellyn must have seen something close to panic on my face. "Very well." She glanced around us and spotted a side room. "In there."

The door opened into a small, enclosed pool room with mosaic-tiled steps leading down into deep, steaming turquoise water. "Get comfortable. I'll be right back with supplies." She was gone before I could protest.

The sooner I got this over with, the sooner Ellyn would patch me up and leave me alone to stew in self-pity.

I tugged off the coat, laid it over the bench, propped myself on a stool, and plucked off my trousers. Then, slowly, deliberately, I stepped into warm water. The baths were fed from hot springs. The hot, lapping water felt divine around my legs, and when submerged, the heat drew the aches from my muscles. I draped both arms along the cool sides of the pool and rested my head back.

Dripping water and my own steady heartbeat lulled my frayed, feverish mind. Ellyn had been right. I'd needed this. A little pennywort might take the edge of the pain. Some pain, I liked, but bruises were tiresome.

"Do not be alarmed."

I jolted against the side of the pool and looked up. Alarmed was an understatement.

A strange little smirk tugged at Prince Arin's lips, one I hadn't seen from him before. He plucked his white cloak from his neck and hung it on the rack of hooks above the bench.

"I met the serving girl you are known to be familiar with and asked after your whereabouts," he explained.

My thoughts raced, my chest heaved, and heart thumped so loudly he surely heard it. "Your Highness."

"Ah, now the fool is respectful. It only took a beating to bring it out of you."

He was alone. Why was he alone? And he was here. Searching for me? Hadn't he already punished me enough?

What was this?

His fingers pried at his jacket buttons next, flicking each one open. Surely, he did not intend to bathe alongside me? There were perfectly good baths near his chambers, salted and fragranced for the royals. Unless his punishment wasn't over. I'd play his games, but I was in no condition to do so now.

"I can leave, if you wish." The rumble in my voice echoed around the tiled walls, sounding gruffer than I'd intended.

"Didn't I just say I was looking for you?" He pulled off his fine white jacket and gold doublet beneath, then unlaced the undershirt.

This was a trap. It had to be. Alone, he might accuse me of anything. He'd already tried to have me hanged for murdering his mother. I had to leave. Yet... How many chances would I get to bathe with Prince Arin? And why now, what did he want?

He tugged his laces loose, crossed his arms, and pulled his

shirt off, over his head, revealing a stunning torso, with enough muscle that he'd outwrestle me, if it came to it. Flawless skin gleamed golden with a hint of his father's desert-touched tone, but most of him was pale, like his mother. The way the light played over his chest reminded me of honey falling from a spoon, and how I might lap it up with my tongue.

I turned my face away and swallowed a rising knot of panic. It wasn't often I lost my voice, or my wits, but Arin had stolen both. The clever thing to do would be to climb from the water, throw on my clothes, and leave. But if I left the water, he'd see the scars, and the bruises he'd dealt me. At least, with my shoulders beneath the surface, he couldn't see the marks he'd made.

Whatever he was here for, it was unlikely to be friendly. I'd dealt with worse than him, but few had caught me so unawares. Or vulnerable.

"You implied, the other day, how I might be watching you," he continued. Where my voice had grated in the quiet, his flowed with a lyrical quality.

I kept my gaze fixed on the patterned tiles across the room and not on the prince who had by now removed his trousers, because he was already descending step by step into the water. I didn't need to see him naked, or close to it. Of course, there was nothing unusual about men sharing baths. Unless one of them happened to be a prince, and the other his pet jester. Not least because of the rumors.

He'd been so careful not to be seen, and now he was everywhere.

None of this made any sense. Arin's behavior was not how I'd imagined, or been told, in his absence. The Prince of Love was kind and caring, everyone had assured me, since I'd asked in the absence of meeting the man for myself. He certainly did not beat his court fools and then bathe with them afterward.

He disturbed the water. It sloshed against my chest. Did he want to see the evidence of his beating, was that why he was here?

"What if I am?" he asked, gliding into sight and resting himself against the opposite side of the pool. He reached back and pulled the tie holding his hair free, then gave his head a shake, spilling golden locks to his shoulders, exactly how I'd imagined.

By Dallin, the man was made of honey and sunlight and was far too pretty.

He gazed back, waiting for me to speak. I'd forgotten what we'd been discussing—something about him watching me? He waited patiently for the answer, blinking slowly, but I'd lost my voice.

He raised a wet hand and swept his fingers through his hair, upsetting its perfect gleam, leaving darker, damp streaks behind.

I swallowed, doing nothing to smooth my throat's tightness. "I fear your arrival has rendered me speechless."

There was that little tease of a smile again, and despite the pain he'd dealt me, or perhaps because of it, delicate tendrils of lust shivered down my spine. His being here alone, that new, teasing smile, and how he'd stripped off his layers of royalty, leaving them outside the pool... This was a side of Arin I hadn't seen—unsurprising since I hadn't witnessed much of the prince. But the beating, and now this... I sensed he might be trying to manipulate me for reasons yet unknown. The Riddle of the Prince Behind the Door had just become more fascinating. And alluring.

"I know you are not as dimwitted as you would seem in

this moment," he said. "So allow me to be clear. We are not so different, you and I."

That was anything but clear. "How so?"

"We'll come to that, but first, tell me of Draven."

"Draven?" My thoughts stuttered. He couldn't know I'd seen the attack, or the aftermath of it. Could he? Did he think me responsible? "Draven...?" I attempted to shrug and deny I knew the lord.

"Lie to me, and our little tête-à-tête is over."

I wanted this to end, didn't I? He had me tied in knots, I *should* want this to be over, but as I stood in the warm waters, the prince within reach of my fingertips, I'd rarely been more exposed. And aroused. Blood thrummed through my veins, and my cock was halfway to revealing exactly how stimulating Prince Arin's company was.

"We met at the ball, Draven and I," I said. "I know little of the man, just that he has an appetite for the male form."

Arin's gaze skipped over my face. I suspected he didn't believe me. "He asked for an audience with me, to speak to me regarding my fool. Why do you think that is?"

Had Draven thought to tell Arin all he knew? *You're the traitor's son. I hadn't been sure, until now.* "I cannot fathom. Perhaps ask him?"

"Yes, well, I would, but the attack left him speechless." Arin peered through golden lashes, and that glare burrowed inside, beneath all my many layers. "As you well know, Lark."

A second thrill surged through me, conspiring with the thrill and fear of his alarming arrival.

The assailant leaning over Draven, the twig in the prince's cloak—the same plant that made up the hedge maze. I'd been blind not to see it before. He'd been hooded and masked, but I'd seen his eyes, both beautiful and haunting. His gait when he'd run, fast, light, and how he'd known how to vanish inside the hedge maze.

It all pointed to one fact.

Arin had attacked Draven.

He'd cut his throat, almost killed him. Would have, if I hadn't interrupted.

My heart thumped harder, quickening my breaths. This was not how a Prince of Love should behave.

Arin's hint of a smile grew. He pushed from the side of the pool and within two steps, he stood close enough to fill my vision. Water dripped from his damp hair, over eyes sparkling with intelligence. He waited. I imagined the throb of his heat washing over me. If he shifted another inch closer, and he'd feel exactly how hard I was for him.

Prince Arin knew a whole lot more about me and his court than I'd thought possible. And right then, he had me in his grasp. I had to do something to trip him up, knock him off his stride and give myself room to think and breathe around him.

"What was it about you Lord Draven wished to discuss, Lark?" Arin asked.

It seemed he did not get the answers he'd hoped for before trying to kill Lord Draven. And now, I was under his scrutiny. Was that why he was here, to cut my throat too? I didn't see a knife, but I hadn't seen one when he'd knelt over Draven either.

"How are we alike, Prince?" I raised my hand from the water, fingers curled beside his cheek—not yet touching. Would he strike me again, if I did? As he blinked, dislodging droplets of water from his lashes, I dared touch his temple— so warm—and skimmed my fingers down his face, under his jaw, following its fine line. I'd expected him to stop me, but he hadn't moved, and now the natural bow of his mouth drew my fingertips toward them.

By Dallin, his lips were peach-soft.

I ached to taste them, to slip my tongue between them. My cock throbbed, and my whole body burned for the forbidden, the untouchable, the riddle of the prince who cut throats. What would his kiss be like? Hard and fast, or soft and slow? Would he hurt me? I might ask him to.

He caught my chin—as he had when I'd lain in my bed—stepped forward, and pinned me to the side of the pool. Lean, hard muscle pushed in, his thigh, his hip, his... cock, erect and against mine, trapping it to my hip. A gasp shuddered through me, almost a moan.

His gaze searched my eyes, and all his lofty princeliness faded, softening his face. It seemed he battled with something, perhaps his own desires. I hadn't known he preferred men, but his dick made that fact very clear. If he kissed me, I wouldn't be able to hold back. I wanted him, his hands on me, his mouth under mine, wanted to hear and feel him moan, his body slick against me. I wanted his hand at my throat, holding me down, his cock in my grip, my ass. I breathed hard, lost to a new scorching agony he'd ignited inside me.

His beautiful lips parted—

The door to the pool swung open, letting in a blast of cold air, and one of the men who'd beaten me the day before.

"These bathing pools are unbecoming of..." The brute trailed off at the sight of us. "Prince Arin?"

Arin huffed a dismissive laugh and moved away. "My mistake." He strode up the steps. Water cascaded down his body. He made no attempt to hide his jutting dick.

I wet my lips and forced my gaze away, trying to wrestle rampaging desires back under control. It was rare for someone to fire me up like he had. I couldn't remember the last time I'd been so aroused. Not in the last four years.

The prince dried and dressed himself. "Good day, Fool," Arin said, back to his cold, hard, distant self.

In moments, Arin and his guard had gone, leaving the echo of his farewell in my mind and my dick demanding to be satisfied.

Alone, rattled, confused, inexplicably enthralled, and painfully aroused, I stared at the wall. He was playing me. I should hate him. I did, but also... didn't. It was a madness. The madness of the Court of Love.

I grasped my cock in my right hand, clung to the poolside with my left, and pumped. Faster, harder. Someday soon, I'd hold him down, on his knees, and slide my dick between his peachy lips, and he'd take it, gag for it, his hard cock all the proof I needed he'd wanted it too.

Pleasure trilled, lighting up my spine, singing through my veins. More, I needed more. I lifted my left arm and bit down into my bicep. Pain sparked, danced through my veins, and I came, gasping free of the bite and shuddering hard, lost to the dream of seeing my cum on Prince Arin's soft lips.

But with desire sated, and my heart slowing, reality clawed back in.

What if I'd met my nemesis in Prince Arin? What if he knew who I was, but even more than that, what if he knew why I was in his court?

Until now, I'd been the one in control of the Court of Love. I sensed that was about to change.

And if Draven had told Arin anything of my past, then I'd lose more than a finger. I'd lose my head.

CHAPTER 6

*I*t rained the day of the queen's passing ceremony, as though the skies grieved, their tears seeking to dampen Katina's pyre.

I hung back from the guests, royal and common alike. My presence didn't seem fitting. I wasn't of their court, my family wasn't from this land, and there was no place for an entertainer here, at a time of grieving. Yet, I couldn't seem to bring myself to leave.

After retreating under the cover of a large gnarled oak, I watched the procession of people march toward the flower meadows, where the pyre was stacked and waiting for its flame.

Countless brightly colored umbrellas bobbed, like a field of primroses. The passing ceremony was joyous in its colors, but solemn in its silence.

Rain soaked my hair and clothes, and a chill gnawed on my bones, although the weather wasn't cold. The cold was within me.

Days and nights had come and gone since the tete-a-tete with Arin in the bathing pools. I hadn't seen him since, or much of anyone. I'd kept to my room, waiting for the bruises to fade. Ellyn had dropped by, checking I hadn't found more trouble. After Arin's timely appearance at the baths, I'd begun to suspect Ellyn might have Arin's ear as well as mine. It would explain how Arin had known where I'd be, and possibly knew more than he should, for someone who'd been hiding for years.

I'd have to be more careful around Ellyn. I should have known better than to make a friend. They were always weaknesses, in the end.

A torchbearer lit the pyre. Flames raced up toward the black skies. Some spluttered under the deluge, but the fire took hold. The crowds parted a little, easing back from the heat, and there, lit by the fire's glow, Arin stood beside his father, head bowed. The grieving son. The heir. Not so kindly and innocent as I'd been told.

Had he tried to kill Draven, could he have killed his mother? Why though? What drove him? Who was he, really? So many questions.

Questions were all that prince ever gave me.

"You're overdue," a gruff, familiar voice rumbled over my left shoulder. I didn't need to look to know who it was. I'd been expecting Danyal days ago. I'd been due to meet up with him after I'd first taken Draven into the gardens as my alibi.

"I've been busy." I flicked my fingers at the constant stream of people marching along the path beside us.

"All the more reason to report." Something cold and hard dug into my lower back. A blade. "Imagine our beneficiary's rage when he heard of the queen's death from careless gossip and not his spy in the heart of their court."

I didn't have to imagine it. I'd felt that rage before, and tucked my mutilated hand out of sight under my folded arm.

"He has waited long enough. Tell me everything you have learned since our last meeting."

"Here? It seems a little exposed—" The dagger's point jabbed deeper. "Fine. The queen was killed, assailant unknown. I was a suspect, spent a night in the dungeon, but managed to escape that unfortunate turn of events and have the king admit to my innocence. You may tell our beneficiary exactly that."

"He's not interested in stroking your ego."

"Hm, no, not my ego—"

"Get on with it."

I kept my gaze fixed on the prince and spilled all the secrets I'd collected from the court. Misbehaving lords, families riddled with debt, the child born out of wedlock, the wrong man beaten, how a lady opened her legs for coin, and how another liked to ride her husband like a horse, reins and all. All the dirty little secrets from behind the scenes and between the sheets. I cherished each one, nurtured them, and gave them up to Danyal, when the time was right.

"Is that all?" Danyal grumbled, dissatisfied. "Tits and dicks?"

"Tits and dicks is what the Court of Love is good at." The words had barely left my lips when the blade dug in deeper, piercing skin. I jerked away, but Danyal's hand locked on my shoulder, hauling me back. "The king is mine!" I blurted. "I control him. Is that not enough?"

"It's a start. And now the queen is out of play. How fortunate. What of the prince?"

Arin, ha. Every time Danyal asked, and every time I told him the same. The prince remained behind his door. "He continues to hide in his room." I nodded toward the pyre. "This is the first time I've seen him."

"Our beneficiary needs more. The prince is an unknown, and we both know how he dislikes unknowns."

Beneficiary. As though saying his name might summon him beneath this very tree. I shuddered at the thought. "Then perhaps he should come to the Court of Love and speak with Arin himself."

"Careful, *Fool*." Danyal's warm breath fluttered over my ear. "Or he *will* come, and sever your tongue as well as your finger."

Prince Arin chose that moment to look up, right through a gap in the people. His silvery gaze locked on mine. At so far a distance, with a lawn, pathway, and many umbrellas between us, he couldn't have heard my discussion, but his eyes narrowed, as though he knew how I conspired against him.

He likely saw the man standing in shadow close behind me. That razor-sharp mind of his would be working to riddle us out.

I wanted him to *see*. Although it went against what I should want. That was it, exactly as he'd said. He and I, we were the same. Both of us locked in a race to figure the other out first. He knew I wasn't just a fool, and I knew he was so much more than the Prince Behind a Door.

"Our beneficiary wants you to return," Danyal said.

Ice encased my heart. "What?"

"Close your matters here. You are to return in three days."

Three days... No. It wasn't enough. Three months, three years. It would never be long enough. I couldn't go back. I couldn't step back into darkness when I'd been so long in the light. "There's more to discover, more secrets—"

"No, you've been given his instructions. It's over. All of it. Come home."

Arin's gaze narrowed further. He'd seen my expression, seen the shock, then the horror. I flung a smile onto my face, but it was too late. Arin said something to his father, and without waiting for his reply, Arin swept through the crowd, white cloak bellowing—coming straight for me.

"Go, Danyal," I whispered. "Now."

"Three days, *Lark*."

I glared over my shoulder, fixing the old man in my glare. He was riddled with scars, each one a gift from our beneficiary. Eight short slashes marked his cheek, one for every man he'd killed. I didn't plan to be among them. "I can't go back, it's not done."

"You don't get a choice. Three days." Danyal hurried down the slope, unhitched his horse from a fence rail, and swung into the saddle. His mount's hooves still thumped the ground as Arin marched across the lawn and squared up to me under the tree. Mud sullied his cloak, staining all that pristine white. Such a terrible color to keep clean.

I bowed low. "Prince Arin."

"Who was that?" He scanned the road, but Danyal was long gone.

"Who was who?"

"Which one of us is the fool?"

"Oh... that man, just now? Yes, a hapless vagrant, I think. Not of your concern."

"With a horse?" Arin frowned.

"His only companion. Truly, a sad tale of one man's descent into drunkenness and poverty, his horse his only company."

Arin huffed. He stumbled some in the mud, stomping on the corner of his cloak, then cursed when he saw the stains. "Your lies insult us both," he snapped.

"Why would I lie about a man and his horse, Your Highness?" I chuckled, drawing several disapproving glares from the passing crowd. Enough to ruffle Arin's feathers. He noticed them glaring and stepped away from me.

He didn't like to be seen with me. But alone, he was happy enough to get up close and very personal. Interesting.

"Why, indeed." He hesitated, torn between interrogating me further and returning to his father's side, where he should be. "Are you going to lie and tell me how that man didn't threaten you?"

"Threaten me?" I laughed. "I think I would have noticed. He was asking for the way to the inn, you see. That terrible drinking habit—"

"Then I suppose that is not blood there, on your coat?"

I followed his gaze. A dark patch had bloomed through my sodden coat. Now that he'd mentioned it, the burn from the dagger against my back hadn't faded, despite the blade having departed with its owner. "Ah yes, a fall... earlier. The rain has made the paths treacherous. You should be careful, my prince. Your cloak is already stained. That is the trouble with white, no? So easily sullied."

He glared, all fierce and angry, his cheeks flushed, making those freckles stand out. Rain had plastered his hair to his face and neck. He looked just like he had in the bathing house, damp and hot, although clearly not aroused this time. "You can't help yourself, can you? The lies fall from your lips like rain from the skies."

"I am but an entertainer, a story teller, an artist, if you will." I bowed again. "If you'll excuse me, I have this evening's passing feast to prepare for."

I left the prince standing alone in the rain, and almost made it back to the palace gates without glancing back. Almost. When I did turn, seeking his gaze, he stood with his back to the palace, staring the way of Danyal's departure.

Arin was too quick, too clever, too ruthless. And in three

days, I'd have to leave his rotten court for one a thousand times worse.

Three days were not enough to know the Prince of Love.

But three days were all I had.

And Danyal was right. I didn't have a choice.

CHAPTER 7

"*E*llyn, my only true friend, do you have some time?" I'd caught her moments after her shift, her hair messy, clothes ripe with kitchen smells, and her eyes heavy-lidded.

She unlaced her apron and hung it with the others in the pantry. "If it's a favor you're after, I surely have none left to give."

"I promise, it's not that."

She left the pantry and headed back into the main kitchen with its long preparation table and several other staff, kneading dough for pies or bread, I wasn't sure. "What is it then?" she asked.

"A stroll into town, my treat. Dinner, some mead? It's been too long since we've let our hair down."

She stopped at the table's edge and glowered. "No strings attached?"

"I... well—"

"Lark, catch!" One of the other kitchen staff tossed a potato. I caught it, and the two more she threw my way, juggled them for a few cycles, and flung them back. The woman squealed, attracting the attention of a few of the other staff about to retire for the night.

With all eyes on me, I picked up a paring knife, and two others that lay nearby, and flicked all three into the air, juggling them. Chaos controlled, the stakes were high. If my timing failed, I'd potentially lose another finger. The little knives spun. My onlookers *oohed*.

"Stop," Ellyn said, a plea in her voice.

"How can I, when you haven't given me your answer?" The little knives danced between my hands.

"Why do you want to go to town?"

I kept the knives spinning, catching each by their handles. Their weight, their length, their speed. Beautiful, and deadly. One wrong move, one ill-timed throw—

"Lark, stop, please," Ellyn whined. "Before you get hurt." Her concern was genuine; such a shame the rest of her wasn't.

"Say yes." I juggled faster, until they were a blur of steel.

"Ellyn, make him stop!" Someone squealed in delight and horror. What a wonderful combination that was.

"All right, fine! I'll go."

The first knife, I caught and flung at the wall, and the second and third flew as true. All three thrummed in the wall, in one tight spot. Applause exploded. *"Oh Lark, you're crazy. Lark, you tease."*

I bowed and hooked Ellyn by the arm. "Come, then. An evening of merriment with your favorite jester is afoot."

ESCAPING palace life was not as easy for me as for the rest of the staff, or the royals. At the beck and call of those in the palace, every hour of every day, I rarely had time to visit the local town and sample its many delights. In fact, the whole town was a delight. The people here didn't care who I was. They didn't demand I sing and dance, or perform for them in any way. In fact, they may even have loathed me, which was a refreshing change.

Ellyn and I strode beneath flickering streetlamps and wove through early evening revelers to get to our favored inn. Here, I often played and won at cards and pried coins from drunken fingers. I was not the palace fool here at Overlook Inn, just another man, trying to get by.

Ellyn and I joined a few familiars playing five-finger, and with the wine flowing, we eased into the evening, winning some, losing others. As time wore on and the night darkened outside, the tavern grew warm and the voices loud. When Ellyn sagged in her chair, I scooted her away from the card game and propped her at a booth, this one at the back, where it was quieter. Sliding in beside her, I topped up her cup, then my own, and we both sat back, boots up on the opposite bench.

"Why have you brought me here, Lark? Tell me the truth."

"To have some fun, why else? And to thank you, for caring." Even though it had been lies.

"But I know you." She wagged a finger. "This is not that," she slurred, making it sound like *thish-ish-not-thad*.

I was not often the betrayed, more often the betrayer. So learning she had Prince Arin's ear, and was in all likelihood telling him my whereabouts, was a new sensation for me. "I may have an ulterior motive."

She smirked. "I knew it. Out with it then."

"Arin."

She blinked. "The prince?"

"The very same."

"What of him?"

"Tell me about him."

She slumped back in the booth and sighed. "What do I know that you don't?"

"Indeed, what *do* you know that I don't?"

"Oh... I see. You're trying to talk me around in circles. I've heard that about you. Clever tongue, they say."

I laughed at that. Clever tongue, indeed. "Would I do such a thing to a friend?"

"Are we friends, though?" She sobered a little, but sipped her wine to hide it. "Because I don't know with you. All this..." She waved a hand at my face, as though unveiling a mask. "I don't know what's real."

"And I thought I couldn't be fooled." My tone shut her down. She blinked large eyes, perhaps hearing or seeing something in me she hadn't seen before. "He asked you to spy on me, didn't he."

"Asked?" She snorted and harrumphed back in the seat, losing her smile. "A prince does not *ask* anything."

"You did tell him." It hurt some, that she'd betray me. I'd trusted few among the Court of Love, but she'd been among them. "He's been watching me through you."

"I told him... some things, yes. But it's not as though I had a choice."

I picked up my cup and downed my wine, sour as it was. "How long?"

"A while," she said, sulkily.

That was how he'd known so much about me when I knew nothing about him. That was about to change. "Why me?" I asked. "Why did I catch his eye?"

She chuckled. "You're you... Whose eye have you not caught?"

"No, with him, it's different. He's using me," I admitted.

"And I need to know why." I had three days to know what he was planning, if anything.

"Arin is... He's not like the rest of them."

Someone at the bar laughed loud and hard. When I looked back at Ellyn again, she was watching the men and woman jest. Market farmers, most of them. Fruit and flower sellers. "How is he not like the rest of them?" I asked.

"His aides say he barely talks to them. He doesn't have company. Sometimes he's..." She trailed off, possibly wondering too late if she'd already said too much.

"I promise not to tell," I lied. "Go on."

"I don't know if I should."

"Ellyn, this is me. We are friends, are we not?" A friendship she'd betrayed. "Trust me."

"The lords and ladies think he hides in his room, y'all think he's behind his door, like a recluse. But he's rarely there." She'd whispered that last part, as though anyone here cared where the prince was or wasn't.

"Then where is he?"

"Where else can he go, but here, in town?" she said.

No, that didn't ring true. Arin would draw too much attention. I'd have known if he'd visited the inns and taverns. But she clearly assumed it. "Do you know why?"

"No, of course not. He doesn't tell me anything. He just... he asks about you. Maybe he comes here, like us, to drink and make merry, to be someone else?"

"He can do that at dinner every night, like his father." No, there was more to the man, more to all of this. Arin was too clever to tell Ellyn more than he needed to. I wouldn't get anything else of use from her.

"He always asks about you, what you're like, who you spend time with."

"And what did you tell him?"

"The truth, I suppose."

I chuckled and peered into my drink. "Well then, is it any wonder he hates me?"

She gave me a strange look, a look of confusion and disbelief. "He doesn't hate you, Lark—"

"No?" The remains of my bruises declared otherwise. "He is not what he appears, Ellyn. I cannot get the measure of him. He's dangerous. You should be careful around duplicitous men like him."

She blinked, then frowned and tilted her head, studying my face. "He said almost those exact words about you."

"He thinks *me* dangerous?" I laughed to cover the fact he was right. "Why?"

"I don't know, precisely, just that he said..." She teased her cup, rolling its contents.

"He said what, Ellyn? You cannot leave me hanging."

"When now I've said too much... So, what's one more? He said you are 'a beautiful lie.'"

My thoughts tumbled over themselves and slammed to a halt. "'A beautiful lie'?" I echoed. "He said those words, referring to me?"

"Well, yes, so you see why I don't think he hates you, hm? In fact, I think you fascinate him. It's all that pretty. The both of you." She pulled a face. "By Dallin, I'm surrounded by hopeless, pretty men who think with their dicks and not their brains."

I chuckled and refilled my cup. The prince had surprised me again. This was becoming a theme with him.

"What...? Why do you laugh?" She giggled.

"It's as though you speak of an entirely different man to the person he's shown himself to be."

"I've worked in the palace since my twelfth year. I may not

be Arin's aide, but I know him well enough. He wasn't always so aloof and distant. Something happened, I fear, not long before you arrived and charmed your way among the court."

"Something like what?"

"The previous jester..."

"What of him?" I knew they'd had one, and he'd left, but little else. He'd been my predecessor, and the past was not my focus. The past could not be changed. But the future was always fluid.

"Oh, well. I suppose, he was meant to have just left... But some of us think he may have dispatched himself."

"He what?"

She mimed drawing a blade across her throat.

"Why am I just hearing about this now?"

"You never seemed that interested."

"No, because I believed *he'd left*." I should have loosened Ellyn's tongue with wine more often.

"Maybe he did." She shrugged.

"Wait... Don't tell me he and Arin were... close?"

She shrugged again and hid a smile behind taking a drink. "It's all just rumor. And he was a terrible jester, not like you. You're the best." She patted my shoulder, then slumped against my side.

"Oh, well, that's all right then. I'm sure he deserved his end." By Dallin, what if Arin had been the one to dispatch him? Was that my fate? But again, why? And now I had a mere three days to discover the man's deepest secrets before my own fate caught up with me. What if Arin did kill the previous jester, then went into hiding, and only now reappeared to try and kill Draven, and perhaps his own mother? And me? No, that seemed a stretch, even for my imagination. "I am far too drunk for rumors and heresy," I muttered. "Tell me, Ellyn, if you know him so well, do you think Arin is a bad person, or a good one?"

"Good." She didn't hesitate. "He's good, but he's got muddled up," she slurred.

"And me?" I asked, levering her back a bit so I could see her face. "Am I good?"

"Of course!" Well then, she was wrong, and a terrible judge of character. "And I'm sorry, for telling Arin things about you. We're still friends aren't we, Lark?"

I didn't have friends. I had pawns, each one put in play where I needed them to be. "Shall we return to the palace?"

"I did enjoy this."

"You were with me. What's not to enjoy?" I pulled her from the booth and we stumbled from the Overlook together. The sweet-smelling evening air cleared some of my tipsiness. I'd learned a great deal about Prince Arin. He hadn't always been this icy, somewhat distant prince. The death of his previous jester, or another event around that time, prior to my arrival, had forced him to hide behind his chamber door. I'd also learned he'd been curious about me for a long time.

His beautiful lie.

Ellyn could only have told him what she knew about me, and none of that was real.

I still had the upper hand, the control. I just needed him to know it.

WE CAME upon my door first. Ellyn tripped, fell against the wall, and almost collapsed in a heap of giggles. I propped her up. She flicked my nose. "Why have you never propositioned me?" she asked.

"Ah, well my dear, for one, you have no interest in what's between my legs—despite its magnificence." She snorted. I pretended to be offended and reached for my door. "And B—"

"Two."

"What?"

"You said one, so the next is two—"

I swung the door open, revealing the striking outline of Arin standing at my window—and slammed the door closed again, sealing him inside and us outside.

"And two...?" Ellyn prompted, slurring.

"What?"

Arin was in my room. Again. But without his guards this time. When without his guards, he didn't seem as inclined to have them beat me senseless. Was this a replay of the pool then, or was he here to deliver a second slap to my face?

"You said there was another reason you haven't, you know..." Ellyn made an alarming grasping motion with her hands.

"Well, if that's how you think it's done then I made the right decision not to seduce you." I slipped an arm around her shoulder and scooted her along the corridor, away from my room. "I haven't propositioned you because I know there's a woman you're fond of and I do not wish to complicate our friendship." I gave her a small shove in the general direction of the servants' quarters. "Good evening, now. Off to bed, you go. Do not blame me for the headache you will surely get..."

She threw a wave over her shoulder and swaggered out of sight. Which left me in the corridor, and Arin in my room. I'd swallowed a great deal of wine. Speaking with Arin now was a terrible idea. Perhaps I could sleep in the gardens? No. I had under three days remaining. I couldn't afford to squander this opportunity.

I opened the door, strode in, and peered into the prince's cool blue eyes. "We really must stop meeting like this or there will be rumors."

"Is that a threat?" Goodness, his smooth voice was delicious.

An ill-timed urge to laugh twitched my lips. So severe, this prince. Did he ever jest? Perhaps I should poke his nose and see.

"Are you... laughing?" he asked, golden brows digging into his smooth forehead.

"Not yet, but give me a moment... I'm rather drunk. And you'll find my tongue and a great many other parts of me exceptionally unrestrained while intoxicated—more unrestrained than usual." I circled my hand in the air. "Shall we just assume you're here to threaten me behind a veil of thin insults, after which we can both retire for the night?" I slumped to the edge of my bed and sighed with my whole body.

He hadn't moved. Still stood by the window, peering down his nose.

If I looked up, would I find him amused or furious? When I was gone, I'd miss our little games, despite not knowing the rules he played by.

He stepped closer, stopping directly in front of me. I stared at his buttoned middle, his jacket pinched over his hips, and his crotch, which was far less interested in me than the last time I'd seen it, although not without a noticeable presence behind the white fabric. If he tipped my chin up, I might do something foolish, like kiss him.

"This is rather perfect," he said, then strode for the door. "Follow me, Lark." He tossed a devilish smirk over his shoulder, the kind of suggestive smile I'd be a fool to follow. "You seem the sort to live without regrets. And you'll regret missing this."

The prince was likely responsible for several deaths, possibly even his mother's and my predecessor's. Yet, even sober, after that look he'd flung at me, I'd have gone with him. I supposed that did make me a fool.

CHAPTER 8

*A*rin lifted his hood and strode along the palace corridors, through archways, leading me on a merry chase through the palace after midnight. He didn't slow, didn't glance behind to see if I followed, just kept on moving.

When we came to the palace library's huge oak door, he pushed through, swept down dark aisles, and stopped at a bookcase tucked away in an unlit corner. I caught up, breathing fast, and spun, wondering why on earth he'd dragged me into a corner of the library. Perhaps I was about to sample that delightful cock of his. Hm, him on his knees, or me on mine? Although, he wasn't paying attention to me, preferring instead to be staring at the books.

He pulled one from among the others, and the shelf clicked, jolting outward on hidden hinges. Another secret. The palace was full of them. Arin caught my eye, smiled, and slipped behind the bookcase, disappearing in a swirl of white cloak.

To show me such secrets, he surely trusted me. This was good.

Or was it a trap?

Damn, I couldn't think.

In too deep and too curious to turn back, I followed him into a cool, dark tunnel, its sides hewn from rock. The prince's steps echoed ahead, guiding me through the heavy gloom. A downward slope tilted underfoot, and the tunnel corkscrewed back on itself, spiraling down. Then a rumbling began, like that of a sleeping dragon.

In all likelihood, I followed a dangerous man into the dark. A man who appeared to be one thing in one moment, and quite the opposite in the next. Excitement, and the thrill of the unknown, set my veins ablaze.

Beautiful lie... He thought me beautiful, and a liar, a thorn on the stem of a rose.

The tunnel spun. I reached out, bracing myself. So very drunk. This was a terrible idea.

I moved on. Down and down, we went. Where was he taking me?

Distant light flickered ahead. Arin walked toward it, hands outstretched, stroking the walls. He'd been here so many times he hadn't needed the light to guide his steps.

Salt dried the air, and as we emerged from the dark into moonlight, the rumbling made sense. Dallin's great ocean shimmered beneath the moon and beyond a small, pebbly beach, the ocean's waves thundered, smashing over enormous jagged rocks. By the time those waves reached the shore, they were tamed, gentle things.

It was... beautiful.

My steps slowed as I tried to absorb the sight.

Arin strode down the beach, toward where the waves lapped at gleaming shingle, as though he meant to walk right out to sea.

I jogged after him, uncertain, enthralled, maybe dreaming.

He waded into the water up to his knees and stopped,

cloak swirling around him. The moon had bleached the whole world white and grey, so that he stood in monochrome and was all the more dramatic for his lack of color. His smile, when he tilted his head and allowed me to see it, belonged to a free man. A man I was just now meeting. The true Prince Arin, revealed here, under moonlight, like a spell had been lifted.

I was dreaming, asleep, drunk in my bed. It was the only explanation.

Or Arin had been replaced by another man altogether, one made of starlight and dreams. He was... spellbinding.

His grin bloomed, turning sly. He waded back out of the water, up the beach, and stopped in front of me. "Where's your voice now, Lark?"

"I fear you've stolen it." Perhaps along with my dark heart, but certainly my wits.

He laughed and the soft roll of it was new to me too. This man was a stranger again, and in that moment, together on his secret beach, I ached to know him.

"Who *are* you?" I asked.

His laughter lessened to a chuckle, as he shook his head. "I am the fool, and you are the prince." I frowned, and he laughed at that too, so freely I envied him. "No questions, hm. Let's not ruin this with unwanted truths."

"All right." Whatever game this was, my racing heart revealed how eager I was to play it. "Then if you are the fool, you should entertain me, no?"

He eyed me sideways, then relented with a chuckle. "Very well."

I hadn't expected him to play along.

He untied the cloak from around his neck and tossed it on the shingles. He pushed up his sleeves and rolled his hand in a bow. "What would you have me do, Your Highness?"

What trickery was this? Prince Arin had a sense of humor now? "Forgive my delay, I'm trying to fathom if I've lost my mind."

"I can see you're struggling. Allow me to aid you..." He studied the pebbles at his feet and selected three that were around the size of an egg, then, weighing them in his hands, he tossed one in the air and tried to follow it with a second, but instead, dropped them all.

I fought a laugh. "Are you trying to juggle? I fear you may have chosen an ill-suited profession."

"Wait..." He pointed. "I have this." After scooping up the stones, he rolled his shoulders and tried again. All three pebbles thumped into the shingle.

Folding my arms, I watched him try again, and again, until all the laughter snuffed out of his silvery eyes and frustration settled there instead. He wasn't going to surrender.

After another failed attempt, I lunged and snatched the three pebbles from their tumbling, juggled them with ease, and then launched all three into the waves, one after another.

He stared. "I almost had it."

"No, you really did not. But truly, your failure was spectacular. You should be very proud."

Laughter glittered back in his eyes. "You make it appear easy."

I arched an eyebrow. "I make a great many things appear easy, but many of them are exactly the opposite."

"Yes, I imagine they are."

His tone had changed, quietened, becoming thoughtful. Close enough to be scandalous in court, but here, on his beach, nobody saw. Just the stars and the moon, our permanent voyeur. We were not prince and fool, but two men, two almost-strangers.

My heart was a drum in my ears, hot blood in my veins, everywhere, all at once. "Why am I here, Arin?"

"I said no questions, didn't I?" he teased, eyebrow arched.

I dipped my chin. "Very well."

"If I cannot juggle, then I'll tell a tale of two kingdoms. You like stories, Lark, do you not?"

Hm, a story? "I do."

"Then you may judge mine." He stepped back and rolled his shoulders, as though freeing himself of another skin. "On the surface, all is well between these two kingdoms, but beneath, an old rift grows wider. We'll call them the Court of Flowers and the Court of Storms. How does that sound?"

My heart fluttered, but the thoughts in my head? They were dagger-sharp and focused all on Arin. "Delightful."

"The Court of Storms churns with chaos, and the Court of Flowers, well... They are the flicker of hope in the darkness." He paced, and his boots crunched in the shingle. "How am I doing, so far?"

"Suitably dramatic, but lacking a figure your audience might sympathize with."

"Ah yes, the protagonist. If we can call him such." He turned his face toward the sea. "A prince, although few would know it. He is afraid, you see? Afraid for so long, it's a part of him, in his veins, his bones. He hides it, hides all of himself, so the world won't know, so the Court of Storms don't sense weakness. But it's already too late. The storms have spread far beyond their borders, raining poison down on all they touch. It happened so slowly nobody noticed."

My heart thumped louder and louder, his story so keen, and so true, he might as well have been calling me out right there. "Alas, I fear the story is too bleak, it needs a happy ending or your audience will not return for more."

"Well, it's not over. There is hope..." Arin threw me his

89

radiant smile. "Our prince is not alone in his fear. There is one other. The most unlikely of heroes. Always observed but too easily overlooked. Seen in one breath, dismissed in the next. The perfect distraction."

"A beautiful lie?" It was out before I'd thought to keep it from my lips. Arin's glare cut to me.

His eyes widened, then narrowed as he regained his storytelling composure. "Yes... The beautiful lie."

My heart thrashed behind my ribs. "I fear fools can never be heroes, only pawns in a prince's game."

"Not this one, for you see, he is a fool in one court, but quite something else in another."

He knew.

He knew everything.

He knew my life among his court was a lie, but worse, he knew where I came from. The so-called Court of Storms from his tale—the Court of Pain. All my efforts to fool everyone, my endless games, dances to distract and delight, kisses placed on the backs of fingers while I picked their pockets for secrets. The Court of Pain was the approaching storm, and I, its silent lightning.

He should kill me here and let the ocean take my remains. If I were him, I wouldn't have waited this long. How was I still breathing?

The knowledge shone in his silver eyes, playing along the edge of his soft, honest smile.

I turned on my heel. It was over. I couldn't stay a moment longer. The net I'd feared had been tightening, had snapped closed. Arin had me.

"Lark," he called, raising his voice over the sound of the crashing waves.

I could have ignored him, pretended I hadn't heard, but while my head told me to run, my heart ached to stay. No matter the consequences. Or perhaps because of them. He'd brought me here to tell me he knew.

I was a fool.

"Run, and I can do nothing for you," he said, now just a few steps behind me.

But I was running, and he gave chase. If I turned I'd see his face, and I'd want to believe whatever he said next, take whatever way out he offered. But nobody escaped the Court of Pain, least of all me.

I stopped at the tunnel mouth, not yet venturing into its darkness. This beach, this prince under moonlight, whatever was said here was special. He'd hinted at that. A magic thrummed around us, the magic of secrets. Perhaps, in this moment, I could speak as me, the real me. Not as Lark... but someone very different. "How long have you known?" I asked, without looking back.

"From the moment you arrived in my court."

Four years. My chuckle echoed down the tunnel until the rumbling waves swallowed the sound. He'd known everything this whole time? How was I still alive?

I turned, and his beautiful eyes were full of misplaced sympathy. "Then why let me continue?" I asked. "Why stand back and watch me seduce my way through your court? Why not take my head?"

"Because you are not like them. And neither am I."

Them. Those from my court, my home. "You don't know me," I snarled, and tried to turn and flee a second time.

His steel fingers caught my arm, hauling me back. "And you don't know me, Lark. But we can change this—"

I yanked my arm free. "It's too late." Fewer than three days, and all of this was over anyway.

Arin squared up to me, his gaze searching mine for all the truths he was so sure he knew. "You did what you had to."

Then, I was a victim? Is that what he thought? "I didn't think you had it in you to be so naïve."

He grabbed my right hand and held it between us, the missing digit a horrible reminder of who held my reins. "You would go back to a man who does this?" Arin growled.

"You speak as though either of us has a choice. I am your enemy, Prince Arin." I tore my hand free. "Invite me into your bed, and you truly are a fool."

"Yes, you are my enemy. But that is not all you are. The same as I am not all you see."

I snorted and backed away. "The Court of Love... You might be the only one left in your court who believes in hope."

"I know they're coming. I can stop this," he said, following. "I'm trying to stop this— stop them, but I need your help, Lark. I've been trying... Behind the scenes, I've been working to undermine everything they've had you do. We don't need to be enemies—"

I turned again and headed into the tunnel. This man he'd become, the truth of him here on this beach... He'd turned into a naïve, hopeful fool right in front of my eyes.

"Don't walk away from me."

I strode back into the cool darkness. This was insanity. Work together? He was absurd.

"Lark, damn you!"

His fingers dug into my shoulder, and he flung me against the tunnel's jagged stone walls. His hand spread over my chest, holding me at arm's length. His golden hair spilled wild about his shoulders, its tie lost somewhere on the beach.

"Damn you, listen... They killed my mother, drew a dagger across her throat and made it appear as though she took her own life. They tried to kill Draven, because he knows about you. I arrived too late, but there's a chance he may recover... But, Lark, you alone did not poison my court. Someone else undermines everything I'm trying to save. I need you, I need your lies, I need you to dance for me, to fuck and tease and dazzle while I watch, and discover the traitor in my midst."

Then there was another killer among his court? Someone who had attacked Draven, someone who killed the queen? It didn't seem possible. I would know, I knew everything.

Arin drew a dagger from behind his back and pressed its edge to my throat. Cool steel burned hot. "I cannot allow you to return to the Court of Pain."

If he expected fear, he would not get it from me. I smiled. "Then cut my throat, Prince. Because I have no choice."

He wet his lips and breathed hard, the man on the beach, the man he was now. He wasn't a killer, I saw that now. He truly was the only honest person left in the Court of Love, and all this time he'd been trying to fix the loose threads I'd been tugging on. That was why he'd shied away from me, kept himself behind his chamber door. All this time, he'd known I was his enemy, and we'd danced around each other. He was clever, I'd give him that—I closed my hand around his and eased the blade from my neck—clever, yes, but Arin was no killer.

I, however, was.

I shoved, toppling him off balance. As he reeled, I grabbed his jerkin in a fist and pushed him against the far wall, then held him there, his blade tight against his throat. I leaned close, like we had in the bathing pool, as close as lovers. His body trembled, his heat soaked my clothes. Every panting breath pushed his chest against mine. He smelled of the night meadows, and sea salt.

Use them, abuse them, but do not kill them, the memory from four years ago teased, so clear it was as though my beneficiary, the Prince of Pain, whispered in my ear now.

"You won't...hurt me." Arin panted, pale lashes fluttering. "I know you. You're good."

"'Good'?" I laughed and stepped back, keeping him pinned under my hand. Hate glittered in his eyes, but hate wasn't all he felt. Desire burned there too, forbidden, wicked, and very real. I brought his dagger to my lips and licked the length of its blade. "The Court of Pain knows nothing of *good*."

With his free hand, he grasped my neck and yanked. I whipped the dagger aside moments before his soft, warm lips slammed into mine, delivering a bruising kiss. All thoughts emptied from my head. All but one: need. His tongue thrust in, demanding mine, but I pulled, and with the knife returned to his throat, he had no choice but to wait. Who was this prince that he could so thoroughly brand himself on my body and mind without my permission? I should have known he'd do something so un-princely he'd leave me speechless; it was, after all, his preferred method of distraction.

Real or fake, I no longer cared.

I nudged his mouth, skimmed his lips with mine, and when he tried to bite, I pulled back, eliciting a moan. He wanted this, me, all of it. I dropped the dagger with a clatter, and he lunged. His hand—the one not clamped on the back of my neck—twisted in my hair. He hooked a leg around mine, trapping me close, and pulled me into a devastating kiss. His tongue lured mine, hips grinding, and it was all I could do to meet his ferocious attack with my own unhinged response. Shock, hatred, fear, desperate lust burned the truth of me—of us—away. We were two men again, two strangers, whose bodies sang for the other.

He writhed, tore from the kiss, and tilted his head back. I

skimmed my tongue down his offered throat, over where I'd held the blade moments before. He shivered, moaned, and his hips bucked, rubbing his stiff cock against my thigh.

"Yes..." I moaned. Needing this, needing him so much I couldn't think. Arin, under me, in me, I wanted that more than I'd wanted anything.

Just as I began to think I might get my hands on that princely cock soon, he thrust his hands between us and shoved, driving us apart.

Breathless, ablaze, painfully erect, I wiped a thumb over my lips and looked up at the riddle that was the Prince of Love.

Blood dribbled from a cut in his cheek. When he'd lunged for the kiss, I hadn't moved the dagger away fast enough.

I swept my fingers under the cut, collecting a scarlet drop, and licked it clean. Arin stared, eyes wide, breathing hard. Whatever was going on in that pretty head of his, he couldn't deny his desperate need to fuck me. He'd been the one to begin this between us, not I.

Heat flushed his face and with a flutter of lashes, he glanced away. He'd be even more beautiful on his back, legs spread around my hips. That startling image stole my breath. I needed space to clear my head of his sweet scent. He knew who I was, knew why I was here. Yet he'd offered help, or at least to use me to find the imposter. Such a thing... unexpected.

"What do you truly want from me?" I whispered.

"Just your help. And I'll keep you safe, here, in my court."

"So sweet, those princely lies." I scooped up his dagger, tossed it in the air, and caught it by the handle, then tucked it up my sleeve. "I'm keeping this. Call it a promise, from you to me." I had to leave, to get some distance between us, before these emotions churning inside became a weakness.

Walking away from all he offered, from a man who'd made me want to forget who I was... It was the hardest thing I had to do. But he'd already proven he could not be trusted. I couldn't fall into this trap, because that was surely what it was. Princes made of honey and sunshine did not want creatures with darkness in their heart.

"Lark?"

I glanced back. His hair and clothes were a mess, his face cut up, and his cock hard. "This did not happen. You and I, it doesn't exist outside of this beach. If we're to catch the Court of Pain's imposter, this must be our secret."

I remained unconvinced there even was an imposter, besides me, but someone had killed the queen. "Of course there is no us. In what world does a fool fuck a prince? It was all a dream, Your Highness." I bowed a farewell and stumbled back along the tunnel, convincing myself over and over that I couldn't go back there, take him back to the beach, and kiss him, stroke him, make him quiver and moan and beg.

The time would come, and when it did, I would savor him like a fine wine. Because he knew almost everything about me, held all the cards, but one. He wanted me, more than he'd wanted anything in his life. He always had, even knowing what I was. In his honest heart, the man he truly was believed he could save me, and save his court.

We didn't have long. When the Court of Pain came for me—which they would—the Prince of Love's fantasy would be over, and so would his court.

CHAPTER 9

I was supposed to dance and lie and distract for Arin to help expose the imposter, those had been his demands in exchange for him *keeping me safe*.

But Arin didn't attend dinner that night—not unusual, for him. Nobody spoke of the queen, as though she'd never existed. It was easier to live in denial. The king grumbled on, his gaze on the serving girls. And the courtly dance continued without the prince.

But as my final night in the palace came around, and Arin continued to be elusive, I wondered if I'd dreamed the beach, the moonlight, his desperate kiss, and our prickly truce.

If I was going to be his distraction while he searched for the imposter, then I'd need more from him than his absence.

But it wasn't just our apparent deal that had me questioning what I'd agreed to in that tunnel. Hope was a dangerous thing.

I'd done without hope for a long time. But Arin, the real Arin, not the icy, aloof, beat-me-to-prove-a-point Arin, had sparked a tiny fragment of hope in my heart. What if we could do the impossible, and somehow work together to stop the imposter, or perhaps go so far as to stop the Court of Pain from undermining the Court of Love? I'd never hung my hopes on anyone but myself. And now the prince had seeded hope inside me, like a weed.

What if this silence was his plan? What if his game was to give me hope and then forget me? Perhaps he was as cruel as he'd had me believe?

Done with waiting, I swept through the royal wing, to Arin's chamber door, and slipped a written poem beneath.

I was needed back in the ballroom, to spin and dance and charm anyone who cared to listen. But the riddle of the Prince Behind the Door had sunk its claws into me. And so I lingered, like a kicked puppy. Eager for its master's love, no matter the shape it took. As time ticked on, I paced, then leaned against the wall and picked at my nails.

This was my final night. Tomorrow, I'd leave. Or not. That decision hinged on one infuriating prince.

The door opened, and Arin regarded me as though we were strangers. "Yes, Fool?"

Of course, we weren't meant to be on familiar terms. Outside the beach, he and I were strangers. "Come to dinner."

He raked his lofty gaze over me. "Had I wished to attend, I'd be there." He attempted to close the door.

I thrust my boot out, bouncing the door back open, and pushed inside. White and gold drapes swathed every column and hung from every arch. The gleam hurt my eyes. No wonder he was rarely here.

My poem lay open on the nearest sideboard. I picked it up and read aloud as Arin marched through his room. "Once upon a time, in a kingdom of flowers. There lived a prince. He made a promise, his heart full of grace. To his people, he'd create a brighter place." Arin sent a raised eyebrow over his shoulder. "But time passed by, and the prince did not keep his promises, buried deep. The people waited, with hope in their hearts. But the prince's vow, forever departs." He stopped at his large dresser, leaned against it, and folded his arms in silent judgment.

I hesitated, but I'd begun, and so the poem must end. "The kingdom fell into darkness and woe. For the prince, their trust, did not bestow. His name, forever tarnished and vile, For breaking his promise, the people's trust defile. Learn from this tale, oh young and fair, Keep your promises, with care. For a broken vow, leads to a ruined plight, and a kingdom, forever lost in the night."

He smiled without amusement. "Lost in the storm, would surely be more appropriate."

"Storm does not rhyme with plight." I closed the distance between us and slapped the poem to his chest. As I let go, it fluttered to the floor. "Which one of us is the fool? Remind me, for I have forgotten."

"Indeed, you have," he smirked.

I'd spent all my ire on the poem and could only think of insults. "You are infuriating."

"As are you."

My pulse raced. I barked a sudden laugh. "You have me, as you wished, now do with me as you please. Else tomorrow, I'll be gone, and you will be alone in your *plight*—"

"Stop," he snapped, then snatched up the fallen poem and headed for an oil lamp beside the washstand. "We are enemies, and to the imposter working against my court, we must be seen as such. This—" He held the poem over a lamp's naked flame. "—is a mistake." Fire galloped up the paper. When it was half consumed, he tossed it in the nearby washbasin and watched it burn to ash. "No more poems and notes.

They could be used as evidence we are familiar." He sighed. "I should burn them all."

Wait, he hadn't? "I thought you had."

He smiled, coyly this time. "Ah, caught in a lie."

That little smile spoke of the things he could not say. His gaze roamed over me, drinking me down and drawing me toward him. Our kiss was supposed to be a dream, but it burned very real between us now. "Come to dinner," I purred. "Watch me play them, as you so wished. But this time, I'll do it for you. Every tease, every whisper... It will all be for you."

He closed the distance between us, coming at me with purpose. I braced for a second brutal kiss, but instead, he tucked a loose lock of my hair behind my ear, fingers skimming my cheek. "You believe being seen gives you worth," he said. "And if you're not seen, then you are nothing." His delicate touch trailed along my jaw.

"As you so kindly revealed during my time behind bars."

His fingers skipped down my neck next. The touch was soft, featherlight, and all the more devastating for its gentleness. "The things I did to you were a necessary act, just like your performance over the last few years. I did not..." He swallowed and skimmed the tip of his tongue over his lips. "I did not relish hurting you. That is not who I am."

Fire sizzled through my veins. Did he even know which of his lies were true? I'd seen his face as his men had beat me, and he'd liked it. "Then who were you performing for? This imposter? Who is he, or she? Tell me what you know so I can better help you."

"I have my suspicions, but you know I cannot tell you, not yet, Lark." He pressed in, closer still, his body firm in all the right ways. The sumptuous four-poster bed was a tease in the corner of my eye. Would he submit if I bent him over it?

"The fact remains you have damaged my court," he said. "I'd be a fool to trust you."

His words made sense, but while he spoke, his gaze stroked over my face and down my neck, perhaps while he imagined what could have happened had he not stopped our kiss in the tunnel—could still happen between us.

"I cannot fathom the wrongs done to you in the past," he whispered.

"Wrongs can seem right from differing perspectives." I caught his hand, stopping its slow adventure south. If he knew the horrors I'd endured, and inflicted, he would not look at me as he did now, with tortured longing. Only disgust. "I need you to be at dinner," I admitted, briefly baring my soul. "I need to be seen *by you*. You demand I stay, but I cannot do so alone. I need an anchor, or I'll be gone."

The side door into his bedchamber clunked and groaned open. His aides trailed in, three in a row, carrying bundles of fresh clothes.

I danced away from Arin and pretended to adjust the nearby flower arrangement while Arin strode for the dresser, so quick on his feet he was already half a room away.

I'd have to ask Ellyn to suggest the aides knock from now on. And Arin needed a lock on that door.

I plucked a deck of playing cards from inside my jacket and shuffled them between my fingers. "Are you satisfied with my suggestion, Your Highness?" I fanned the cards and smiled as one of the aides caught my eye. Rumors would fly. I'd been seen with the prince, alone in his chamber no less. Oh, the scandal. If there was someone else here, someone from the Court of Pain, working without my knowledge, then they'd be eager to hear how I'd gotten close to Arin.

"Do as you please" Arin said. "Oh, and Fool?" He didn't

look up, far too important to meet my gaze. "Tell the king I'll be along to dinner shortly."

"Of course." I plucked the King of Hearts from the deck and placed it next to the vase of flowers, leaving it for him as a promise and a tease.

~

ARIN ATTENDED DINNER.

I danced and sang and played tricks. I listened to rumors and gossip, stoking those fires while adding fuel of my own. I did what I'd been put inside Arin's court to do—sow the seeds of chaos—but now Prince Arin *knew*. He watched, discreetly, from the top table, playing his part of the aloof royal. Perhaps he'd assumed I'd be ashamed of my actions, now I'd been "found out." Oh, but the opposite was true. His knowing gaze fueled the added bounce in my step, the extra flare in my gestures.

It was like being caught while having sex and having the observer *watch*. A thrill, a dance, a performance.

He'd so rarely attended the dinners that his presence drew attention.

I mingled, and the guests wondered aloud, *where had he been?* Grieving for his mother, most assumed, but his absence had begun long before her death. They spoke of rumors of how he sometimes left the palace. Some were adamant they'd seen him in the taverns, drunk and high, eying tavern girls. But Arin was not his father. The ladies of the court admired him, lusted after him, several asked me if I knew how to gain an audience with the prince. I smiled and laughed and teased such possibilities. Arin was *my* secret. One of many I kept, but a new and exciting one.

The evening wore on, I performed, and when I caught a

moment to myself, I skipped a glance his way. His pale blue eyes lifted and locked with mine, sparking lightning down my spine. With his gaze on me, the banter and laughter, the endless jeering and demands of the court, all fell away. The ballroom may as well have been empty, the guests all gone. Just he and I stood alone. As we'd been on the beach.

I broke the connection and fell back into step, only missing a moment. Nobody noticed our secret dance.

After dinner, with the guests' bellies full, wine glasses empty, and feathers wilting, I approached the prince. It would have been unusual for me not to at least acknowledge him, considering how new his presence was among us. King Albus glowered but made it seem as though he was the overprotective father and not a jealous dolt.

Arin ignored my approach, the same as he'd done for years.

"A card trick, Your Highness?" I asked, plucking a deck from my pocket.

He lifted his gaze. "If you must."

The ice in his tone and his eyes proved how good a liar he was. This Prince of Love was so very cold, but I knew the truth to be the opposite. His secret was mine to keep.

I fanned my cards, told him to pick one and remember what card he'd seen. A few of the lords and ladies had fallen silent to watch us; the king too. "Return the card to the deck, facedown." He did, and I shuffled the entire deck with flare, then slammed them facedown on the dining table and swept them in a great arc. I hitched myself onto the edge of the table, crossed my legs, and bumped my boot against his elbow. "I cannot possibly know which card you chose. They are all facedown, are they not?"

The crowd agreed. Even the king begrudgingly nodded.

Arin studied the backs of those cards, searching for any

tiny imperfection, any crease, that might suggest I could pick his from the rest. But they were all pristine. "There's no way," he agreed.

"My boot, dear prince?"

He smirked and leaned away, only now realizing how I'd been resting my foot against his arm. "What of it?" he asked.

"Unlace it."

Gasps and excited giggles simmered. Oh my, how dare I demand the prince unlace my boot.

Arin's glare turned suspicious. I was skirting the line we'd agreed not to cross.

"It surely does not bite." I wiggled my foot, in its boot. "At least, that part of me doesn't."

Our audience tittered, and a smile broke through Arin's expression, shattering his stoic mask. His grin was a thing of true beauty, and for a few heartbeats, its appearance stunned me into silence.

He tugged at my boot's ties, intrigued, and considering his jerking efforts, probably irritated by the attention we'd garnered. Peeling back the boot's edges, he found a card folded against my calf muscle. Our twittering audience simmered with delight.

"Well?" I asked him. "Take it out?"

He held up the card and laughed. "How did you—"

"The King of Hearts, no?" I prompted.

He showed the card to the crowd, and they burst into applause. My work done, I scooped up the deck, hopped off the table, took a bow, and retied my boot as the audience filtered away, leaving just Arin and I. The king was nearby too, but his focus was already elsewhere.

Arin offered the card back, pinched between his fingers. "Very good, *Fool*."

I took the card, taking the opportunity to stroke his

hand. The gesture was so quick, nobody noticed. The trick had bedazzled him, and he made no attempt to hide it from his expression. Or if he did, then he'd failed. No wonder he hadn't dared come to dinner before; his wide smile and sparkling eyes belied any attempt of his to pretend he was cold and hard. It was rather endearing.

I bowed. "I live to please my Prince of Hearts."

His smile cut off. He blinked, remembering his act, and slammed the shutters down over his expression. "Hurry along now, I have business to discuss with my father."

After leaving the royal table, I continued the same dance around the ballroom. A glance back, however, revealed his vacant seat at the table. He wasn't among the dancers either.

Someone tugged on my arm. "Lark, won't you spin us a tale?"

He'd left. And the feasting hall, with all its flowery decorations and bright colors, was all the duller for his absence.

"Lark...?"

It took more effort than it should to pin a smile to my lips. "Of course."

THE NEXT NIGHT, when Arin attended dinner, any attempt to catch his eye failed, and when I tried to tempt him with a trick, he dismissed me with a flick of his hand. The next night was the same, and the next... He watched, presumably gathering information on his imposter. But I'd overstayed. My return home was overdue. Whoever Arin believed worked against him—this assailant who had killed the queen—they could get to me. And it wouldn't be a beating.

I'd lose another finger, or worse.

I'd been safe while I'd danced to the Court of Pain's tune,

but that was no longer the case. If the killer was brazen enough to kill a queen, then he or she wouldn't hesitate in killing me.

After another evening's entertainment, I sought Arin in his chambers. A knock at the door yielded silence. The prince had a knack for disappearing. He didn't go into town, I knew that much. Then, he was likely at his secret cove.

It was the only place he could go where nobody knew to follow. Except me.

I retraced our steps from that night, using the servants' corridors to arrive at the library, and hurried down the book aisles.

Muttered cursing and the rhythmic clanging of bouncing balls sounded from the back of the room. I might have ignored it, had I not recognized the prince's voice. I snuck behind a bookcase aisle, parted the books on the shelf, and peered through at a prince attempting to juggle.

He threw the balls, managing to cycle them in the air for several seconds, but just when it seemed he'd gotten the flow, a ball skipped from his fingers, and the rest went tumbling, springing off nearby bookcases. From his messy hair and disheveled attire, he'd been here a while. Probably since leaving the dining hall.

He picked up the balls, muttered some rallying words, and tried again. His skin glistened, damp from perspiration. He had muscle enough to swing a sword with gusto, but apparently, he'd met his match in three balls.

The balls escaped him again. One rolled under my bookcase and came to a halt next to the toe of my boot.

"Who's there?"

I picked up the ball and ventured around the end of the bookcase.

He flicked his damp hair back and straightened. "How long have you been watching?"

I tossed him the ball, and he snatched it out of the air. "Long enough to know my position as court jester is not in jeopardy. At least not from a juggling prince."

"You could help," he sneered, "instead of gloating." He swept a sleeve across his cheek, dislodging the hair stuck to his skin.

He'd continue to fight those balls all night if I let him. And he would master them. He wasn't the sort to easily give up.

"I'll help, if you tell me what you know of your suspected imposter."

"I can't do that." He tossed a ball, then the next, but by the time he'd launched the third, he was already playing catch-up with the first. Two escaped his grasp. He snatched one back but the other bounced free. He swore and flung his head back with an exasperated sigh. "How did you do it?"

I picked up the two escaped balls and sauntered over. "I'll show you."

"Not this, the trick with the King of Hearts? How did you know which card was mine? And how did you get it in your boot?"

"Well, I left a King of Hearts in your room, so it seems likely you'd pick the same from the deck."

"No." He grinned, but the smile was a skin over frustration. "I didn't see the deck before I chose that card. I couldn't know what card I'd pick. So how did you do it?"

What was he angry about? The fact he couldn't juggle, the fact I'd tricked him, or something else? I circled around behind him. His damp shirt clung to his smooth back, leaving little to the imagination. It was all too easy to imagine licking up his spine and making him arch for more... Would he fight

107

me between the sheets too? I hoped so. "Arin, you don't really want to know how it's done."

"But I do." He glanced over his shoulder, glare spearing into me.

I stepped close, against his body, gathered the two juggling balls in my right hand, and reached around his waist to hand them over. "The magic is not in the trick." He took the balls, freeing my hand. I laid it gently on his hip, testing for any resistance. "The magic is in the feeling."

"Magic doesn't exist."

"Wrong again. Magic is the surprise, the wonder, amazement. This world is dark enough, it needs a little magic to light the way."

He turned his head and now my mouth was at his ear and my hands on his hips, our bodies once more pressed close. Butterflies danced low, stuttering my breath. I didn't know Arin, not who he truly was behind his thin acts. I'd tried to put the pieces of his puzzle together but most didn't fit. He didn't know me, either. We were two strangers, both playing games, but I liked our games, and so did he. So here we were, the prince and the fool, standing far too close where anyone might stumble upon us, my breath at his ear, my touch branding his skin, while his heart raced and his blood quickened.

"Tell me how it was done, Lark," he said again, voice gruff with the order.

He couldn't stand not knowing, or rather, he knew it to be lies, and that infuriated him—my prince of hearts, wearing his heart on his sleeve. "No." If he knew, he'd think he'd won, but deep inside, he'd lose the magic. It was better just to believe.

"Fine. Don't tell me. But teach me how to juggle."

"That, I can do." I slid my hands along his warm forearms

—his sleeves rolled up—over his wrists, to his hands. "You need to be ahead of the balls, not behind them." My chin brushed his jaw, scratching over rough stubble. "Master them or they will master you."

"They're just balls." Arin chuckled.

"Respect the balls."

He laughed, then caught my raised eyebrow in his over-the-shoulder glance. "You're serious."

"Do you want to learn or not?"

He sobered and shifted on his feet, for which I had the fortunate pleasure of having his ass rub my crotch.

"Fine." He raised the balls again. "Master the balls," he repeated.

I refrained from suggesting I might master his balls later, despite it being on the tip of my tongue. "Measure their weight," I told him, freeing his hands so I could bracket his hips again and hold him in place. "You need to give yourself time to catch and release. Throw them higher to begin with."

He threw the balls and immediately, all three escaped him. His laugh filled the library and my heart. At least he *was* laughing. When I'd arrived, he'd looked as though he'd been ready to tear the library to pieces.

I let him go to retrieve the balls, and when he returned, he turned his back once more. "Well?" he asked, inviting my touch.

I slotted myself close again, resting my hands on his firm waist. This was surely foreplay. And as he prepared to launch the balls again, I breathed the ghost of a kiss on the back of his neck. Not even a kiss, more the promise of one. Arin stilled. He sucked in a breath and tried admirably to refocus on the task of juggling.

When he tossed the balls again, he lunged from my grasp and managed a whole three cycles before sending the balls flying. "Yes! Did you see?! I had it!" He tracked down the balls and hurried back. "Again, Lark."

"Very well."

This time, when I tucked myself close, I eased a thigh astride his and skimmed a kiss lower, tasting his saltiness mixed with the scent of clean linen and the flower meadows.

A tremor shivered through him. "I do believe you are deliberately distracting me."

"Never." With that, I tilted my hips and dug my cock against his firm ass, leaving him in no doubt.

He gave a small, pained moan. A sound that begged for more. "Lark—"

I skimmed my hand around his right hip, stroked down the front of his trousers, and grasped his rapidly hardening dick through the fabric. "How long has it been since someone pleasured you?" I whispered, easing my fingers around as much of his length as his trousers allowed.

He sighed through his nose and dropped his head back against my shoulder. "Too long."

Years, then. Probably before I'd arrived and he'd shut himself away. Years, starved of pleasure, except his hand. But that could never be the same. Four years was too long. He was going to spill right here for me, right into my palm, and neither of us was leaving this library until that happened. The sound that growled out of me had his dick twitching in my grip.

A door clanged. Footfalls sounded, at a distance, somewhere near the front of the library.

I smothered Arin's mouth with my left hand and muscled him face-first against the bookcase, pinning him still. "You're going to say we can't do this," I whispered at his cheek. "You're afraid to be found with me, I know. But trust me. It's been so long, my Prince of Hearts. You want this, you'd prefer

I fuck you right now, but we do not have the means and I daresay, when it happens, my hand will not be enough to silence your demands for more."

He panted through his nose and writhed, trying to fight me off.

I had him trapped facing the bookshelves, and at my mercy. The footfalls continued, moving back and forth. Whoever they were, they'd never know how a fool tempted a prince a few aisles away. I couldn't undo his trousers, not here. But his dick was so hard, it didn't matter. I sunk my hand between his waistband and the hot dip of his hip, then clasped him through his undergarments and stroked.

His breaths sawed, too loud. He writhed, hips jerking, trying to plunge himself into my hold.

"Hush." I pressed in, plastering my body against his back, and nipped at this ear, then growled as he moaned behind my hand. Books thumped far away, someone busy collecting their reading material.

I rubbed my own painful erection against his ass. He writhed in time with my thrusts, giving himself over to my control. "You feel me?" I rubbed against him again. "How hard I am for you? Soon, I'm going to fuck you—going to hold your hands behind your back and bury myself inside, and you will beg for more. You want it." He shuddered, moaning behind my hand. His thrusting stuttered. "No, not yet... Wait, hold it... You do not come until I allow it. Four years, prince, you've wanted this. It hurts, but there is pleasure in holding back. You want to surrender, to chase the pleasure, but don't let it ride you, make it yours." I pumped harder, faster. He whimpered—the sound dragged a moan from inside me. I wanted him under me, his hole spread, slick and tight around my cock. I'd fuck him until we were both wet with sweat, our veins burning, bodies bruised. "Fuck my hand,

Arin, fuck me like you hate me. Ruin me like I know you've dreamed—"

His muffled cries turned ragged and breathless. I yanked my hand tighter over his mouth, and his hips jerked, spasming under my grip. Wet heat dampened my palm on his cock. "Yes, spill for me, Arin," I whispered. He bucked, shuddering every last precious drop of cum into his pants.

By Dallin, I might have spilled along with him had I not stopped pleasuring myself against his ass. He was too damn good, too brilliant, and everything I'd ruin, spoil, destroy.

I eased my hands away from his mouth and cock, and braced against the bookcase over his shoulder. His shuddering skimmed my dick, his touch like a hot iron. Neither of us spoke, not in words. He clung to the shelf, kept his head bowed and had enough strength to hold himself up and *breathe*.

Footfalls thumped across the library floorboards, fading away. The door closed again, sealing us back inside the library, alone.

"This..." He cleared his throat and tried again, and this time his silvery glare stopped my heart. "This did not happen."

He should know by now, none of this was real. I pushed off, freeing him. In the absence of his body against mine, a cold, hollow sensation tried to swallow my heart and a chill shivered through me. I brushed the sensation aside, scooped up the balls he'd dropped, and juggled them a while, trying to clear my head. Fucking Prince Arin was a game, like all the rest. Games ended. And I survived. I always had. This was no different. I couldn't go home, so if he wanted me to stay and root out his mystery murderer, so be it. If he wanted me in his bed, I'd play that game too. It didn't matter anyway; whatever we did, fate was coming for both of us.

But none of it could ever touch my heart.

Including the prince who liked to hide, the prince who wanted to juggle, the prince trying to bring hope back to his court. The prince who had fooled me.

"You need to leave." His tone carried an element of disgust, but was it for me, or himself, for letting me tease his desires out in the open?

I caught the balls, stalling their dance, and bowed low without meeting his gaze. "Of course, Your Highness."

A game. Nothing more. No matter what my heart tried to tell me.

I threw him the balls, which he caught, along with my careless smile, and turned on my heel.

"Lark?"

My name on his lips reined me in, like a snap on a leash.

"Tomorrow, you won't attend dinner," he said.

But I always attended dinner. Dinner was when I came alive, it was my time.

I was being punished. For not telling him how the trick was performed or making him realize how he needed some cock, mostly mine. "Very well."

AFTER I RETURNED to my room, Arin consumed my thoughts, how he'd trembled in my arms, spilled in my hand, and then dismissed me like a whore. I laughed, pacing from my window to the door. One, two, three, four strides. And back. I *was* a whore. When had I begun to believe anything else?

My missing finger ached.

Worthless.

Bought with coin.

I hugged my right hand under my arm. *Use them, abuse them... do not kill them.* I squeezed my hand, paced faster... *Killing them is the final act.*

A game.

One, two, three, four. Back.

It was all a game. Court of Love, Court of Pain. Two sides of the same coin. And I was trapped between them, their pawn, their fool. With no heart or home of my own.

The traitor's son.

"Fuck!"

I kicked the bedside table, sending its contents flying, then dropped to the floor and pulled my knees to my chest.

Arin's dagger glinted where it had fallen, mocking me. I could pick it up, go to him, cut his throat and then my own. It would be done, the game finished. The Court of Pain could no longer hurt me or him if we no longer played. It was inevitable.

Only, I didn't want that. I never had.

Arin... damn him, he was right. I wasn't like the others...

I grabbed the knife, flew to the washbasin, and pressed the dagger's edge to my neck. The man in the mirror glared back, his dark eyes full of hate and spite, daring me to do it. *The traitor's son. Dance until you bleed. Prove your worth or die trying.*

There had to be more to this life, didn't there? More than being used by everyone around me? More than being seen to be believed?

My hand trembled. The blade nicked my skin, drawing a dribble of blood. It snaked down the smooth blade.

Who was I fooling? If I'd had the courage to end it, I'd have done so years ago.

The room spun. The dagger clattered into the basin, and I bowed my head, willing the hot nausea away.

I was still in control. I still had all the balls in the air. The Court of Love was still mine. Arin changed nothing. This so-called imposter was a ghost.

If I could discover who they were, I could remove them and begin to fix the loose threads I'd created. It wouldn't save Arin and his court, but it might delay his end. And mine.

But how... Arin had hinted he was working on something, but it wasn't enough. I had to take back control, I had to find the imposter before they found me.

And there was only one man who I knew for certain had met them.

CHAPTER 10

*T*he palace had its own private rooms set aside for medical procedures and patients with minor ailments. Ellyn had informed me the royal doctors had deemed Warlord Draven too fragile to be wagoned back to his lands. Arin's father had offered to host him while he recovered. As the man had no voice, he couldn't have declined had he wanted to. But there were other ways to communicate.

After the male nurse left Draven's room, I snuck inside.

An open fire and a single oil lamp made the space small and comfortable, if a little stifling. His court, surrounded by desert, was always sweltering, so the heat was likely deliberate.

Draven's chest rose and fell beneath the bedsheet. It had been almost two weeks since I'd pleasured him in the gardens. Long enough, I hoped, for his strength to return. Long enough for a beard to sprout, adding a sense of the untamed to his masculine handsomeness. He still had that short plait, trailing down the right side of his face.

I approached his bedside, hoping not to startle him.

His eyes snapped open.

"Easy." I spread my hands. "I'm not going to hurt you." He clambered backwards, climbing into his stack of pillows. "Easy, Draven, it's just Lark. You remember?"

He blinked.

"If I kneel and suck your cock, will you remember me then?"

That didn't seem to calm him any. He wheezed, eyes going wide. If he struggled any more, he'd fall from the bed. Just my luck he'd die of a heart attack without my touching him, and I'd be blamed.

"Look." I slipped the notepad and pencil from my pocket and mimed writing. "See? I'm here to help."

His gaze bounced from my face to the notepad and back to my face. After a few moments, he nodded and reached out, shuffling back down the bed. I handed over the pad and pencil and watched him scrawl at length across the first page.

A bandage covered half his neck, front to back. He was lucky to be alive. Arin had said he'd interrupted the assailant moments before I'd arrived. He'd also said he hadn't been able to get any information from Draven. But Arin could have brought the man a pencil and paper, like I had. Why hadn't he if he was so desperate to find the imposter?

Perhaps Draven hadn't been well enough until now.

Draven thrust the notepad out. His writing left a lot to be desired. He'd scrawled at an angle, the words written in capitals and looped together.

HAVE TO LEAVE. HELP ME?

He dragged a hand down his beard and nodded, big dark eyes full of hope.

"I'll see what I can do. But you have to answer some questions for me. Can you do that?"

He blinked, made a huffing noise, and waved for the pad, then scribbled furiously on the page and thrust it back into my hands.

YOUR IN DANGER

I ignored the urge to correct his spelling. Why would Draven care if I was in danger? He'd all but called me out in the gardens—*"traitor's son."* I was a traitor here too. But now he was warning me, trying to help?

Unless he didn't understand what *"traitor's son"* meant.

Perhaps he didn't know as much as I'd thought, or as much as the imposter had assumed, when they'd tried to kill him.

When I'd first seen him, I'd pegged him as a hapless lord, and my instincts were rarely wrong. If I assumed Draven was still the hapless lord, who knew very little, why had someone attempted to kill him? We didn't know each other. He wasn't a regular in the Court of Love, and was *traitor's son* enough to cut his throat?

Strange that whoever had attacked him hadn't tried again. Strange too, that there were no guards at his doors to prevent that.

"Listen, I don't have long." I handed the pad back and pointed at the paper. "Who attacked you?"

He shook his head and wrote four letters in deep, jagged lines:

ARIN

His memory was probably muddled. "Arin was there after. But who hurt you?"

He shook his head again, dislodging scruffy locks around wide, panicked eyes. He jabbed a finger at the page, and at Arin's name.

"The prince hurt you?"

He nodded and coughed, the sound raspy. He gestured for

119

the notepad back. I shifted to sit on the bed, alongside him, and watched him write.

ARIN CUT NECK

SILENCE ME

But that didn't make any sense. Arin had told me he was fighting to protect his court. How would silencing the truth about me do that? Wouldn't he want everyone knowing who I was? "Did he tell you why?"

CAN'T KILL ME WAR WILL COME

ONLY SILENCE

"Yes, but why silence you, Draven? You wanted to meet, to discuss me, yes? What did you tell him that had him almost kill you?"

He made an effort to speak but the sound left his lips as a muffled croak. Shaking his head again, he flipped the page in the notebook and scribbled:

ARIN DID NOT KNOW YOU

"Wait... He did *not* know about me?"

Draven blinked, shook his head. *FURIOUS*, he wrote.

Oh.

I leaned back against the headboard.

I'd made a terrible mistake.

Arin had told me he'd known I was his enemy from the moment I'd arrived, and I'd *believed* him. Every word. I knew he could lie, knew he was good at it, but in my arrogance, I'd thought I'd recognize his lies when they were in front of me.

But I hadn't.

If he hadn't known about me, then the news would have come as a shock—enough of a shock for the prince to lash out?

But how much did his attacking Draven change things? He claimed to be searching for an imposter. The assassin who had killed the queen. That didn't ring true now either. He'd lied about knowing me...

Unless I'd been right the first time, and Arin had killed his mother, not an imposter.

No, no, no that wasn't right. Arin wasn't a killer. A liar, yes, but not a killer. That was the only true thing I knew about the prince. I'd looked into his eyes, and despite the games and lies, and whatever pantomime he was trying to direct, he could not lie about that.

"Prince Arin vexes me more every day."

I rose from the bed and paced with Draven's gaze tracking my every step.

"The Court of War is far more straightforward. But Arin..." I laughed. "Oh Arin, the hopeful Prince of Love. He is trying to play games with me, and I am not one to be manipulated. Despite finding it painfully arousing." I glanced at Draven. "Forget I said that."

He shrugged and gestured at his throat, *who was he going to tell?*

"Arin, Arin, Arin..." Such a contradiction, a riddle.

He'd attacked Draven. I knew that much. But I did not know why. It was time the prince and I had an honest discussion about his motives and what exactly was going on here.

I scooted back onto the bed beside Draven, jostling him over so I could lean against his pillows too. "This is good, I can work with this. You've been very helpful. You're a good listener."

Draven scribbled on the notepad. *PAIN COMING*

"Yes, I fear it is." I side-eyed the Lord of War. Did he mean the courtly pain, or did he mean generalized pain? Both were likely true. "Who told you about me?"

LETTER, he scrawled. *NO SENDER NAME*

I rolled my eyes. Well, that explained how he could know I was the traitor's son but not know what it meant. I'd had him right the first time I'd laid eyes on him. Handsome, he'd be a great fuck, but not too bright. "If you want," I said, "I can finish what we started in the gardens?"

He smiled and wrote: *SUCKING COCK WILL NOT SAVE YOU*

I laughed at his fine words of wisdom and mirrored his soft grin. "Shame you've lost your voice, but then, it's not like anyone asks warlords for advice, is it?"

ASSHOLE

I hopped off the bed. "Keep the notebook, you're going to need it. I fear I'm rather between a rock and a hard place. I doubt I'll be able to help you out of here."

TRY

"Sad eyes do not work on me, Draven." I backed away from the man's impressive attempt at puppy-dog eyes. "I don't do nice. But hurt me, and perhaps I'll get down on my knees for you... again."

He smiled, then wrote one last thing. *YOUR NOT ALL BAD*

"There's an apostrophe and another vowel in there, big guy." I bowed to the lord, as was proper. "If I survive whatever happens next, I'll finish what we started. Until then, you'll have to get pleasure yourself. Just imagine it's my mouth wrapped around your cock. And make it good. You know I never disappoint."

He soft wheezing laugh followed me from the room.

Now I had a problem. The original problem, in fact. To kiss or kill a prince. Killing him would bring the whole cast of cards down and get me hung, drawn, and quartered. The final act was not mine to make. And despite Arin's torrent of lies, I didn't want him dead. He was a spectacular liar. I could appreciate such a skill, one liar to another.

Fuck it.

It was time for the prince to speak some truths, and I knew how to wring them from his peachy lips.

CHAPTER 11

*T*he lesser-known servants' entrance into Arin's chambers took some bribery to find, but after applying the right amount of pressure and threatening to reveal a few secrets, I found it and snuck inside. He wasn't here, and was likely at the dinner I was barred from.

I shifted a chest of drawers over the side door. This time, there would be no interruptions.

As the night wore on, growing darker with every hour, I flitted about his rooms, skimmed his books, admired his clothes. Oil lamps flickered, and the fires burned low.

He was usually back by now.

I dropped onto the end of the large, four-poster bed. My black trousers, shirt, and waistcoat contrasted with the white and golds draped over the bed's canopy and all around the room. The courts loved their colors, and wore them with pride. Justice, blue. War, black and red, and Pain... black and purple. So stuck in their traditions, their ways.

I stroked the golden silk drapes, tied to the bedposts. Luxuries like this were the reason the Court of Love was coinless. It didn't matter though, as long as they were seen to prosper, or so Albus believed. The king was a blind fool, and his son... His son was about to discover who I was beneath my smiles.

The main chamber door opened. I ducked out of sight, tucking myself into shadows alongside a large dresser, and caught sight of Arin striding through his chambers, peeling off his cloak, then his jacket. As he passed by, the air around him smelled of sea salt and flowers. He'd been to the cove, the place he went to think and be his truest self. His long hair, tied up in a tail, swished down his back, damp from mist. Even knowing how he'd lied, or perhaps due to it, I couldn't shake the desire to have him moaning, his ass slapping my hips and his back arched under my hands.

He stopped by a standing mirror and loosened his shirt. If he shifted a little to his left, he'd see my hiding place.

"How was dinner?" I asked, stepping from the shadows.

He froze, fingers on his shirt buttons. Irritation snuffed the surprise out of his eyes.

"Dull, I presume, without the entertainment. Did they ask after me?"

"You should not be here." He continued unbuttoning his shirt but tension kept his shoulders rigid.

He gleamed in gold and white, so brilliant next to my darkness. Two sides of that same coin, pain and love. Surely, one did not exist without the other.

"Tell me to leave." Stopping behind him—not yet touching—I freed the dagger I'd taken from him on that secret beach and kept it low at my side, out of his sight. "Tell me you don't want me here."

"What's gotten into you?" He fiddled with his cuffs, head bowed, exposing his smooth, pale neck.

"I spoke with Draven."

Arin shot right, as fast as a bow from an arrow. I caught a

fistful of ponytail, spun him around, and flung him against his mirror, then pressed the point of the dagger to his chest, indenting his shirt, right over his heart, holding him there. He spluttered and tried to pry me off him. I leaned in. "Strange, I wondered, while with Draven, why there were no guards at his door. What if the imposter were to try again?"

His eyes shone with their beautiful, silvery hatred. "Unhand me."

I freed his hair, but as he slumped with relief, I grasped his neck instead. Its lithe length fit so perfectly in my hand. "But why would you need guards, when you know no killer is coming for him."

"Lark?" he questioned, becoming concerned. Was I playing or not? What was this, he hadn't seen me like this before. It felt so good to be the one delivering the surprises.

I plastered myself against him, with just the dagger between us. Loosening my grip on his neck, I pushed my thumb under his chin, tilting his head back. "You were born into the wrong court, my prince." I gave the dagger a slight turn, knowing he'd feel its sharp point dig deeper. He bared his blunt teeth in a snarl. "Pain suits you."

"Love and pain are not so different," he said through his teeth.

Adrenaline, fear, rage, and lust—being close to Arin summoned them all. I'd felt the same in the tunnel when we'd first kissed. But oh how he wanted me. Even now, while he looked death in the eyes, if I were to drop my hand I'd find his cock hard.

Fear, I could smell it on him. "You've been lying to me."

He bucked and shoved at my chest, trying to lever me off. His fist got free and flew at my face, skimming my jaw. I laughed, and Arin bolted from my loosened grip.

I snatched his sleeve, yanked, and spun him into my arms.

He pivoted and used that momentum to swing for me a second time, knocking us both backwards—through his dressing mirror. Glass shattered. My back hit the wall, his fist slammed into my middle, stealing the air from my lungs, but breathing through agony was child's play.

He expected me to buckle, instead I slashed the dagger up, zipping open his chin.

He recoiled, swept a hand cross his face, then sneered at the blood collected on his fingertips.

"You look dashing in scarlet," I quipped.

He lunged, locked hot fingers around my throat, and threw me against the wall, but in his rage, he'd forgotten I held his dagger, now poised under his chin. Arin stilled.

"Ah, I'd rather not take your head just yet."

With the both of us locked together, panting hard, he stared, and I stared back. His punch had landed well. Its bruising heat thumped through my middle. The problem was, I liked it. The cut on his chin wept blood and blue eyes glared their fierce accusations.

"If I didn't want to fuck you, you'd be dead," Arin said. And there was the *real* Prince of Love. The little bitch who wanted my cock and lied through his teeth. "Take the knife from my throat, Lark."

"I think not."

He pushed *against* the blade—into it, making it cut him. I eased off, reeling a little. Had I not eased off, the blade's razor edge would have sliced into his neck as it had Draven's.

He was insane, he had to be, and every inch of me burned to devour every inch of him.

His pretty mouth sneered. "Did you come here to kill me?" he asked, his lips brushing mine.

I still had the knife at his neck, and his grip remained on my throat, but the rest of him pressed close hurt more.

"My life would be so much easier if I had. I came for the truth."

His mouth hovered over mine. Our breaths mingled. "What did Draven tell you?" he demanded.

"Nothing, since *you* cut his throat. Like you cut your mother's—"

He recoiled violently, as though I'd struck him. He even staggered, losing his balance.

I stalked forward, pressed the tip of the blade to his chest again, and walked him backwards across the room. He stumbled and tripped, looked down at the dagger, then up at my face. "You don't know anything, *Fool*."

I marched him by the point of the blade to the end of his golden and white fluffy bed. "Strip."

"What?"

"If we're going to kill each other, we should relish it, no?" A quick glance down, and yes, indeed, the evidence of his interest poked from his trousers. The prince was as aroused as I was, even though he likely hated himself for it. So terribly conflicted. I was going to enjoy this. "Take off your shirt."

He tore at the remaining buttons on his shirt, flicking them open, then yanked the garment off and flung it aside. "You're not going to kill me," he sneered, so sure.

I chuckled, eyeing his ripple of golden abs. "You still believe you know me? Why, because you've watched me dance?" I pushed the dagger against his chest, a little to the left, and indented his pert pectoral, just right from his nipple. "Because we kissed on your beach? Because a maid said I was *nice?*"

His eyes widened. Oh dear, Prince Arin *did* think he knew me.

"Lark, listen... I did lie. But not like you think. Draven would have ruined everything... I had to silence him."

"There is no imposter, is there."

He blinked. "No."

Then it was all him. All of it. He'd manipulated me. Fuck, the slippery sense of betrayal knotted around my heart, painful, but oh-so good. I wanted to taste that snarling mouth, taste the hate there. "You're a fine liar, if a poor juggler."

"My mother killed herself." His snarl twitched. He dropped both hands to his trouser ties. His arousal jutted impressively behind the trouser fabric. "Ask me why," he said. "Why she killed herself. *Ask me!*"

So angry, so fierce, like a lion with its claws clipped. "She didn't," I said. "She was lost, but not so far gone to end her own life."

Arin's quick laugh belittled my apparent facts. He yanked his ties looser, slipping his trousers down his hips so they clung on, held up by his erection. "And you think you know my court, my family? My mother knew what was coming for her. She had no escape. Certainly not my father. She heard the weeping girls through the walls, you know. She'd heard the rumors, knew what he was like. Rumors that were *your* doing." He snarled, true hate beginning to boil inside him, yet he still fought with his trouser ties, eager to get his hands on himself. "You told your tales and your twisted little secrets and ruined my life, my court, my everything. With your thousand little secrets, spilled each month for the man who comes to collect them from the Court of Pain, bleeding blood from my veins!" He pushed at the dagger, and the blade gave a little, sinking into his skin. Blood welled.

So, he knew about Danyal. Knew it all. Draven had been wrong. Arin had kept his fury so well contained; I'd seen glimpses, but I was seeing it all now. He might impale himself on the dagger if I let this go on.

"So dramatic, Arin. Are you sure you weren't born into Pain?"

"I've had to be like them—like you—to get through this."

"Oh stop." I flicked the dagger away and stepped close, pinning his legs to the bed. "You don't give a shit about any of this. You could have left your room and comforted your mother, you could have called your father's sins out. But you stayed hidden behind your door. You're cold and afraid. If you have a heart, it hasn't beat in years."

Silvery-blue eyes flicked over mine. "You're wrong, I feel *everything*. But if I let it in, it will break me. So I don't. I keep it out. All of it... except you."

I tilted my head and dragged the tip of the dagger down his naked, heaving chest, leaving a jagged scratch behind. "Except me? Then you feel this?" I looked up, and he was watching my face, not what I was doing with the knife. Good. Flicking the dagger around, I pointed its tip downward, pushed it lower, and nudged cold steel against his dick.

His heavy breathing hitched.

"I watched you," he whispered, golden eyelashes fluttered over desire-wide eyes.

"So you say." With my free hand, I worked at his trouser ties, jerking the last of them loose.

"I saw such pain in your eyes the first time we met."

I remembered that moment well. Nineteen years old. I'd dropped to my knee, kissed his hand, and thought him beautiful, even then. His life, his court, it shone with hope and brilliance, and the task of undermining it from the inside out had seemed insurmountable.

I'd vowed to begin with the prince. But he'd vanished the next day, as though I'd dreamed him up, and he'd remained out of reach ever since. Until now. I had him in my hands now.

ARIANA NASH

"I watched your lying smiles," he said. "Your sleight of hand. And I knew I couldn't stop you, not without alerting my enemies—but I could *use* you, Lark."

"Well, there's a surprise," I drawled.

"I planned to let your scheming continue, and your actions would reveal my enemy's hand in my court's affairs."

I plunged my left hand into his undergarments, still holding the dagger in my right hand against his cock, and captured his length in my grip. His sigh brushed my cheek. "While you watched, I dismantled your court," I whispered. "You knew and did nothing to stop me."

"My court has long been broken," he rasped, lashes fluttering low as I stroked my fingers down his eager dick. "You saw it, and so did I. The Court of Love without love is no court at all."

I wanted to believe him. I had believed him, but it had been lies before, and now I didn't know what was real around him. His desire was real, there was no denying the firm length sliding between my fingers. Or how his pupils had blown, swallowing the silver in his eyes. Lust was easy; the truth was much harder to find.

He was the prince I couldn't touch, the prince I couldn't fool. He'd lied to everyone, even himself. He'd modeled himself on me, he'd silenced Draven to keep my secret safe, to keep his act going, and all the while his court had unraveled around him.

But why? What could he hope to save if there was nothing left at the end of it?

"Why didn't you tell me the truth?" I asked.

"You know why. You were my enemy."

I worked his cock slowly, leisurely, and nudged his mouth with mine, teasing his lips apart. "I *am* your enemy."

His eyes flashed. "I hate you."

I bit my lip to keep from moaning. "Lie to me some more, Arin."

His hand at my throat hauled me into a furious kiss. His tongue thrust, and I took it, lashing back with my own. Hate was the fuel, and lust the spark, and now there was no stopping this inferno.

I shoved, pushing him backward. He fell onto the bed, knees apart, straining cock half exposed from his undergarments. All that fury and hate simmered in his eyes and strummed through his body—a body I hungered to explore. He reached out, as though to hold me off. I pressed the dagger's flat edge to his chest, pinning him down, then straddled his legs. "Have you ever fucked with a knife at your throat?"

Alarm widened his eyes. "Lark, wait—"

I shoved him back and braced over him. He could speak; I wasn't smothering him now, just peering into his eyes while he panted and panicked and *wanted*. A little fear heightened desire, for some. Arin appeared to be the type to enjoy not knowing if it was pain or pleasure about to assault him.

I skimmed the knife's tip down his hip. He hissed, arching under me, and moaned his need. Those peachy lips parted, and he glared his hate right through me.

"Touch me," I suggested, or ordered. There was little difference.

He hadn't, not yet. Not now, not on the beach, and not in the library. We'd kissed, groped, I'd stroked him to climax, but he hadn't touched the part of me we both knew he wanted to feel and grip and taste. I needed him to touch me, ached to have his mouth on me, for him to feel how damned hard I was for him.

He dropped his left hand between us, and when his

fingers skimmed my cock, their featherlight touch lit a dozen more sparks down my spine, twitching my dick.

His eyes widened, his sneer softened, and now he searched my face for permission. So fierce, this prince of love, but so willing to submit. I still didn't know if I was here to kill him, or fuck him, or punish him. Maybe all three.

"How many times have I featured in your dreams?" I asked, my voice a smooth rumble. "How many times have you woken hard and fucked your hand, thinking of me?"

I tilted my hips, grinding against his dick, trapped between us. He rolled his eyes and clutched my ass, so willing that I struggled to hold myself back from tearing his trousers down and plunging into his tight hole. He'd claw at me, demand I stop, but he'd take it, want it.

I returned the knife to his throat. His glare sprung back to me, accusing and full of hate all over again. "How many times?" Definitely a demand, this time.

"In the beginning? Once or twice. Lately? Every night. And I hate you for it. I hate that I can't think about you without wanting you to touch me. I hate how hard I am for you, right now."

Fuck. A moan slipped away from me.

"I hate how much I want you." He grasped my dick, pinching hard. I gasped and took the blade away from his neck to brace over him.

"I always have." He palmed my length, rubbing through my trousers, each rough and desperate stroke a lick of bliss. "I hate what you've done and who you are," he sneered. "I hate where you come from." Faster, he rubbed, driving all reason from my thoughts. "I hate that I cut Draven to keep *your* wretched secret within these walls. And I hate myself for needing you, like this. For wanting to taste..."

"Taste what?"

He turned his flushed face away. "Your cum."

It took a while for his words to sink through the madness of lust.

I couldn't stand it. Any more of his rage-filled talk, his angry touch, and I'd lose control. I pulled free, scooting low, and yanked his undergarments down, over his hips. His dick sprang free and I had it in my mouth, sucking him deep, before he could draw breath to demand I stop.

It was just sex. Just pleasure between two men, nothing more. But even now, with his hate all over me, my excuses felt like lies. Just sex was what I'd engaged in with the rest of the Court of Love; this—with my mouth on Arin's dick, his hand twisting in my hair—was something else.

This felt like... freedom.

CHAPTER 12

rin

I KNEW LARK, knew how he lied with every breath and cheated behind every flick of his graceful hands, and how he loved every moment of it. He'd ruined my life. But he'd also made it worth living. That was the contradiction I fought against.

Because as I'd watched him for years, I'd learned to be like him, how to lie and misdirect. I'd stolen what I'd needed from the spy in my court to win this hidden war. And I'd hated every moment of it, hated what it had turned me into, hated myself.

Lark believed he was my downfall, my obsession, but I knew, when the end came, he'd be my savior.

And in the years I'd watched him laugh and dance, I'd seen the pain he carried inside him, like a second beating black heart, and against every instinct, every rational thought, I'd vowed to save him, whatever the cost.

Foolish thoughts, made even more ridiculous while he sucked my dick and held a dagger to my middle. But by Dallin, he was my beautiful lie.

His finger slipped between my ass cheeks and skimmed my hole. I bucked, sinking my cock deeper between his lips, stroking the back of his throat. The dagger nicked my hip, leaving its stinging bite, and pleasure pulled tight—too much, he was too much, everywhere, all at once. "Lark —wait."

He looked up, his sharp mouth sealed around my thickness. *Wait...* There was nothing in his eyes to suggest he'd do anything I said. Dark, beautiful, catlike eyes promised he'd hurt me, and I'd want it. I breathed too fast, and the words telling him to stop stuck in my throat. His finger stroked below my balls again, but this time, it pushed in, through my hole, widening me as it dove deeper.

No, this was—

He lifted his head, sucking up my length, then keeping my dick between his lips, he tongued its head, shocking pleasure down my back. That might have been enough, but he did something with his finger, stroked some part of me, and a different ripple poured through my body. I flung my head back, grasped the sheets, and stuttered an agonizing moan of pleasure. But it didn't stop, and as his finger stroked, the sizzling ecstasy came in wave after wave, and his tongue flicked, lapping the tip of my dick.

I was going to come, didn't stand a chance to stop it. I'd come in his mouth, down his throat, and I knew his smile, having seen it a thousand times in dreams like this.

Lark suddenly pulled away, both finger and mouth, gone in an instant. I was too close to climax. With my head spinning, I looked for him. My dick lay against my belly, leaking, proud, flushed. But he wasn't there... Desire strummed me like a bow. All I had to do was think about his mouth on my cock and I'd—

He flew back in, pinched my dick, and white-hot fire shot up my spine. "Gah—stop!"

He grinned, his long black hair wild about his pale face, eyes shining their wicked glee. "You come when I give you permission."

No, this was too much, I couldn't... I hadn't... Not with anyone. If I didn't stop him, he'd be the first to take me, and that couldn't happen. He couldn't be my first. Could he?

"Wait..." I panted.

Something cool, soothing, and wet touched my hole.

"Lark, wait..." I gripped the bed and tried to writhe away.

He slapped the flat edge of the dagger against the plane of my lower belly. "Don't tell me you don't want this. I will not believe you."

I did, that was the problem. I hadn't ever done this. I was the Prince of Love, and I'd never fucked anyone, or had anyone fuck me. It was a joke, or a tragedy. I wasn't ready, or prepared; I didn't know what this was, what we were doing.

Lark's eyes narrowed. Damn him, he probably saw the fear on my face. His smile tipped half off his glistening lips. He withdrew his finger, set the dagger aside, tore his waistcoat off, then the shirt.

He was all tight, lean muscle, a dancer's physique. And the scars, so many, just tiny things, like stardust on his skin. He dropped his hands and expertly whipped open his trousers, wasting no time in freeing himself. And he was... endowed, in that regard. Warmth heated my face and chest. I couldn't take my eyes off the slow stroke of his hand over his veined length.

Of course, I knew the rumors, knew he had a reputation as an amazing lover. A dancer in bed too, they said. Whatever that meant. But to have a man inside me, and for that man to be him... I couldn't do this.

I tried to sit up—the dagger was gone, lost somewhere in the sheets. If I was going to stop this, it had to be now.

He shoved me in the chest, knocking me back down, then spread my knees.

"No, wait." I reached down. "I just..."

He fell forward, bracing over me, pinning me under him. All his black hair fell from his shoulders, stroking my chest with his every movement. His gaze searched mine. "If you trust me in nothing else, trust me in this, Prince of Love."

He reached down between us. I feared he'd try and enter me again, feared a lot of things, like whether I could do what had to be done when this was over.

His slick grip collected my dick and trapped it against hard, silky, soft muscle. He rubbed with smooth, slick fingers—he'd found some oil from my dresser moments ago, when he'd left me teetering on the edge of orgasm. His little smile danced as his expert hand stroked me back toward the precipice. His mouth hovered over mine; his sly, dark eyes were all I could see.

I reached up to clutch at his arm, but he reared back, propped on his knees, straddling my hips, our dicks trapped together in his oiled fingers. A strangled, desperate moan left me, a noise I didn't think I was capable of. His stroking hold quickened suddenly, and my breaths raced with it. This again... It was too good, damn him, and he knew it. I bucked, shuddered, moaned, so close...

He slowed, and I whimpered, clutched the sheets, then grabbed his knee and dug blunt nails into his skin.

"Harder," he purred.

I didn't understand. And then he slapped his hand down on mine and crushed it down on his knee.

"Harder, Arin."

I dug my nails into his thigh, and he flung his head back, pumping our dicks together. He rocked, fucking his hand, sliding his dick along mine. He could be quick and sharp, like a whip, or soft and slow, like a caress, like now. His cock stroked mine, the motion easy, rocking me toward the edge. His eyes, their lashes so soft, demanded answers. He'd sauntered from the dark this night with murder in those eyes, more than capable of seeing me dead. I knew that and somehow I'd still let him into my bed.

I was close again, riding the same bright wave, needing to breach, but desperate to hold back. Lark dropped, braced over me. Our chests touched, slick with perspiration, hair clinging.

"I'm going to bite you, Arin, and when I do, you will come."

"I... What?" Bite me?

His head dropped, teeth pinched into my shoulder, and then he pumped so hard, so fast, and so smooth that the maddening mix of pain and pleasure tore me apart. I wanted his cock then, wanted it inside, fucking me deep, couldn't speak to demand it, and it was too late anyway, because the wave broke, pulsing down my lower back, and I spilled hot cum with his teeth in my shoulder and his hand on my dick, in complete control.

I'd resisted this, us, even as I'd ached for the touch he'd given so many others. I'd watched him from the shadows while he'd danced in the light. I'd envied his laugh, so bright it filled a room. Everything I felt for Lark was a muddle of madness, all of it probably wrong. And here, now, he had me pinned under him, and I'd given up fighting my feelings. Fighting him.

I'd needed to be someone else, and he'd taught me how to live that lie.

His grip vanished, eliciting my small, needy moan. His smile slanted sideways, heavy with knowing. He'd liked that sound. My cock twitched between us, slick and messy. Had he come? I didn't know. I wanted him to, wanted to do that for him, but I had no idea where to start, or what he'd like.

He dragged the tip of the dagger—my dagger—down my neck. He'd snatched it up again without me seeing. Pain sizzled in the blade's wake. If he hadn't cut me, he was close to it. He stroked the blade over my left pectoral and encircled my nipple. His lips parted, his tongue slid over his teeth.

Where he came from, they took pleasure from pain. Four years ago, I'd thought such a thing abhorrent. Now, desire scorched my veins and made my sensitive dick twitch, drawing Lark's smooth gaze.

By Dallin, if he...

He pressed the dagger into the nest of golden hair, up against the base of my cock. My panicked breaths stuttered again. Was it wrong to like this? It didn't feel wrong. I didn't think he'd cut me, not there; he liked it too much to hurt me there.

Lark scooted lower. His smooth chin skimmed my quivering abs, and then he licked at the cooling cum pooled in the hollow of my hips.

I gave up second-guessing him and myself, dropped my head back, gazed at the bed's golden canopy. His swirling tongue tickled. I chuckled, making him purr. This man... He was insane, he had to be. And I was insane for letting him get so close.

"Hm," he growled. "Despite appearances, your cum does not taste like honey and sunshine."

Would he say *anything*? Although, I'd been the one to

mention tasting cum. I'd told him I'd wanted to taste his. I'd been angry, but I'd definitely said those words.

Yes, I was insane, and getting more insane by the second. But no longer angry. That had vanished when he'd pleasured me, making my skin tingle and heart flutter.

Had he come? Should I reciprocate somehow? That was how this worked, a give and take. I knew the act of sex, but I hadn't participated, too young, too cloistered, and then I'd removed myself from court. There hadn't been the opportunity. Only my hand, and dreams of Lark.

He settled against my side, propped his head on a hand, and stroked circles on my chest, just the right side of tickling for it to be soothing.

"You vex me, prince."

I captured his hand under mine, stopping his stroking, and curled my fingers around his. "The feeling is mutual."

His hand tightened, squeezing, and he leaned in, whispering in my ear, "Which of us is the villain in this tale?"

If only life were that simple. "Neither. There are no villains, nor are there heroes. Although, you could be one—"

He laughed and dropped his head onto my pillow. "Me, a hero? You jest. And jesting is my role, prince. Next, you will be juggling, although there's still some way to go there—"

I rolled onto my side, hooked my leg over his, and braced my head on my hand, our positions now switched. His black hair flowed across the white pillow behind him, as dark as spilled ink. He blinked, his smile still on his lips. The shallow humor in his eyes covered a thin veil of softness, and behind that, perhaps a troubled soul.

The traitor's son.

I knew what that meant. Draven had told me before I'd been forced to silence him.

Lark had escaped the Court of Pain, but they'd discovered

him begging for coin in the slums and dragged him back, put him in chains, and called him the traitor's son. And that was scratching the surface. Draven would have told others. I'd had to stop him, temporarily. The Lord of War would heal. Until then, I'd ensured Lark's persona remained intact for a little while longer. His court couldn't know he was compromised or they'd have come for him.

Lark's actions in my court would both save and condemn me, which explained why I hated how I'd grown to care for him, despite my best efforts not to.

That was my heart's curse, I supposed. I cared too much, and none of my lies could change that.

"What's it like?" I blurted. "Where you're from?"

He studied my face, perhaps wondering why I'd asked, or how much he should say. The Court of Pain... I knew so little of it; they were careful with what knowledge they leaked. King Umair ruled the court, but he'd been absent for years. His son, Razak, ruled in his stead, with the help of a close-knit council.

I'd met Razak, once. Four years ago.

"I don't like to talk of it, in truth," Lark said, and it was the truth. He made it difficult to tell, but when he was being honest, he looked away, not into my eyes. "It's like how describing a nightmare makes it real."

"Forget I asked." It didn't matter anyway. I'd heard enough to know he came from a dreadful place.

"I... No, it's..." He sighed and let his eyes flutter closed. "The skies are always dark," he said, softly. "There are no flowers, and every thin smile is full of teeth."

I wasn't sure I wanted to know more. It didn't seem possible someone who could sing and dance and laugh like him could come from a dire place like that.

His eyes opened and he focused on me. "Do not pity me.

It's not all darkness, although it looks that way from the outside. There's pleasure to be had. Pleasure is pain's cousin, after all." He turned his face away and his smile slipped from his lips. "Stare too long, Arin, and all beauty fades."

My beautiful lie. I should never have told the maid my thoughts, should have known he'd discover my secret. But beauty couldn't fade when it came from within, from his heart. As the Prince of Love, I knew hearts, and his wasn't as poisoned as he believed. No man could bring joy to hundreds of faces, the way he did, if his soul was rotten.

He peered at me from the corner of his eye. "Your smirk is unnerving." He sat up and pulled his knees close to his chest. "I know you less now than when I entered. Just that you've been playing me. Although, I do know how you taste." He combed his fingers through his long hair, drawing it away from his neck. He'd leave soon, collect his clothes and walk out, and tomorrow, or the next day, we'd be enemies again. I didn't want that. I never had.

I pushed up and placed a kiss on the back of his neck. "Stay," I whispered, and skipped my fingers down his bare arm.

He peered over his shoulder, his face unsure, perhaps even surprised.

What was I asking? I didn't want to be alone, and he was here, and warm, and I couldn't resist touching him now I'd had a taste. I placed another kiss at the top of his spine and stroked over the tiny silvery scars, like distant stars on his skin. I didn't know what had made them, just that they were a strange kind of beautiful, like him.

Another kiss.

He was Lark, the dancer, the player in my court, and this wasn't supposed to happen. But it had. And I didn't regret it.

"Arin—"

On my knees, I straightened behind him, gathered his hair in one hand, and nuzzled his neck, below his ear. "Fuck me again, Fool."

"Arin," he said in that deep, smooth way of his—how I loved to hear my name on his lips. "The Court of Pain plans to destroy your court and I'm the tool it's used to do it. I am not a good person, I'm not nice. You hate me, as is right. You've used me, I've used you, used your people. We've lied, relentlessly, to each other, to ourselves. Lied so much I'm not sure what's true anymore."

I nipped at his shoulder, feeling the burn from his earlier bite in mine. He was right, in all of it. I hated him, who he was, what he'd done. But I also understood him, perhaps more than he understood himself. And the truth? He was my enemy, and I knew that. It really was that simple. The only thing I didn't know was *why*.

"What am I doing here, in your bed?" he asked.

I slid my hand around his waist and grasped his lagging cock. A few eager strokes summoned it back to life. He leaned his head against my shoulder, giving himself to and to me. "Making magic," I whispered in his ear.

He turned his head, and now his mouth was close to my cheek. His smile had vanished, and he stared at me as though I was a trick, one he hadn't yet riddled out.

He swept my hand off his dick but collected my fingers in his, so it wasn't a complete rebuttal, just a temporary one.

Didn't he want this—me—again? Had I done something wrong? I'd watched enough couples fucking in the gardens to know what had happened couldn't have been bad for him—

"Arin," he said, cutting off my thoughts. He tucked a lock of my hair behind my ear. "I do not know what to make of you, or this, and that is the truth."

Then I'd succeeded in fooling my enemy? But it didn't feel like victory. It felt like a betrayal. "Rest with me a while?"

"Just rest?" He arched an eyebrow. "In your bed?"

"Yes, in my bed. Right here. You and I." I scooted down the bed, grabbed the sheets, and held them open, indicating the space beside me. If he didn't want sexual pleasure, then perhaps I could offer company instead. I certainly needed it.

"Very well." He lay back and I threw the sheet over him, and now we were together in my bed, resting. That was a thing two people could do, without sex.

I looked over and found him smirking. His pupils widened, darkening his eyes.

"Are you going to kill me while I sleep?" I asked, not entirely jesting.

He shrugged one shoulder. "I've considered it. Not this night."

Was *he* jesting? "Oh, then... rest," I said again, firmer.

"I've never slept in another's bed—actually *slept*," he said. Sex was another way for him to spin his little lies and gossip, another way to make people do what he wanted them to do. Once it was over, he probably left right after, as he'd been about to do with me. "I don't know if I can."

"We'll see." I shuffled onto my side and studied the man beside me while he stared at the bed's canopy draped high over us. I'd watched him for so long from afar, it was a rare treat to be so close, to study how his smile melted away and the shallow lies faded from his eyes, leaving them softer. His eyelids fluttered, dark lashes shuttering. And then he was gone, asleep. He really did look innocent and vulnerable like this.

"I'm sorry, Lark..." I whispered. "For everything you've endured, and for the pain yet to come."

CHAPTER 13

ark

I SKIPPED the fiddle's bow across its strings and sang the song Mother had taught me. My voice sailed down rain-soaked streets, over the stream of marching passersby, all dressed in black. A few of them flicked coins into my upturned cap, but nobody stopped.

They heard me though. And sometimes, when they thought nobody watched, I saw their smiles.

This was a dream, one I hadn't had in a long while.

I knew what came next, but as a prisoner of the past, I could no more stop fate than I could force myself to wake.

A man stumbled from the procession, drawn to my voice like a moth to the flame. He probably thought himself the flame, and me the moth. "I'll give you coin, boy." His mouth twitched. He dragged his thick, gnarled hand down his whiskered chin.

I stopped playing, with the bow balanced in my fingers,

and my song ended, half sung. I was no boy but perhaps appeared to be one in ragged clothing, bones jutting.

"Well?" he grunted. Not even the deluge could wash away the stench of mead on his breath.

The procession marched on, their umbrellas held aloft against the rain like shields. Water dripped from my hair and ran down the back of my neck. The cap would have helped, but I needed that to collect coins.

A gold coin winked from between the man's thick fingers. I had a few silver ones in my cap, but no gold. Gold would help fill my belly for a week.

I peered through wet bangs. Raindrops on my lashes blurred any details from the man's face. He didn't want me to sing, didn't care for the music, although that was probably how he'd found me. *Go to the boy on the corner, he sings and plays other things for coin.*

"Pretty one, aren't you?" He thrust the shiny gold toward me. "Take it. You want it. So take it."

What I wanted was to play my fiddle and sing, and for people to drop a few coins into my cap as they passed by. It really was that simple. But others kept making it complicated.

The man grabbed my sleeve in his fist and hauled me forward. My boot caught my cap, scattering the few coins I'd already earned. "Don't pretend you don't know what I want, boy."

His rank breath brought tears to my eyes.

He hauled me away from the street, away from the people, deeper into the narrow alley, where rain spilled from gutters and ran across sunken cobbles.

He was strong, stronger than me. And angry, for reasons I couldn't fathom.

He flung me against a wall, grabbed my hand, and shoved

the coin into my palm. I looked at it, at the water pooling around it. Gold never tarnished. It didn't rust, it remained unchanged, no matter the time or trauma it endured. It could be reshaped, made into other things, but it was always gold, always bright.

"Don't say much, do you?" He groped at his belt, unlooping it from the buckle. "Eh? You got a voice, I heard it. A sweet voice." His voice grated, thick with greed.

All I wanted was to sing. It was all I'd ever wanted. *You sing like a lark, my precious boy. One day, we'll fly free from here, just you and I.* Mother was gone now. She had freed us, but we couldn't have known the world outside our cage was worse.

The man tore the fiddle from my hand and flung it aside. It clattered across the cobbles and came to rest in a puddle.

He reached inside his trousers. "Turn around, boy."

All I wanted was to sing.

He wiped his hand across his mouth and stepped in.

The knife I'd taped to my back, under my shirt, slipped easily into my hand. It slipped easily into the man too, time and time again, until the rain turned red, and he lay on the ground, no longer moving. The air tasted of metal, like spilled coins in the rain.

I picked up my fiddle, shook off the water, and strode back toward the street corner. Once there, I righted my cap, collected my coins, and played the song Mother had taught me, and I sang like a—

"Lark?"

The dream vanished, swept aside in a blur. I blinked awake, looking up into Arin's pale blue eyes. His hand burned against my chest. Sunlight poured through the chamber's many windows. "You were thrashing," he said, his expression so full of concern I almost believed it. "I wasn't sure if I should wake you..."

The memories swirled, like water down a drain, water from broken gutters, bloodred...

"It's fine," I croaked, and reached for my head, as though to steady the stream of images, memories, dreams. "Thank you." I wasn't back there, back then. But I needed more, I needed my anchor to tie me down here, in the now, in this moment. I grasped Arin's worry-filled face and pulled him into a savage kiss. His brief resistance melted away, and the prince moaned into my mouth, then brought his knee over me, mounting my hips. I was already hard: he didn't ask how, or what I'd dreamed to make me so. Instead, he took my cock in his hand, hitching my breath and pausing my heart.

How did he know I needed this, needed to fuck, with no words, no questions? We were strangers... so how did he know my heart?

Arin moaned again, his kiss turning sloppy. He rocked, pumping my cock, while his bounced between us. His naked body gleamed in the bright golden morning light. His hair shone a messy mane of gold—never tarnished, never changing, but it could be reforged into something else, like he'd tried to reforge himself. A contradiction, a riddle. I'd begun last night hating him for his lies, but that hate had been lost among kisses and quivering thighs.

I spread my fingers over his firm ripple of abdominal muscles, unsure if he was real. He felt real, hot, and hard and soft all at once. His breaths and mine sawed in the quiet of his chambers.

This couldn't be real. I didn't trust him, knew he'd lied, used me, and he would again. But like the fool I was, in that moment I didn't care. Torn from the dream, I was vulnerable and open, at his mercy.

Fierce determination pulled a snarl onto his lips. He wanted me to come... wanted to be the one to make it happen. He'd clearly noticed how last night I hadn't. It would take more than his savage strokes for me to spill my seed, but this pleasure was enough. I'd noticed a few things about him too. For a Prince of Love in a court infamous for its sexual freedom, his bed had been a lonely place long before I'd arrived. Was he saving himself for someone? A special lady? Or a lord, given his eagerness for men. I could not have been his first, but the thrill at the thought left me breathless.

If I asked him to hurt me, would he?

"What is this?!" Albus blustered from somewhere near the door.

Arin stopped rocking and pumping, although he kept his grip on my cock—so firm, in fact, that when I pulsed in his fist, his fingers flexed a little, and I bit my lip to keep from moaning. Perhaps his father would like to watch? Hm no, that was a step too far for this court.

Arin stilled and lifted his chin, so damned proud that he had me under him. And so fucking gorgeous for it. In the morning light, all of Arin's new, tiny cuts blushed on his honey skin. There was one at his chin, another at his hip, my bite in his shoulder—that one had turned into a startling purple bruise. There was no hiding it from his father.

I'd have laughed, but the king's expression made it clear he was far from amused.

"Father, kindly knock before you enter my rooms—"

Albus surged toward the bed with new purpose in his stride, a purpose I hadn't seen in him for years. The dagger in his hand might have had something to do with that—Arin's dagger. I'd tossed it at some point during the night. He'd found it. Albus swooped in around my side of the bed.

Arin called his name, and now the prince did dismount, probably fearing he might be about to witness a murder.

I shifted upright, covering my cock—a vital part I'd prefer to keep.

Albus didn't have it in him to kill me. But rage made men do desperate things.

He drew to a halt. "Get out, Lark," he growled. "Get away from my boy, you... you, whore!"

If only he'd shown such passion and fervor toward his wife, she might have still been with us.

"I rather think I should dress, or would you prefer I stride naked through the royal wing?"

"Father," Arin interrupted, throwing on a shirt. "Lark's presence here is none of your concern."

"Do you know what he is?" Albus waved the dagger toward me but glared at Arin. "He will use this, he'll hold it against you, he'll make you pay for it in ways you can't imagine. He recently showed me how manipulative he can be."

"I know what Lark is." Arin sighed, already tired of his father. What Albus had recently discovered, his son had known for years. "You're the one who needs to leave." A thin warning wove through Arin's tone.

"'Leave'?" Albus blustered.

"Lark stays." Trouserless, wearing just a shirt, Arin's icy calm made it appear as though he didn't care about me or his father, or any of this, but it was a thin veneer. He'd told me how he felt everything, and I saw it now, reined under control but there. If pushed, his icy veneer would shatter.

The king glanced from me to his son. "All those cuts? Did *Lark* cut you? Did he hurt you?"

Arin marched to his dresser and snatched a pair of trousers from its drawer. "Father—"

"Did he cut you?!" the king shrieked.

Arin whirled, and all that restraint shattered. "How dare you enter my chamber and demand answers of me when I've spent the last half a decade propping up *your* reign! You have no right to judge when you drove mother to madness, force girls into your bed, and lose your mind to pennywort while your kingdom crumbles."

Albus blinked, stunned, and lunged *at me*, assuming I'd been the one to spill his secrets about the girls.

The dagger slashed the air too close for comfort. I danced up the bed, rolled off the opposite side, and then Arin lurched between us, his hand clamping on his father's wrist, holding him back. "The Court of Pain slithers around our feet and you do nothing!" Arin roared. He snatched the dagger out of his father's trembling hand.

"The Court of Pain?" the king stammered. "What do they have to do with any of this?"

Arin's laugh sounded hollow, but I knew that to be a ruse to hide the pain. "Your ignorance is proof of your incompetence. If only you'd cut your own throat, instead of mother's."

So sharp, Arin's tongue, when he wanted it to be. I backed away but didn't leave—couldn't leave. Arin was ablaze with righteous fury, his passion only matched by that which I'd summoned last night.

"She...? She what...?" The king swayed on his feet and reached for the bedpost.

I shouldn't linger. I picked up my clothes, discarded beside the bed last night, and tugged them on.

Arin was dressed now too. He slammed the dagger down on the dresser and yanked his hair back into a tail, his every movement as sharp as any blade. "It's time you abdicated," Arin said, like the final thrust of the knife to his father's chest.

"No." The king slumped. "No, I cannot..."

"Under me, our court—our kingdom—will survive. I've been working to save it. To do what you cannot."

His father's mouth fell open and closed, open and closed, his jowls loose. "By fucking Lark?"

"Forget Lark!" Arin snapped. "By Dallin, I am ashamed of you. It is because of you we are weak!"

His father's shoulders folded in, and he buried his face in his hands. "It was never supposed to come to this."

I'd moved away, to the periphery, unseen and forgotten for a moment. And what I saw before me was a portrait of decay. Pain would tear Albus apart; in many ways it already had. Arin though, he stood over his father as the king in waiting. And he might just be the only hope the Court of Love had left.

The king stared at his own trembling hands. "Where did it go so wrong?" He curled his fingers into fists and looked up at his son. "Yes, you are right... we will discuss this, later. We have guests... It's what I came to tell you, unannounced guests..." he mumbled. "When you wouldn't answer the door, I... came in..." His face crumpled. "Oh, my Katina." Sobs spluttered out of him. "A fool... I've been a fool..."

Arin's backhanded slap rang like a bell through the chamber. The blow whipped his father's head aside and knocked him off the edge of the bed, to the floor.

Arin stepped back and shook his hand, flexing his fingers. The blow must have *burned* him. I felt it too, felt its sting, and wanted more. "For mother, you selfish, rancid excuse for a husband, a father, a king."

Hm, the Prince Behind the Door had teeth. He truly did know pain, and that made him a formidable ally, and a worthy enemy.

This was what I was here to uproot and nurture, sowing the seeds of discontent, pathing the way for Pain. A few weeks ago, I'd have taken everything I'd witnessed to Danyal.

But now... now Arin's secrets were mine, and watching him come alive like this, I'd gladly keep them for him.

Arin knelt and peered up into his father's flushed, tear-stained face. "Compose yourself." He straightened the man's clothing, suddenly tender. "For now, you remain our king. Tonight, at dinner, you'll announce your intent to abdicate. We'll deal with the formalities after."

"What will become of me?" Albus asked.

"Frankly, I do not care. Now get out of my chambers, *Father*."

The king looked to me as though I might help him. I had, in the past, for a secret or a promise, but I couldn't help with this. He stumbled toward Arin's chamber door, mumbling and choking back sobs.

Arin had ruined his father in a matter of moments. But what his father missed, and I saw now, was how Arin's face crumbled in pain. He hadn't wanted to be like this. He still didn't. But love was sometimes cruel. My unfeeling heart tripped behind the bars I'd placed around it. Arin... He staggered, reached for the bed, needing it to hold him up. I almost ran to him, almost betrayed my own weakness. Wouldn't it be ironic if the only heart that loved in this rotten Court of Love was mine?

Arin glanced over, and a small, bruised smile wiped the pain from his face. "Father?" he called, catching the king as he dallied in the doorway. "Who are the unannounced guests?"

"The guests, the guests?" Albus wiped his face and smoothed down his clothes. "Oh yes." The king cleared his throat. "Prince Razak," he said. "From the Court of Pain."

rin

LARK'S FACE turned to ice. He'd been smiling. Not in his brash, look-at-me, entertainer's way, but in the small, secret way that was far more honest than the rest of him. But at the sound of Razak's name, his smile froze on his lips, and all the soft warmth I'd discovered in him drained from his face. Fear widened his eyes. I almost reached for him, but everything we'd shared while lovemaking vanished now as Lark fled out of the door.

I hurried after him, pushing past my wretched father.

"Wait...Lark?" The corridor was empty.

"That man is made of trickery and spite," my father grumbled. "He tried to bribe me—"

I spun on my father and almost struck him again. "Then do not give him the fuel with which to burn you."

He blinked and nodded, backing down. "Why did you demand I have him arrested if you knew your mother had...

159

knew what she'd done to herself? If you knew the jester had nothing to do with it?"

A lie. I had to think of one. I couldn't tell him I'd arrested Lark because I was trying to make Lark believe I was the *vicious prince*, to further use Lark's secrets against the Court of Pain. Father was beyond knowing the intricate moves of this dance Lark and I were trapped in. "Because I wanted to punish someone, anyone." And I'd despised every blow he'd been dealt.

"I'm sorry, son." He reached for me, as though an embrace now might heal years of absence and the knowledge of his sickening behavior.

I brushed him off and returned to my chamber.

"Look at you, at what you've become." He followed. "This is not the way we conduct ourselves. We are creatures of light and hope. I hardly know you anymore, my son, my prince. I barely recognize the anger you harbor—"

My laugh startled him back a few steps. "It's too late, Father. All of it, everything we do is too late. You killed Mother, with your wretched desires and selfishness. You let our court rot around you. You let the enemy in and all you care for is pennywort and what girl you can fuck next. Get out. I cannot bear the sight of you."

"I have failed you, son."

I waved away his pathetic attempts to garner forgiveness, waited for him to stagger out, and slammed the door behind him.

Finally alone, I fell against the closed door and blinked at the floor.

My father was the least of my concerns. Prince Razak had arrived, unannounced. In all likelihood, he'd come to witness how far we had fallen and to retrieve his disobedient spy. I knew one thing—Lark could not go back to that world. He did not belong among them. I'd free him, whatever the price. I had to... for all our sakes.

Tonight, Razak would see how Love wasn't yet on its knees, despite his best efforts to put us there. We were not his pawns. "This night, everything changes."

~

FLOWERS AND PAPER streamers decked the feasting hall. Bright blooms sprouted from enormous vases, ivy climbed marble columns, and sweet peas draped from glistening chandeliers. The guests too, lords and ladies wrapped in silk, were a riot of colors.

And Lark moved among them, startling in his black and white attire.

He'd painted half his face black, half white, and half his hair was painted white too, then plaited down his back. He wore one black and one white glove. The black tailed suit fit him perfectly, and the white shirt gleamed. He swept from guest to guest, dazzling them with card tricks or by pickpocketing their sparkling jewelry, only to pluck their rings from behind their ears or their bracelets from between their breasts, in the case of many women.

I tried not to stare, not to watch him, but in truth, he was too much of a delight to ignore, and on a normal night, I'd have been planning all the ways I'd have him in my bed later. But not this night. This night, we had a guest. The Prince of Pain.

Razak entered the feasting hall late in the evening. He wore black and purple, the colors of his court. He'd slicked back his short, black hair, leaving it ruffled on top. Small silver studs gleamed at his ears, and silver rings sparkled at his fingers. His eyes drank in the color we'd splashed around the dining tables—like a crow admiring shining things it might later steal—and his smile seemed to say he enjoyed it, but that smile was a thin lie. I knew because I'd been wearing the same smile for four years, since he and I had last met.

"Prince Arin," he greeted, bowing and taking my hand for a kiss. "A pleasure."

He took the seat beside mine, graceful and refined. He behaved just like the rest of us, but where a soul should reside behind his eyes, there was only darkness.

Four years felt like four days.

It had been four years since Razak's last visit, during which he'd killed a man—a friend—in front of me. He'd drawn his blade across my last court jester's throat and promised it was just the beginning. He'd thought me weak, he'd believed I'd let him spill the blood of my people in my palace and wouldn't retaliate. His dagger, the same one I had up my sleeve now, he'd left as a gift. Nobody knew about the threat, and the promise. Only he and I.

A few weeks later, the entrancing entertainer Lark had arrived and woven his purple threads of deceit through my court... and my heart.

Four years ago, everything had changed. And this night, everything would change again.

Four years of preparation.

Four years, planning for revenge.

Four years of staring into a mirror and changing who stared back. Four years watching Lark run circles around us all, of learning to lie, and of waiting for Razak's return.

"My dear Prince of Love." Razak leaned closer, his shoulder almost against mine. He was older by a few years. We likely made a startling pair, him in his black and purple, and me in white and gold. "You seem a little... tense. Won't you forgive my unannounced arrival? I do so hate the fanfare. It's far easier just to walk in, without the parade."

"We are a court of forgiveness."

"And such a beautiful court, so... bright. You must be very proud."

"Naturally." I had been, once. But not for a long time.

"Lords, ladies, nobility..." The band ceased playing, the crowd's dancing and twittering stopped, and my father rose from his seat to my right. He wore the golden, pearl-encrusted crown of Love, as was customary during another court's visit. "Please join me in welcoming our esteemed guest, Prince Razak."

Applause filled the hall, so like thunder that it was no wonder Razak smiled to hear it. I scanned the crowd for Lark, but his black and white attire wasn't among the colorful meadow of guests. My heart fluttered. He'd be close by. He was *always* close by. I hadn't spoken with him since he'd fled my rooms. Not even the maid, Ellyn, could find him for me. But nothing had changed between us. He'd want to be here, and he had no choice.

"I have presided over this court with, I hope, delight and wonderment," my father went on. "It has been my honor to serve as your king for these past forty years. But after my beloved wife's... departure—"

"My sympathies," Razak whispered, smiling into his wine.

"The time has come to pass the crown on to my son, your beloved prince." My father gestured for me to stand among a chorus of gasps and mutterings. I stood, smiled at a king I'd come to hate and the father I was ashamed to call my own, then bowed to a surge of applause.

My father sat and groped for his wine, spilling some as he gulped it down.

I lifted my head. "Love is ever enduring," I told the court. "It is the light in the dark."

Lark was suddenly among them, appearing between one blink and the next. His gaze burned so fiercely I almost forgot my words. "Love will overcome and I will ensure the prosperity you have all enjoyed continues." I raised my cup. "To our home, our court, the Court of Love!"

"To the king!" the guests responded, even Lark, with his teasing smirk.

"Well, I am honored to be seated beside a King of Love," Razak purred the moment I sat down. Irony thickened his voice. "Although, I wouldn't get comfortable. Love has a tendency to turn sour."

"What would you know of love?" I asked through a thin smile.

"About the same as you, I suspect." He tugged at his purple gloves. "*The Prince Behind the Door.* Four years is a long time to hide, alone, in your room."

"That must have made it difficult for your spies to collect secrets on me. No?"

He laughed. "One man does not make a court, even if that man is a prince. For all his flowers and finery, he's still just a man playing a fool's game."

"Speaking of fools." I nodded toward Lark, dancing scandalously with a woman in a blue dress. "What are your thoughts on mine?"

"That one?" Razak scooped up his cup and pretended to study Lark as he danced and flirted, making the woman blush. "He dances well." Razak's gaze lingered, implying more to his words, hinting at secrets he shared with Lark.

Razak had sent Lark to my court. He had a hold over him still, but how far and how deep that hold went, I could only imagine. "He sings too, I hear," Razak said nonchalantly, as though bored.

Had Lark sung in the Court of Pain? Had he danced among my enemies? It seemed likely. He'd learned his craft somewhere.

"What is his name?" Razak asked.

"Lark."

Lark was spinning the woman now, and with his typical dramatic flair, he tipped her backwards, catching her in his arms, to the delight of the people around them. "He is a man of many talents," I said.

"Hm... 'Talents,' you say. Not least those between the sheets?"

"I wouldn't know," I lied, even as I could still feel the bruises from his fingertips and the ache from his bite in my shoulder. "Although, honestly, most of the guests here have likely sampled his pleasures."

Razak smiled. "You are quite the mystery Prince Arin."

I'd made sure to remain a mystery. Razak didn't know me, which meant he couldn't predict what came next. Lark had fed him secret after secret. He probably had something on every member of my court, because Lark knew them all intimately. But he did not know me. Or he hadn't, until recently.

Razak's arrival was perfect timing. He thought he held all the cards. But I had one, the most important one of all.

I had Lark.

Razak stood, scraping his chair back across the floor. "Fool! I say, Fool..." The Prince of Pain's smile grew as the band ceased playing, missed notes clattering. The dancers all twirled to a halt, Lark among them. He turned toward us and lifted his chin, the epitome of poise. With half the feasting hall between us, he was too far away for me to read any slip in his expression, but I doubted there'd be one.

"You play the fiddle, no?" Razak enquired, ensuring we all heard. He likely already knew the answer, which made this a game he'd begun to play.

Lark stepped forward. "I do, dear prince."

"Won't you play us a song?"

Lark swept his arm low in a bow and bounded toward the band. The violinist handed over his instrument. Lark propped it beneath his chin and glided back across the floor. He plucked a few notes, familiarizing himself with the strings.

The crowd backed away, giving him room, and a shiver of excitement rippled through them, as though they sensed they were about to witness something special.

He breathed in, flicked his gaze up, and began to play.

At first the music flowed slowly, the notes delicate. He swayed, his body teasing what was to come. I glanced away, pretending to be uninterested, but it didn't last. He should have been nothing to me, a leaf on the wind, like any other, but as his playing sped up, as he skipped the bow over the violin's strings, he began to dance. Music poured through him, coming alive at the tips of his fingers and beneath every light step. He teased the instrument, making it sing.

I couldn't have taken my eyes from him had my whole kingdom depended on it.

I didn't stand, though I wanted to, if only to see more of him. My heart raced alongside his galloping pace. The feasting hall, its people, and my place among them, it all faded away. Until there was just Lark and his violin, a ray of sunshine in the storm.

He'd never played like this before, never danced as though exposing his soul.

The music flowed and spilled, he danced and played, building to a crescendo and then suddenly, breathlessly, it ended. He stopped, arms spread, violin in one hand, bow in the other, and he breathed as hard as he had last night, when he'd had his cock grasped against mine and his teeth in my shoulder. His crescendo was another kind of climax, one that left his audience spent and breathless.

Silence rushed in, filling the absence of music, coming so fast and so thick that it seemed to last for an age. And then the applause roared like a crashing wave.

Razak clapped, on his feet. "Stunning, truly!"

Such was my awe for Lark's performance, I almost missed the sly delight shining in Razak's gaze. Lark was more to him than a tool. The evidence of it shone alive in the prince's otherwise dull eyes. Had Lark danced with such passion and heart for the Prince of Pain in *his* court?

Jealousy soured my thrill.

Of course they were lovers. Who *hadn't* Lark fucked?

It didn't matter. None of this mattered, and certainly not Lark's performance.

I downed my wine, and with the applause still raining down on Lark, I left the table and swept across the dance floor toward him. Lark's eyes widened.

"Dance with me," I demanded.

"What?" The alarm on his face was the first time he'd let slip his real thoughts all evening. We were not meant to be seen together, and never engaged in anything that could be seen to be intimate.

I clicked my fingers at the band. "Music, please." And offered Lark my hand. "Dance with me?" I said again, but this time making it a question.

He surely wouldn't refuse, but as I feared he might, he smiled, jogged to the violinist to return his instrument, and hurried back to my side. The band picked up a similar tune to his, but now with a full musical accompaniment, and Lark swept me into his embrace.

"What are you doing?" he whispered, breath tickling my cheek.

"What I must."

We danced and the crowd watched, including my father, and Razak. Rumors would fly, the shock and surprise of the aloof ice-hearted prince dancing with his fool. It didn't matter. Nothing mattered other than the feel of Lark pressed close. He always smelled so good, of some kind of exotic flower I did not know. I allowed myself a moment to vanish inside the sound of the music and the feel of Lark's body pressed close to mine. It wasn't so different from last night, his breath at my ear, his hands on my hips.

I should have let him fuck me and done all those things he'd promised in the library, let him have me the way his dark eyes had demanded when we'd been tangled on my bed. I'd wanted it, but I'd been afraid, and now...

"Razak is planning something," Lark said. "He did not come here to drink your wine and watch me play the violin."

"Oh, I know."

We spun and stepped, and I breathed too fast. My heart thumped as loud as the music swirling around us. Lark pulled me close. We swayed as one, just he and I, alone in a crowd. A horrible ache began to hollow out my chest, a pain I'd known would come, and the sting of guilt with it. "I want you to know"—My jaw brushed his cheek, stubble scratching—"The prince I was before, the one you met on your first day, he would have loved you with all his heart."

Lark's steps faltered, but he recovered, managing to keep us out of the nearby flower arrangement. He leaned back, peering into my eyes, searching for the truth. "And the prince you are now?"

"Is so very sorry for this—"

I let go, pulled the dagger from my sleeve, grabbed Lark

by the hair, and shoved him to his knees in front of the royal dining table, and in front of Razak.

My father yelled, someone screamed, and the music died.

With a fist in Lark's hair, I yanked his head back and held the dagger's edge to his throat. He panted, twitched, his fingers dug into my arm, but I had him.

Now was the moment to show the rest of the shatterlands and its courts how Love was not weak, how we would not suffer fools sent as spies, and how every broken heart had its price. Including mine.

Razak's lip curled, then twitched into a smile. He slowly rose to his feet. "Prince Arin, it appears you have a traitor inside your court."

"You know I do."

His smile grew. "Then what are you waiting for? My permission? Kill him."

ark

I'D DANCED for Arin as though it was my last performance, and played the fiddle fearing that chance was also my last. Music was my sanctuary, dance, my soul. And I'd known this night would be my end.

But I hadn't expected its final blow to come from Arin.

My knees struck the hard floor, darts of pain shot up my legs, and heat burned down my scalp, where Arin's fist twisted in my hair. And then the kiss of cool steel touched my neck. This was no foreplay. No game. What had I expected? Had I blinded myself so thoroughly to Arin's scheming that I hadn't seen this coming? Was I so in love with the idea of Arin's hope that I'd forgotten who I was and where I came from?

Of course, this had always been Arin's plan. Why else would he have allowed me to live?

His betrayal burned more than all the other hurts combined.

Screams erupted, the king yelled for the guards, and Razak stood, saying something about a traitor. I smiled, because it was all I had left in me to give.

"Four years ago, Razak, you gave me a gift. You killed a friend, a courtly fool," Arin said. "And then you sent me another. So, here's my reply."

Finally, the Court of Love was showing its teeth. I'd have enjoyed it more if its teeth weren't in me.

Razak slow-clapped, then laughed. His laugh slithered over my skin, igniting old scars, making them burn anew. I hadn't seen him in so long, but he never changed.

"I'm *impressed*!" The Prince of Pain grinned and waved a finger at Arin. "You are quite the performer." He strode out from behind the table but remained on the royal dais, elevated above Arin and I. He leaned against the table, legs crossed at the ankle, so relaxed, like a snake in the grass.

"Guards!" Albus boomed. "Guards, stop this at once!"

Razak tilted his head.

No guards came. Nobody moved to stop Arin, or arrest him. The king's commands fell on deaf ears.

The crowd murmured and tittered, uncertain what they were witnessing. If any of them survived, they'd tell their children they were there the day the Court of Love fell.

"I am still king of this court! Where are my guards?" Albus blustered.

Satisfaction brimmed Razak's grin, and dread sank like lead in my gut. Arin believed he'd turned the cards on Razak, thought he'd won. Arin would cut my throat in front of Razak—a show of strength the Court of Pain would recognize, in the language of blood—and Arin believed that would be enough.

But Arin had made a mistake. He'd played his hand too late, because this game had been lost long ago.

Razak gripped the edge of the table and leaned forward. "Do it, Love's Prince. Bleed that man's life from his veins."

I couldn't swallow, or speak, and the blade's edge burned. Arin's steady hand had cut my skin. But I could still breathe... and my heart still beat. I still lived for a few moments more, precious seconds.

"Kill him," Razak urged Arin again. "He is your traitor, no? So, do it, prince!"

Someone in the crowd whimpered.

Arin had to do this, and really, the betrayal must have been the hardest part for him. After that, killing me should be easy. He'd twisted himself up, made himself anew, turned into the villain to stop Razak. This was his moment, his grand finale. He had to kill me, or his transformation, the lies, the hurt, would be for nothing.

"You put this viper in my court to feed you secrets," Arin accused. As he talked, the blade burned deeper. Blood dribbled down my neck.

"Yes, I did." Razak studied his nails. "Your *Lark* was always mine. And now I own every person here. I own their fears, I own their failures. I know how weak you all are. You're slaves to your secrets. Most of all, I own the king, who is the weakest of you all."

Albus had fallen into stunned silence, his face screwed up in confusion. Without his guards, without power, he was a man wearing a pretty crown and nothing more.

"I am not my father," Arin said.

Delight sparkled in Razak's eyes. "Yes, I see that. You are the wild card. Lark failed to mention *you*." Razak took a deep breath, and all around, the court breathed with him. Waiting.

"Well." Razak sighed. "This has gone on long enough." He marched back behind the table, past the royal seats to where the king stood, hopelessly ill-prepared.

Razak didn't slow, didn't miss a step. He drew a blade from his wrist bracers and slashed, opening the king's throat in a great gush of blood. Albus groped at the wound, mouth gaping. Screams burst alive. Albus collapsed over the table. Blood ran, soaking into white. He clawed with bloody hands at the cloth and then slumped and dragged it with him, thumping out of sight to the floor.

"No," Arin breathed. Defeat lived in that one, soft word.

Razak bent down, picked up Love's golden crown, and spun it on his fingers.

The feasting hall erupted in chaos.

"Guards, lock the doors!" Razak boomed. "Nobody leaves!"

I heard the doors slam, heard the screaming. But the knife at my throat held me on my knees, unable to look away from Razak.

My secrets had done this, given him their weakness so he knew where to apply pressure. He'd had control of the court long before tonight.

Arin's arm trembled, shaking the knife at my throat.

With his father slain, he had every reason to kill me. He'd want to do it. He had to do it. My death was all he had left.

Cries and whimpers rose up. People banged on doors, trying to hammer them down.

Razak climbed the king's chair, stepped onto the table and kicked Albus's fallen cup toward the crowd. He raised the crown in his hand and cast his gaze out, over my head, across the sea of terrified people.

Gradually, the panicked crowd calmed, waiting for Razak to speak, still hoping he'd let them go.

"How..." Arin muttered.

Razak crouched on the table and pointed the bloody dagger at me. "You hold the *how* under your blade, Arin. The man you call Lark was instrumental in your downfall. Yet, you have not killed him. I ask myself why... Could it be, you fell for his act?" He laughed. "The question you should be asking me, Prince, is not how but *why*, but as you neglected to ask, I shall not tell. *Love endures!* Love is weak, as evidenced here, by you and your cowardly king and all these foolish people clinging to all this finery as though it will keep them from drowning in moral and financial debt." He straightened and raised his voice for the crowd to hear. "Do not fret. Your torment ends here."

He scooped up a candlestick with its three lit candles. Bloodred wax spilled over his fingers, and delight flared in Razak's eyes. He jumped from the table and sauntered toward us.

"Kill him, draw that blade across Lark's pretty throat, and perhaps I will end this here, sparing you and your people their fate. How is that? Hm? Lark's life for all these people. A fair trade, no?"

Arin trembled from fear, adrenaline, hate—whatever the cause, it shivered through me too. He had to do it, end it now, because whatever came next would be so much worse.

Razak laughed and turned away. "Love, indeed. Love is a pretty distraction. As Lark has shown." He strode to a column and held the candles under the paper streamers. Flames bounded to life and raced up the paper, devouring the flowers and fabric in seconds. "I appreciate the effort, truly, Arin. I can see you mean well. But you're not a killer, and we both know this court was lost long ago."

Arin flicked the blade away from my neck, shoved me forward onto my hands, and raced for Razak.

"Don't!" I cried, too late.

Arin slammed into Razak. They spilled against the table, grappling for the dagger and each other. Razak's scattered candles rolled. Their flames licked at the tablecloth. Arin had him pinned, the dagger pointed down, toward Razak's chest. But Razak had his own blade.

"No!"

Razak stabbed Arin's side once, twice.

Arin stuttered, gasping in shock.

No, not Arin...

Razak kicked Arin back. He stumbled, touched his side, saw blood on his hand, and his legs buckled.

I bolted toward him, to catch him, hold him. He'd be all right, if I could just—

"Lark," Razak snapped, his words yanking me to a halt.

Flames boiled up the walls behind him, too vast and fierce to stop.

Razak straightened his clothes, picked up the crown again, and smoothed his hair. "So much preparation, so many years, and it all fell within moments. It is done."

Done?

Arin braced on an arm, breathing hard. All around, his people screamed, desperate to escape the heat and thick smoke. Lords and ladies I'd frolicked with. I knew their mistakes and their regrets, but I knew their hopes and dreams too. Some were vicious, but many were just... people. They did not deserve this, yet I'd known it would happen. I'd always known.

This was my fault.

Razak snatched a fistful of my hair, spun me around. "Look!" He laughed. "Look how they dance."

Fire dripped from above, setting their colorful clothes alight. Some lay still, thoroughly ablaze. Others ran and clawed at the walls.

"Take a bow, Lark. This would not have been possible without your cunning." Fire danced in the Prince of Pain's eyes. "Treachery is in your blood. I was right to place you here."

I fought in his grip. I had to get to Arin; if I could somehow get him out, then it wasn't over, it wasn't done. Razak laughed and dragged me toward smoldering drapes. He yanked them aside, flung open a pair of terrace doors, and pulled me into the cool night air. Behind us, the drapes fell back, hiding the doors again and the terrified people.

Arin... I had to go back. The people could be saved if they knew about the doors.

A great rumbling groaned from inside the feasting hall and the vivid screams faded behind a howl of fire. "The doors, tell them—"

"Tell me, Lark," Razak said, cutting me off. He eyed the quiet moon suspended above the Court of Love's endless flower meadows. "How easy was it to make him love you?"

I struggled, buckled under his grip, but there was no escaping him. There never had been. No longer fighting, I slumped on my feet, and Razak freed my hair. "Four years," I said, sounding cold again, sounding like the stranger in my mirror, the man I'd left behind to come to the Court of Love.

I thought of Arin trying to juggle balls in the library, Arin bathed in moonlight on his secret beach, of his promise to keep me safe in his court, his passion to save his people. His tender touch had reached into parts of me nobody else had exposed. He'd lied about what he'd wanted me for, of course. He'd always planned to kill me. And now he was dead too. Dead like the heart in my chest.

Guilt twisted my insides in knots, trying to choke me. I breathed in and wrestled the horror and regret back into the far corners of my mind.

Razak descended the terrace steps to a group of his own men waiting by a black carriage. "Burn it all," he ordered.

He climbed into the carriage, settled into the seat, and placed Albus's crown beside him.

I sat opposite, present in the moment but strangely detached from it too, as though moving through someone else's dream. The carriage door closed, sealing me inside a thick, pregnant silence with just the muffled sound of roaring flames and breaking glass.

Razak stared out of the tinted window at the meadow's swaying flowers, lit by dancing firelight. "By morning, there will be nothing left of Love."

No, I thought, and let my gaze settle on the blood-splattered crown. *Just its jagged pieces in my heart.*

ark

RAIN STREAKED THE WINDOWPANE, melting the view of the towers outside, although there was little to see in the darkness anyway. Always grey, always raining. Gone were the brilliant flower meadows and ocean views. The Court of Love's sweet pollen could not reach me here, in one of many towering buildings the Court of Pain called home. The smell of smoke haunted me, wafting from the same clothes I'd worn for days. I'd slept once, and dreamed of playing the fiddle while the world and all its people had burned. Ellyn had been there, Danyal too, his face marked with dozens of scars.

Ellyn was likely dead, caught in the fire.

I hadn't slept since.

Four years I'd been gone from Pain's court. Two days I'd been back, if my grumbling stomach was any indication, and already Lark's brilliant life had begun to fade like a dream on waking.

I wasn't Lark anymore.

He didn't exist. I'd burned him down too, left him in Love's ashes.

I had another name here. My true name.

The door lock snicked over, and Razak entered.

Nerves clenched my gut. I schooled my expression and stayed at the window. He clicked the door closed, flicked the lock, and stood with his back to me, measuring what to say. Razak's moods turned like the lash of a whip. He might be furious or jubilant. He might praise or punish, and sometimes his praise *was* punishment.

I swallowed what felt like glass in my throat and waited.

"Lark..." He finally turned and approached, stroking his thumb along his bottom lip. Intelligence sparkled in his eyes. Amusement too. He wore purple, the dark kind that turned black in soft lighting. No crown, no lace, nothing to detract from the man. "Interesting name. However did you think of it?"

You sing like a lark, my sweet boy. We'll escape one day, just you and I... "It came to me."

He huffed and stopped in the center of the room. The bed was little more than a collection of blankets on the floor, and the fireplace gaped, cold and empty. Love's dungeon had been more comfortable.

After he'd appraised my living conditions, he deigned to see me. "Are you proud of what you've done?" His smile was the slash of a blade, sharp, fleeting.

One wrong answer, a single wrong step, and I'd pay. Before I'd left—before he'd sent me to the Court of Love—I'd have asked him for forgiveness for whatever I'd done to displease him. I'd been nineteen then, a boy on the cusp of maturity. I stared back at him now, four years later, a man. We were almost of the same age, he and I. But he wore a crown of obsidian, while I flipped my cap for coin.

He'd hurt me soon. Oh, how I wanted to deny him that pleasure.

But like the fall of the Court of Love, his victory was inevitable.

I knelt, bowed my head, and closed my eyes, remembering my place. His fingers settled on my hair, then skimmed down my face and hooked under my chin, tilting my head up. "You did not tell me all you knew of Prince Arin. You kept secrets."

Fear parted my lips in a silent gasp. "Forgive me."

"Forgiveness is not for the likes of you." He grabbed my right hand, separated my fingers. A blade flashed. Pain danced up my arm. I knew not to scream; it would satisfy him. The sound choked me instead. What was another finger lost anyway?

"Welcome home, Zayan." He smiled. "Brother."

rin

"You should have cut the fool's throat," Ogden, the king of War, grumbled.

"What I do in my court is of no concern of yours." I stood in the center of a vast, horseshoe-shaped table, flanked by two guards. War's council of advisors sat around me, along with several faces I recognized from my fleeting visits to Justice, many years ago. This felt like a trial. Perhaps it was. After my spectacular failure, I deserved to be judged.

"Your court?" The king chuckled, making his thick braids bounce. "There is nothing left of your court, young prince." Only the king of War would laugh at a massacre. His large, shirtless chest and shoulders heaved beneath a heavy, decorative gorget.

I kept my chin up, even as shame and disgrace tried to bow my head. A few days had passed since my court had fallen. Days that were a blur of hot pain and maddening dreams. I barely had the strength to stand on ceremony here, but this display was necessary.

Ogden eyed me now, his face full of disappointment.

My father had always respected him. I could never understand why. The brute of a man considered violence the answer to everything. Nothing could defy the swing of Ogden's axe.

Weapons hung on the walls of this great hall, all kinds of curved swords and jagged spears crossed behind spiked shields. Red and black banners draped from the high ceilings. Occasionally, a blast of hot desert air rippled over them, bringing some respite from the cloying heat, but it soon gasped out again.

Sweat dripped down my neck and glued my shirt to my back. Sickness churned in my belly and the wound in my side throbbed. The council chambers were vast but the air stifling. I'd remembered War's palace as a furnace as a boy. Little had changed.

"Justice, here, want to see you tried for treason against Dallin's accord." Ogden gestured blindly toward the three blue-robed visitors. "But you assaulted a lord of this court, which means the decision is—"

"If Draven's tongue hadn't been so loose—"

Ogden slammed his great fist down, rattling numerous cups. "Silence! A prince you may be, but here, now, you are in my debt, and the debt of Warlord Draven."

I clasped my hands behind my back and clenched my jaw. It was true, I owed the Court of War much, even my life. Draven had found me outside the palace's smoldering remains, delirious, bleeding to death. I remembered little of the next day and night, just that he'd found help, patched me up, and brought me here. To War. Considering what I'd done to the lord, it was a surprise he hadn't left me for dead among the flowers.

Ogden's gaze narrowed. "I didn't think you were stupid, quite the opposite. But why you allowed that vicious little serpent, Razak, through your doors is beyond me."

I'd made a mistake and underestimated how deep Razak had sunk his claws in my court and its guards, taking control long before he'd arrived. I'd underestimated his insanity too. And my own feelings toward Lark, as complicated as they were. The whole event had been one mistake after another, and I was far from proud of it.

I should have killed Lark. It would have been a small victory, but a victory nonetheless. "My *father* hosted Razak."

"Your father was a kind and gracious man who will be sorely missed. You, prince, I have yet to get the measure of. I have given your testimony to the representatives of Justice and will discuss your fate with them." He clicked his fingers, dismissing me.

"May I speak?"

The man growled low. "Go ahead, then."

"If you believe for a single moment the Court of Pain is not among you, then they have already won."

Ogden's chortle rumbled through the room. The council members chuckled with him. "Yes, well, we have no jesters here, and we are not so easily fooled as those who put their trust in Love."

They'd always laughed at Love, as though we were the shatterlands' joke of a court. Perhaps we had been, because now we were nothing. But what had been done to us wasn't isolated. "They will not stop at destroying Love's court. Razak wants blood."

"Why?"

"I..." I didn't know why, and that was what made all of this so infuriating. "How do you guess the reasoning of a madman? Because that is what he is. He wants to spread pain, to make us all his subjects." It was a guess and seemed plausible, but there was more to it than that. There had to be.

"What the little prick wants and what he gets are two very different things—and what he'll get is my sword up his ass!" Ogden surged to his feet. "You have said and done enough, Arin. Your court is ashes. Your family, slain. Your people spill over my borders, desperate mouths to feed. I have half a mind to give you to Pain just to see the matter done—"

"That would be unwise." A woman in a blue hooded robe spoke up, her tone like ice-water poured on Ogden's fire. Much of her face was hidden, as Justice preferred, but I saw thin, unsmiling lips form the next words. "Justice will not support such actions."

"I suppose you'd suggest diplomacy?" Ogden grumbled.

"Of course. Balance is all. We should reach out to Pain, opening lines of communication, instead of barring them behind weapons and talk of war."

This was insanity. Razak had no interest in talking. I'd seen the rabid glee in his eyes as the flames had raged. He wanted the rest of us to writhe on his hook. "You cannot negotiate with insanity. Trying to speak with Razak would be a mistake—"

"A mistake?" Ogden huffed another dry, dismissive laugh at my expense. "He speaks of mistakes... The only mistake here is the fact you're not in chains, Arin. Do not make me regret it. Until we can determine your true motives in all of this, you have no voice among the courts. Guards, escort Arin back to his rooms and make sure he stays there."

Ogden may not have had fools, but he was one. War was blind, more so perhaps than my court had been. He couldn't

186

see past the tip of his blade, and as I was escorted back to my room, I feared the fate of my court might soon be his.

LORD DRAVEN LEANED against the wall outside my room. Gold rings gleamed at his ears, and like most of the desert-dwellers I'd seen about War's sprawling palace halls, he'd lined his eyes with a sweep of gold paint. A loose black shirt gaped at the neck and billowed at his wrists, while a red sash hung low on his hips. The affect was a dramatic one. He looked like some untamed wild man and nothing like a lord from a civilized court. Which was how War seemed to prefer things.

He nodded at my guards and rasped, "I have him." His voice sounded like sand grating over rock. I winced. That was also my fault.

"King Ogden says he is to remain under guard at all times," the guard declared.

Draven nodded. "Very well." He opened the door to my room and stepped back as I entered then followed me inside. The guard attempted to join us, and Draven held out a hand. "No need, he's not going anywhere. Wait outside."

"Regardless—"

"What's he going to do, leap from the window only to die in the desert?" Draven slipped something into the guard's hand that gave him pause. Whatever it had been, he left moments later.

I headed for the open balcony window, where the endless desert wind rippled through gossamer drapes. A generous canopy shaded two seats. I gingerly lowered myself into one and waited for Draven. The stab wounds pulsed with dull throbs. I'd been told to rest, but if I'd stared at the sandstone walls a second longer I'd have gone out of my mind.

187

Draven settled in the chair next to mine, remaining silent. Beyond the palace, an enormous wall dotted with watchtowers separated us from the shifting dunes and turquoise skies of War's unforgiving desert land. I tried not to think of the cool ocean breeze of home, or the scent of flowers, or the salty mist on my lips. All things I could not go back to. Things that had no place here.

"I thought, if I waited, you'd apologize," Draven said.

We'd exchanged only a few words before I'd almost severed his vocal cords, forcing his silence. I barely knew the man, but I did owe him my life after almost taking his. It hadn't been deliberate. I'd lashed out... "I had a plan for Lark. Your reckless gossip threatened to expose him, ruining everything," I snapped, and winced as a surge of heated pain rolled up my side. "Damn." I shifted in the chair, trying to alleviate the ache.

"The plan to cut his throat in front of the Prince of Pain? That turned out well for you."

The wind pushed a fan of sand over a distant dune. I watched it instead of Draven's arched eyebrow and judgmental glare.

"Does your side hurt?" he asked.

"Yes."

"Good. There's a saying in the Court of War that the endless winds always come back around. Do bad things, and they come back on you, Prince Arin."

"Yes, I am aware." I clamped a hand to my side and grimaced at the wetness. The bandage was already soaked through. I may have broken the stiches. Damn it all to Dallin's bottomless ocean and back.

I shoved from the chair too fast, making the balcony spin. Draven's firm grip caught my arm. "You were told to rest," he said, and I couldn't tell if he was angry or if that was the tone of his broken voice.

"Yes, well..." The nausea waned and I brushed him off. "Thank you, I just... I can do this." After pulling off my jerkin, I removed the shirt, stopped in front of the mirror behind the washbasin, and peeled back the bandage. Razak's two stab wounds had gaped like two puckered mouths. They'd been sewn shut, and the stiches remained in place, weeping some from strain. My head spun. I gripped the washstand.

"Why didn't you kill Lark?" Draven asked from somewhere behind me.

The representatives of Justice had asked the same. Why hadn't I killed the traitor among my court? They'd heard the rumors from those who had escaped the feasting hall. I'd held a blade to Lark's neck, but even after my father's death, I hadn't killed the man Razak had admitted to being a spy.

"Why?" Because despite his lies, his game playing, despite years of his manipulation, I knew the taste of his lips, the feel of his body quivering against my own, and I knew his heart, beneath all of that, was good.

"Because." I sighed, looking up at Draven's reflection behind mine. "Despite my best efforts, I cannot change who I am." I wasn't a killer, and even if I had been, Lark had danced his way around my heart. "I am the Prince of Love, whatever that means now. I am not capable of killing, not even someone who betrayed me... as Lark did."

"You knew who he was, even before I told you?" Draven persisted. "Didn't you?"

"I suspected, yes." I poured water into the basin and splashed it over my face.

"Then why were you so enraged by the truth that night in my chamber? Why did you attack me?"

"Not for the reasons you think." I could say no more. If the Court of War learned how I'd spared Lark because I *cared* for him, they'd think me Razak's puppet too. I'd known Lark hailed from the Court of Pain, but I hadn't known the details Draven had imparted that night. I hadn't known how Lark had once escaped his court, or how he'd been found in the slums, singing for scraps, and other things... It wasn't right, Lark being used like that. Draven's information had shocked me into a rage. The Lark I knew to be hiding beneath all his flamboyant layers did not deserve that life. I'd had to keep his secrets hidden, and in my fury, I'd perhaps cut Draven a little too deep.

I patted my face dry on a towel and turned to face the warlord. "Your voice is returning."

Draven touched the small bandage at his neck. "A little more each day."

With my court gone, I didn't need to be the man I'd created—aloof, untouchable, his emotions guarded against all. It would take some time to shake that act, but I could begin here, now.

"I *am* sorry, Draven," I said. "I'm sorry for all of it. I thought I could be as cruel as my enemy, but I was wrong. It cost me everything." Grief tried to choke me. I swallowed it. "I suppose there is a lesson in all this somewhere."

"Don't fuck with the Court of Pain?"

That was certainly one.

"I'm sorry too," Draven said. He approached, and it was only now I noticed his two curved daggers, one at either hip. Most of the warlords and ladies openly carried weapons. But did he mean to use them on me? He stopped and looked me in the eye. "I'm sorry for all the love you have lost. Despite your actions, I would not wish what befell you upon anyone."

A nod was all I could muster. Any more, and I might not

fight my way back from despair. "Despite the name, there was little love in my court. Our family was not as harmonious as we made it appear."

"Few are," he said, as though speaking from experience. "You have wine?"

"Wine? I doubt it. Unless your prisoners are routinely left with wine in their closets?" As with their weapons, the people of War liked to have wine close by at all times. It seemed to be a terrible combination, but in my short time here, almost everything was terrible.

Draven began searching the wardrobes and dressers I hadn't yet had time to open. "Ah ha! Welcome to War." He triumphantly raised a bottle he'd found and then the cups, then set about pouring us both drinks.

Draven seemed like a good soul. He'd saved me when he didn't have to. I owed him more than angry retorts and bitterness. But with my body, head, and heart bruised, I was having a hard time finding much good in anything. "Thank you, Draven."

He handed over a glass of wine. "No need for thanks, Arin."

"No, I mean for... saving me. And I'm sorry, for being an asshole."

He laughed, raising his glass. "Let's drink to that."

I tasted the drink, found it spicy and warm, and swallowed it down. I'd heard how War cultivated enormous vineyards that were half submerged in the ground to keep them from wilting in the sun. I'd heard a great many things about the Court of War. They were warriors, all, men and women alike. Every child was raised with a weapon in their hand.

"What of Lark?" Draven's voice, even broken, held a strange note. He studied his drink, took several generous gulps, and looked up.

191

"What of him?" I asked carefully.

"I assume he survived, and he's among the Court of Pain?"

Thinking of him there, in their towering buildings, like great swords thrust into storm clouds, it hurt my heart. I'd never been to their court, but like the rest, I'd heard talk. A huge city sat at its center, consuming commerce and people, like a black hole in the land. I couldn't imagine anyone laughed there, or danced or sung or did all the things Lark loved. "Where he belongs."

"Hm," Draven said, and with his voice in tatters, it sounded like a growl. He knew what Lark had been through. He'd told *me* the details. We hadn't gotten so far as to discuss what any of it meant. Now Lark was back where he belonged, it didn't matter.

"*The traitor's son,*" he wondered aloud. "One of his parents must have insulted the court, I assume."

"The Court of Pain is careful with knowledge." I set my wine aside on the washstand and rummaged underneath for a fresh bandage. "How is it you know even this much?"

"A letter."

That seemed unlikely. "Someone wrote you and told you Lark was the traitor's son from the Court of Pain?" I found a cotton bandage and tape and straightened, finding Draven next to me.

"The letter revealed the Court of Love's favored entertainer was a spy known as the traitor's son, and the rest I told you."

"Anything else?"

"It said that when I attended your ball, I should seek the traitor's son out, and that I'd know by his... missing finger."

Whoever had sent Draven that letter knew Lark well. "I don't suppose this letter was signed?" I asked, picking up a separate cloth. I rinsed it and began to dab at my side, but the blood welled again, and the stifling heat closed in. Perhaps the wine, combined with the desert air, had not been a good idea.

"You don't like the sight of blood?" he asked sympathetically.

"Who does?"

"Allow me to help? Then, I won't have to watch you almost pass out."

"All right." I braced against the washstand and let him do whatever needed to be done. Cool cotton dabbed my side. I steered my thoughts from how the wounds had gotten there and the feel of the knife punching in. Had Razak stabbed me in the chest, or any higher, I wouldn't have survived.

"No, it wasn't signed," Draven said, wiping blood away. "I thought little of it, honestly. Almost forgot it. Then I saw the jester in your court, and well, he's... unmissable."

I stared into the washbasin's pinkish water. "He was quite the distraction. Do you still have this letter?"

"Yes, I think so."

"Was there a wax seal?"

"Ah, yes..." He sighed, something only now occurring to him. "There was, and now you mention it, the answer is obvious."

I turned my head. "The seal was purple." The color of Pain.

"Yes. I was certainly played. They wanted me to blunder in, I suppose." He taped the fresh bandage to my side with surprisingly gentle hands. He looked up, catching me watching, and stepped back. "There. Now rest, or this will not heal."

"Thank you," I muttered. I retrieved a fresh shirt and shrugged it on, thoughts swirling with Razak's plotting.

"Someone pointed you in the direction of my court and let you stumble into trouble. Were you not suspicious?"

"I thought it a joke." He laughed. "A letter about a traitor's son..." Returning to his glass, he refilled it from the bottle and held it aloft, then hesitated, his gaze on the wall but focused elsewhere. "I thought it nonsense. Until..."

"Until what?"

"Until I saw his face, in the gardens, when I told him I knew he was the traitor's son." Draven downed the entire glass of wine in a single substantial gulp, then winced at its burn on his sensitive throat.

"What did you see on Lark's face, Draven?"

"Fear."

CHAPTER 18

ark

THE COURT OF PUNISHMENT, the court of pleasure, the court of pain... It was many things. But never a home.

Razak had me dance for his council, and if I didn't, I'd gain another scar, just shallow enough to hide in candlelight.

They had me dance and then ignored me when I did. Which was its own kind of torture.

I'd been here before, in this invisible birdcage.

It had been easier to dance before, when I hadn't known another way to live. A way not filled with agony in every step. Strange, how I'd been so blind to my own joy in Arin's court, until it had been taken from me.

Arin, who had told me he'd keep me safe... and then tried to cut my throat.

My ankle buckled. I tripped and fell on the small stage, lungs heaving. My whole body *burned*. Fitting, I supposed. I'd burned Arin's world.

The talking and laughter that had filled the council chamber all night descended into silence.

How long had it been? I'd danced for hours. It had to be enough.

I saw the toes of Razak's boots first, then the rest of him when I lifted my head.

"Get up," he snarled.

The others were shadows at the table behind him, their faces a blur. Only Razak's face was sharp. His sneering slipped into a daggerlike smile. Nobody saw how our smiles were alike, or how we both shared the same sultry dark eyes. A boy who begged for coin, the slave on the end of Razak's leash could not be a prince.

And I wasn't.

Razak had made sure of that.

"Stand!"

I propped a quivering arm under me and levered myself onto my knees, but my legs were shot, every muscle spent dancing for him. The room spun and my heart throbbed as though it might burst through my ribs. Bile burned the back of my throat. I couldn't do this. It wasn't like before. My heart wasn't in it. I didn't want to be here, in this life, this world.

Razak's hand clamped my chin but as he peered into my eyes, his grip softened. "Your performance cannot end on failure." He let go and stepped back, expecting me to rise. The others would be watching too, waiting for the climactic ending.

He was right.

I had to finish. The dance had to end for my audience.

But not the council, I couldn't dance for them, or Razak. They could not take another piece of me. No, I danced for one other.

I blinked, sliding my focus away, and where Razak stood I imagined Arin there in his gold and white, trying to be hard and cold and indifferent, trying to be my enemy. Almost succeeding, until he failed so spectacularly with my hand around his cock and a gasp on his lips.

For Arin, I found my feet. The nearby gramophone continued to play, beckoning me to join it once more, and so I did. I forced my body to move and sway and dip and spin, emptying my heart and mind of everything except Arin.

I wished I had danced for him, just for him. No court, just he and I, on his secret beach.

He would have liked it.

The music ended, the vinyl clicked and cracked, and I flung myself into a bow.

Arin came forward and when he tipped up my chin, tears slipped down my cheeks. "You never fail to surprise me," he said, stroking my tears away. But the voice wasn't Arin's, and in a blink, Razak took his place.

A sob tried to choke me. I clenched my jaw, holding it back.

Razak bit into his bottom lip, then raised his voice. "Council is ended. We are done!"

The rest was a blur of dark palace corridors, a door slamming, a cushioned bed draped in purple, and Razak, his hands on my chest, my neck. My thoughts whirled, as though I still danced somewhere far away... in a meadow full of flowers by the sea. I dreamed while awake, and danced in the flowers, until spotting a figure at the cliff's edge overlooking the ocean.

I thought he might jump.

And that figure... was me.

rin

A WEEK TURNED INTO TWO, and while the wound in my side healed, those in my life did not. Ogden refused any further meetings. The only contact I had from any court was a representative of Justice, telling me no further action would be taken. I'd suffered enough. I was a *victim* of the Court of Pain's unsanctioned attack, not their accomplice. And Draven had made no charges against me.

As for how they planned to retaliate, or if they sought to punish Razak—or Umair, King of Pain, if they could find him —I wasn't told. As a prince without a court, without power, I was worthless.

There were no locks on my doors. I could leave any time I liked. All I had to do was walk out into the miles of desert sands and probably die there. I didn't know which way was home, didn't even know if there were roads beneath all that shifting sand. I might as well have been stranded on an island in an ocean.

Shutting me out was a mistake.

I knew Razak, knew him more than most. I could help determine what he wanted, and what his next move would be. His attack on Love's court must have had a motive, besides madness. But all Ogden saw was weakness that Pain had taken advantage of. To him, it was justifiable. They cut out the weak, killed their wounded.

Ogden probably wished Draven had left me to die.

The warlord was the only respite I had from pacing my room or standing on the balcony, staring at shifting dunes. Almost daily, he came with a bottle of wine, and we'd drink until the sun set. Then he'd go off and do whatever he did in this enormous palace, preferring to work in the cooler evenings.

Today, he was late. The sun was already excruciatingly high, driving me inside, off the balcony. Draven didn't seem to be like the rest of his kind, who appeared to be made of gruff snarls and blunt, three-word sentences. Or perhaps that was how they behaved around me, an outsider.

A knock sounded on the door. "Come in."

Draven shoved open the door and propped himself against the frame, no bottle in his hand today. "A walk?" He'd tied his hair back into a thick, bushy tail, keeping it off his neck to keep him cool.

"By Dallin, yes. Anything to get out of this room." With no need to collect a coat—one layer was too much in this heat—I strode out into the hall and welcomed Draven's substantial presence beside me. We'd walked before. The palace was a sprawling maze of terraces and courtyards interconnected with long, arched tunnels, open at both sides to let the wind pass through. Walking with Draven seemed safer than on my own. Alone, I'd attracted all manner of peculiar looks for being blond-haired and slighter than anyone else.

"Does the heat ever let up?" I asked, plucking my damp shirt from my neck.

"Oh yes, it can get cold enough for Justice to feel right at home."

Justice's lands were well known for their dramatic ice-dusted fjords and snow-capped peaks. *Ice in the desert?* I snorted. "I don't believe it."

Draven's dark eyes held a hint of humor. Was he jesting with me or being sincere? I couldn't tell with him, although the rest of his kin seemed to speak their thoughts, so perhaps this desert frost was true too.

"Stay long enough, and you'll see for yourself," he added, quite proud of the fact.

We walked on, descending multiple outdoor stairs to a sunken oasis, protected from the heat by the towers and battlements of the palace itself. Several aquamarine pools trickled into each other, cascading down a waterfall before plunging back into the ground. It was a wonder the water didn't evaporate the moment it bubbled up from its spring. Around the pools, decorative tiles depicted the desert dwellers in their stepped pyramids, armed for war. One such pyramid loomed off to one side of the palace, connected to the rest of the grounds by a long viaduct. I'd asked what it was, but all I could get out of anyone was how it was used during times of ceremony and all other times it was sealed.

A handful of people milled about around the pools. Walking for pleasure was not something the people of War did. Unless there happened to be an argument at their destination. They liked to argue. Or partake in "robust discussions" as Draven had corrected.

"I appreciate you spending time with me." I shielded my eyes against the sun.

"It's no trouble." His voice still held a throaty rumble that wasn't unpleasant.

He gestured for us to take a seat at the nearby bench, flanked by flowering cacti. Small birds buzzed from the bright red flowers, their wings moving so fast it was as though they hovered without them. The Court of War was a strange place. So very brutal, but beautiful with it, like a well-forged weapon, I supposed. Although this court's savage beauty was no match for Love.

"Thinking of home?" Draven asked.

I sighed and leaned back on the bench, seeking relief in the shade. "I must learn to let it go."

"Give it time."

Time. Something I appeared to have a lot of, yet it slipped through my fingers, like the sands for miles in every direction. My people had perished. Without my court, our lands had fallen into chaos. Most people had fled and were now refugees. I wasn't doing enough to help them, but what could I do if Ogden wouldn't meet with me? "Any more time without a purpose and I might go mad," I muttered.

"Ogden hasn't given you a role?"

"No, and he's unlikely to. He'd prefer to forget about me. And Razak. He doesn't see the threat. Delaying gives Razak time to maneuver. We should be rallying together against him." Draven arched an eyebrow, and I laughed, rubbing my face. "I'm sorry, my rants must be tiresome by now." During every walk and usually halfway through each bottle of wine, the conversation always found its way to Razak. When I wasn't dreaming about Lark and his quick fingers and strong hands, I dreamed of Razak's blade plunging into my side.

Draven leaned toward me. "No. I agree with you. But I

am a mere lord and you are..." He gestured, trying to find a word I wouldn't take as an insult.

"A prince without power?" We could talk all we liked, but neither of us could do anything. "Do you know if there are plans to retaliate?"

"There are always plans for war. Plans aren't the problem." He sighed and squinted across the oasis. "Some talk of mustering an army as a show of strength. That is all I've been able to discover."

It wouldn't work. Razak didn't see strength in numbers. "He's not interested in battles. He won't fight a war, he knows he'd lose. He'll use sleight of hand. He'll trick his way to victory. Poison, assassins. He'll cheat. *That* is how the Court of Pain fights." I'd let my gaze wander too, and now Draven had fallen quiet, I turned my head and found him staring at me.

"How do you know this?" he asked.

"Lark." I clasped my hands together, and rubbed them, needing to move out of frustration.

"He told you how Razak fights?"

"Not explicitly. We didn't talk of his court, or where he came from. I just knew, and then... he knew I knew, and well, that was enough. He showed me, in his way."

Draven nodded and leaned away, half slumped in the corner of the bench. "There is rumor you and he were... involved."

I laughed. "Lark was involved with everyone."

"Yes, I'm aware." He chuckled too, as though he knew what being *involved* with Lark felt like. Had they been intimate? Probably. Lark had said he'd visited Draven. Is that what he'd meant? Somehow, Lark's escapades continued to surprise me. Although they shouldn't. Of course he'd fucked Draven. A debut warlord in my court, as handsome as Draven

—Lark would have been fascinated. He'd have wanted to riddle him out, see what made him tick, and then collected Draven's secrets to tell the Court of Pain later.

What would it have been like had I let him riddle me out from the beginning? Four years we'd have had, instead of just a few weeks.

"Then you do not deny it?" Draven squinted, shielding his eyes. "Caring for him?"

"I suppose you think it makes me look like a fool." I no longer had the taste for lies. And what harm would it do, him knowing I'd been intimate with Lark? He had been, so what difference did it make? "I used him to learn how to be ruthless. To do that, I had to get close to him, make him believe I cared. He'd have returned to Razak if I hadn't, and I needed him. I planned to show Razak how Love was not afraid of Pain." Saying it aloud left a bitter taste in my mouth. I *had* used Lark, right down to those final moments when he'd been on his knees, my dagger at his throat. I'd never wanted that. I'd told myself I was saving him, but really, everything I'd done had been for me.

He likely despised me, wherever he was. Which was probably for the best. He and I, his world and mine, we were too different, poles apart.

"Then you do not care for him? He was just a tool?" Draven asked.

I swallowed, looked away. "Four years I watched him, and I kept my distance. But for all my efforts, I couldn't guard my heart completely. Sometimes I hated him so much the rage was blinding, but there were other times..." Like when I'd stood in the library, his arms around me, hands on my wrists, trying to teach me to juggle. It wasn't even about the sex, or how he'd brought me to the height of passion in that library with one hand over my mouth and the other on my cock.

There was a softness to Lark, hidden so deep that I wasn't sure whether I'd dreamed it. But if it was real, then the Court of Pain would torture him, even if it was his home.

"I see."

"Lark was a tool. My use of him was... complicated. It happened. It's over. And he and I are not entirely relevant when it comes to holding Razak to account for his crimes—"

Draven raised a hand. "You misunderstand. I'm not judging you. In fact, in all truth, I liked Lark, the sly prick. I will confess, that mouth of his is quite something." He hesitated, sensing perhaps my own judgement in what he *didn't* say. Clearing his throat, he added more sternly, "But others have judged you. Your name is ruined, your court gone. They think you weak. Rumors speak of how you fell in love with the fool and he played you like he plays the fiddle."

"That's not— He didn't..." I groaned and buried my face in my hands. "I knew what he was. It was deliberate!"

"A Lord of War would have fallen on their own sword had they shamed themselves so."

I huffed through my nose and glared at Draven's grinning face. "Is there a point you're getting to or would you like to rub more salt in my wounds first?"

"There's a point." He grinned. "Actually, a proposal. Something that might help you and see to it you have a voice among the courts again."

Then why wasn't he speaking it? "Go on." I needed to be heard, I needed a seat at Ogden's court. Like I was, Draven may as well have left me for dead in the meadow.

"It's rather... unorthodox," he said.

"Well, now I'm intrigued."

"Marriage."

"What?" I spluttered.

"You and I. We join as one."

I must have misheard. Or the sun had made me delirious. "...What?" I asked again.

"Your joining with a warlord will legitimize you in this court. As a prince married to a warlord, Ogden will not be able to deny you a seat at his council."

I laughed again, stunned, and a little alarmed. "Forgive me, but in the Court of Love we marry for love, not... whatever this is."

"In War, we join for position," he said. "And the Court of Love is gone."

The idea was absurd. Nobles did not marry outside their courts; such matches would end in disaster. Not to mention the fact that while my court was relaxed when it came to same-gender couples, War did not look kindly upon two men joining. Fucking was fine, as far as I knew, but nothing more formal. War treated marriage like another battle to be won, or lost, and its goal was a child. More warriors for their battlements.

"It's not about us," Draven continued. "It's about winning. If we can lure Razak from his court, he'll be more vulnerable, and what better way than an invite to our joining ceremony? A refusal would look weak on his part. He'll come, and as you say, we might have an opportunity to hold him to justice for all those who perished at his hand."

Yes, having Razak leave the safety of his homeland would be the only way to get to him. And he'd do more than attend our joining ceremony—he'd bring Lark. Because he'd know it would hurt me. Once inside War's palace, he'd believe himself safe, because War did not stoop to subterfuge. But I did.

But marriage to a Lord of War, to Draven...? "War and Love are not the greatest of bedfellows..." I trailed off, the implication of other marital aspects heavy between us, then cleared my throat and hurried on. "I'm beginning to wonder if you're not like the rest of your kin, Draven. Your suggestion to lure Razak here is more subtle a plan than I thought warlords capable of."

He smiled. "And you are not all flowers and sunshine." He touched the scar at his neck. "Both misfits in our courts."

Lark too did not fit among his own kind. It appeared the three of us had that in common. Any more misfits, and we'd have our own court; a Court of Fools, perhaps. A prince, a warlord, and a jester.

"Think on it," Draven said.

The idea of joining made political sense, but my heart recoiled. "Don't you one day want to join with someone you care for? You... had a son?" I'd heard he'd had a young child who had died but knew no more than that, or even who the mother was. Nobody seemed willing to discuss it, least of all Draven. Not even a few bottles of wine had loosened his tongue on his past—I had tried.

"That time has passed," he said stiffly.

"What would you get from our partnership?"

Draven's slow smile brightened. "A prince."

CHAPTER 20

rin

"THIS IS VERY UNUSUAL." Ogden stood behind his chair and gripped its back under thick fingers. The sweep of gold under his eyes shimmered under flickering torchlight. It was night, and the air breezing through the open arches, windows, and walkways had cooled, making the king less irritable.

Draven and I stood before him. Our proposal had been written and lay on the table in front of the king. All he had to do was sign it, thus granting us permission to wed.

"War and Love? I'm not sure what to make of it," the king mused, then came out from behind the table and studied us both.

We were alone; there were no council members or even guards. Not that any guards were needed when the king himself had an axe strapped to his back.

"Of course, this would give you both a seat at this very table and a place in my court. Draven, can you not find a

209

female to fuck? Although—" The king squinted at me. "—he does have womanly looks. Yet he's without the necessary equipment for childbearing."

I rolled my lips together and withstood the king's demeaning appraisal.

"Whereas you are a fine lord, of good breeding stock!" Ogden slammed his big hand down on Draven's shoulder, and while Draven wasn't small, the king still loomed over him. "Find a prestigious female to wed and fuck him on the side," he muttered, not quietly enough.

"I am a prince of the shatterlands—the Prince of Love," I blurted. "Not a whore to fuck 'on the side.'"

Ogden smirked. "You're a fiery one, not like your father at all. Or the rest of your pretty court." He scooped up the written proposal and studied it.

Draven glanced at me and gave a half-hearted shrug. It was hard to tell if this was going well or not. Everything sounded like an argument here.

"Your proposal, little Prince of Love, will give you status, and it puts you in my court, in power."

Draven likely saw the fury building in me and stepped forward. "You're surely not concerned that Arin could be any kind of threat to your reign?" He laughed. "He has no army, his people are scattered. He has nothing but a name. If a mere name frightens you, then I find myself wondering how worthy a King of War you are."

Ogden's head snapped up. "Bold words, Draven. Bold words, indeed." He swept the quill across the paper and handed the proposal over. "It looks as though we're having a wedding. Congratulations." The king breathed in, expanding his huge chest. "We'll need more wine."

CHAPTER 21

ark

I DOZED against the chair leg with my eyes open. Not really asleep, but far from awake. My body was present while my mind dallied elsewhere. A collar—or was it a noose—clung to my neck, its leash loose in Razak's fingers.

Razak's voice droned on and on. His council members stroked his ego, told him how prosperous the cities were, talked of commerce and production, where the people worked to eat in an inescapable cycle that served the higher lords, ladies, and the prince, lining their pockets with gold. They talked of a grand plan, of four crowns, and a key. All of it washed over me.

There was nothing to sing for here.

I missed the sweet scent of flowers in the air, and how the sea breeze filtered through my window's drapes in Love's palace. I missed the laughter and joy I'd summoned in Arin's court. I missed the magic, the warmth, and despite all their mistakes, desires, and little lies they'd tried to spin to make their lives better, I missed the people.

But more than anything else, I missed the control.

"Arin's alive?"

Arin's name on Razak's lips summoned me back from the waking dream. He tugged on my leash, dragging me against his leg. "It seems your pet prince survived the fire. Resilient, isn't he? Aren't you pleased?" he asked, his smile sharp with teeth.

I blinked. Was this Razak's new game? Lift my hopes then dash them? I turned my face away.

He sighed and dropped the leash. "You are tiresome." He tossed a note onto the table, where it lay, half unfolded. Black and red, the colors of War. An invite to a joining...

I saw two names on the paper: Prince Arin and Warlord Draven.

Arin *was* alive? It wasn't a lie.

"Where's your spark?" Razak yanked on the leash again, choking off my air, and sneered at my spluttering. "Where's your flare? You were more entertaining when you fought back." He curled the leash around his fist. "Submissive doesn't suit you." He raised his fist.

Arin was alive...

Hope's bright spark hadn't burned out.

I'd thought him dead, I'd believed he'd burned because of me.

He was alive, and that changed... everything. My heart raced, my body burned, alive and here.

Razak's fist swung down. I jerked away, grabbed the back of his neck, and slammed his face into the table. Something cracked, probably the table. I wasn't lucky enough for it to be his nose. He screeched, and the council members erupted, lunging toward me.

I snatched the invite and read it—Draven and Arin were to be wed? Arin had gotten over our fling, then. But what had I expected? He'd tried to kill me. He'd used me as much as I'd used his court. *But he was alive!*

"You will pay!" Razak roared. He cupped his bleeding nose and swung wildly with his leash-holding fist, missing me by a mile. Blood ran into his sneer, around his teeth. *Blood in the rain... Blood in the gutters as I sang for coin...*

I hooked the leash around Razak's neck, hauled him into my arms and hugged him close. He bucked, wheezed, clawed at his neck. He was stronger; I couldn't hold him for long. Others rushed in, screaming, reaching.

"You want to fight, *brother*?" I whispered in his ear. "I'll happily oblige—"

A vicious blow struck the back of my head. I slumped. The hot, heavy beat of unconsciousness pulled me down. Razak writhed out of my arms, spun, and spat blood. Warm wetness dashed my face. Reeling, dizzy, I had nowhere to go but down.

I dropped, gripped the table, clinging onto its edge. I had reason to cling on... reason to fight.

Arin lived, and the Prince of Love was a fool. Only fools fought battles they knew they couldn't win. He'd fight, because he was fierce and determined.

I laughed.

He'd come for Razak. He'd come, and they'd think him weak, they'd underestimate him, my Prince of Flowers. The room spun. Razak closed in. Blood dribbled down the back of my neck. But I still clung on.

Razak's glare caught mine. His hand locked around my neck. He held me up and smiled. "There's your fire."

The next blow tore consciousness away.

~

RAZAK LAY BESIDE ME, his purple silk gown untied, revealing his nakedness beneath. His eyes were glassy from the pennywort he smoked from a slim black pipe pinched between his fingers. He hadn't spoken since I'd regained consciousness, but his small smile suggested he was content, for now.

I shifted, naked beneath the sheet. The ghost of his fingers burned in places I had no memory of him touching.

This was nothing new. But the bars at the windows seemed different today. I couldn't place why. It was still raining, wasn't it? I tried to twist onto my side to get a better look. My right wrist snapped taut to the bedpost—a steel cuff held me on a short chain.

"Justice has come to question me," Razak said, drawing my attention back to him. "Imagine that. They think they hold sway over my actions." He placed the pipe between his lips and drew the pennywort deep inside, then blew the sweet smoke toward the ceiling. "They are all fools."

"Do they wish to speak with me?" My voice sounded rougher than I'd expected. With my free hand—my left—I stroked my neck. Prickly heat burned under my touch. I'd been choked.

"Why would they want to speak to you?"

I swallowed, softening my voice. "They'll know it was me who undermined Love's court."

"But it wasn't *you*, brother, it was me." He smiled and moved from the bed. His purple silk gown billowed like a cloak. He was graceful, slim and quick, like our father.

He plucked his crown—just a prince's crown, not the king's— from the hatstand and planted it on his head, then smirked and propped his ass at the windowsill. Rain streamed down the panes, like it always did. He drew on his pipe and sighed. "It's a shame the queen herself won't come. I'd be delighted to liberate her from the weight of her crown."

Justice would never be so reckless, not after seeing Love fall. The Court of Justice would be Razak's most challenging foe, Queen Soliel especially. Despite his talk, she was no fool and could be as ruthless as him.

If I could speak with one of their representatives, just a few words, I could tell them about Razak's crowns... I didn't know much, but perhaps enough for them to piece together what eluded me: Why Razak was doing this. The council had talked of four crowns, of their significance. He did have a motive for all this, it wasn't mere madness.

"Perhaps I should wrap you in a pretty little bow and gift you to him?"

My thoughts jarred. We were no longer talking about Justice. "Who?"

"Arin, of course. Who else? Certainly not the worthless warlord he's joining with. Such a strange pairing, obviously political. The warlord has balls, marrying a prince. Albeit one without power. I can't decide if Arin is as naïve as he appears, or if he's trying to outmaneuver me. Naturally, he'll fail."

"Naturally." I flopped my head back onto the pillow. What *was* Arin doing? Love was neighbors with War, but they'd never truly gotten along. Nobody got along with War.

"Are you concerned they care for each other?" Razak asked.

Was I? Even if I was, it didn't matter. "No."

"Hm, someone has captured the Prince of Love's heart. He wore it so obviously on his sleeve that I'm almost embarrassed for him."

"Arin is of no concern of mine." I sounded so sure I almost believed it. I propped myself up on my elbows and met my half-brother's smirk. "Shall I dance for Justice?"

He faced the window, drew in a lungful of pennywort, and exhaled through his nose. "I think not. You'll stay here."

Here... cuffed to his bed, to return to when he was done with Justice and wanted an asshole to fuck. I hid my sneer. If he wasn't going to let me out, I'd have to find a way to escape the cuffs. Pick the lock, perhaps. To do that, I'd need wire. The bed was all soft silks and feathered down. The lamp beside the bed had a wire-rimmed shade. If I could somehow dismantle it, the wire might be flexible enough...

"But I might take you to the Court of War, parade you in front of Arin on his joining day," Razak said.

"You're going?" That seemed like a mistake. Arin had already tried to kill Razak. Surely, Arin wanted him to leave his lands, where he was protected. And Draven... While he wasn't the brightest, he'd know how to swing an axe and take a head. Arin and Draven together might make a real threat.

"It'll be worth the risk, to see his face." Razak sauntered back to the bed. The amethyst gems in his lopsided crown glinted. He flicked the sheet back and his heavy-lidded gaze swept across my nakedness, raking my soul. "I doubt he'll ever get over you. Men like that, they mate for life. *One true love,* and all that shit. You were his *Lark.* I bet he told himself it was just sex?"

Perhaps. I had. Although, Razak's assessment was flawed. Arin didn't care for me. "You've taken his court, his family, his life. Some might say that's enough?"

He laughed. "Enough? No, not for him. Prince Arin's heart is stronger than it seems." He pointed the pipe at me. "And you're going to help me carve it out of his chest."

No, I wouldn't. But I smiled like I would. I'd lie, fuck, and cheat for another chance to escape Razak's court. But I wouldn't ever hurt Arin again—I'd hurt him enough.

Razak's face softened, like it did sometimes, as though there was a thinking, feeling soul inside the monster. He was more dangerous like this. Every time he gave me that smile, a small, hopeful piece of me believed it—the piece that needed to be seen, to be loved. He pulled the sheet up my chest and laid a soft kiss on my forehead. "Don't get cold. I'll be back soon, after I've dealt with Justice." His skimmed his fingertips down my face, and the swell of emotions shuddered through me. He mistook the reaction for lust, and his eyes widened, but it was more than lust. I despised him, hated him so much that it choked me as readily as his hands had. Hate wasn't a strong enough word, neither was loathing. What I felt for my brother came from deep inside my soul. It was dark, oily, and vile.

He left the chamber for his room, to dress. The door lock snicked.

The sound of my thudding heart accompanied that of his footfalls as he moved away. Drawers rumbled, boots clunked, and after several minutes, another door closed. Then there was silence.

If I was going to find Justice, talk to them, then I didn't have long.

First, I had to escape the cuff.

I grabbed the lamp off the nightstand with my left hand, shook off the shade, and used my teeth to try and twist its wire frame apart. It bent and buckled but refused to snap. Breaking it for the wire, and then molding the wire into a lockpick, would take too long. I needed to be out of this room, *now*.

I rolled onto my front, knelt, and tugged at the cuff. The links clattered. I tugged again, trying to snap it. But it didn't give, not even a little.

"Dallin, give me strength!"

If I didn't get to Justice now, there might not be another chance.

I had to get out of the cuff.

I snapped at it again, and again, until my wrist was bloody and raw.

I slumped and stared at my trembling, mutilated right hand.

Razak had taken the little finger long ago, but more recently he'd taken its neighbor. I was down to two fingers and a thumb. At least it wasn't the hand I used to press the strings on a violin. If he'd known me at all, he'd have known to make it so I couldn't play...

My remaining fingers twitched. Two fingers, one thumb. I folded them together and smiled. Razak had given me the key to escape.

Tucking my thumb into my palm, I pulled. Sharp metal dug into the back of my hand, trying to peel off my skin. I leaned back, levering all my weight at the point where my hand was stuck in the cuff. Just a little more, and I'd have it. Blood dripped onto silk sheets. Damn Razak. I was getting out of the cuff, the room, getting away, if I had to break every damn finger to do it!

My hand tore free, and I sprawled flat on my back, breathing hard. I'd done it! I raised my bloody digits. "You are good for something after all." I was out. No cuffs, no collar, no leash. This was my chance, probably my only chance to be heard. I flung on a pair of trousers and a waistcoat, forgoing a shirt and boots.

Now the locked door... The door was easier. Razak always left the key in the lock on the other side, never taking it with him.

I grabbed a rug, crouched by the door, and slid the corner of the rug through the gap between the door and the floor. I grabbed the warped lampshade, molded the bent wire into a point, and jabbed it through the keyhole. The key plunked onto the rug. I tugged, and there was the key.

Everything else happened in a blur. Razak's bedchamber, the corridor beyond, draped in the dark and quiet. Nobody was about. They were all likely in the council rooms, especially if Justice was questioning Razak.

I had to get to the guest rooms.

I darted down the corridor, bare feet fast and silent. Razak's court ran on a small number of staff, all of whom were loyal to him. If any saw me, they'd alert him. There were no discreet corridors here, like at Arin's. Nowhere to hide. Hopefully I had some luck left.

The sound of voices sailed down the corridor.

I ducked through the next door, pushed it almost closed, and waited in the dark for the people to pass by. My heart boomed like a drum inside my head and chest. If caught, Razak might grow tired of taking fingers. He'd take my whole hand, and then there would be no more music.

It didn't matter. I had to get word out, I had to explain who I was, to try and redeem myself, try and balance Justice's scales. But above all of that, I needed them to see me, to know me...

And maybe they'd get word to Arin that I was sorry, even though he despised me. They could tell him I was sorry for us both.

CHAPTER 22

rin

A BREEZE ROLLED over the flower meadow, making the flowerheads ripple like ocean waves. I strode among colorful blooms, stroking them, and my palms tingled with the thrum of life. This was a dream, surely, as my palace, my home, shimmered on the headland by the sea. The towers sparkled under the sun like jewels in a crown. A pang of regret or grief cloaked my heart. I stopped, and as I watched, flames boiled from the palace's foundations, climbed its white walls, turning them black. But the fire wasn't red or even blue. It burned purple, the color of twilight or an approaching storm.

I watched, stranded among a sea of flowers, until there was nothing left of Love, just ash raining down from clear, starlit skies.

As the flames receded, another sound rose. A violin's swift rhythm. I knew its tune. And when I turned toward the edge of the cliff in the distance, where the meadows gave way to endless ocean, I knew the man playing too. He skipped the fiddle's bow across its strings, and behind him, the full moon hung like a lamp in the star-speckled sky. He spun with the instrument tucked under his chin, hair fanned out. So beautiful, like one of his stories, too magical to be real.

The music quickened, the violin's melody so painfully haunting it spoke of terrible things.

I had to get to him.

I hadn't saved my court, or its people. I hadn't even saved myself. But I could save him.

I called out. He played on, the music too loud, too fast, and he danced and spun and played toward the cliff's edge.

I ran through the flowers.

The cliff edge—he was right by the edge, his music building to its crescendo.

He stopped. Frozen. The music cut off, as abrupt as the slash of a knife. He stood on the cliff's edge, face up.

He was safe, he'd stopped playing, he'd be all right. I slowed again and waded through the flowers, so close now that if I called out, he'd hear.

He tipped forward—

"No, don't!"

I bolted awake, wrapped in cold, damp sheets.

The drapes rippled, teased by the desert's nighttime air. "Lark?" Of course, Lark wasn't here. Just a dream. "Damn..." There was no going back to sleep with my heart galloping in my chest.

I climbed from the bed, threw on a gown, and ventured onto the balcony. The moon hung high and bright, so full it lit the dunes in ice-white light, turning them into frozen waves.

Lark was out there, somewhere far away, playing the same games he always had. Like me, he pretended the hurt couldn't touch him. But also like me, it was lies.

I couldn't have saved him *and* my court, but in the end, I'd saved neither.

If only he was here with me. He'd sprawl in the chair, one leg over its arm, so casually flamboyant, then recite a poem about how awful a prince I was, because he could say what he pleased and live how he liked. Because, he'd been free in the Court of Love. As free as he could have been.

And my actions had put him back in a cage.

Someday soon, I'd free him again and I'd keep my promise to save him. "Hold on, Lark." Perhaps, wherever he was, he dreamed of his Prince of Flowers, and perhaps in those dreams, the prince saved the fool.

CHAPTER 23

ark

THE COURT of Pain rarely had guests. Which meant the staff entering one of the guest rooms had to be there for the representatives of Justice. I hung back, behind a corner, and waited for them to reemerge. This was a long shot. All members of Justice might have been with Razak and the council. My escape could all be for nothing. But I had to try.

The maid left. I darted forward through the door as it closed, and froze.

A young red-haired woman sat on the edge of a bed, half-dressed—or undressed in a blue lace vest and panties. Her eyes widened, then her mouth—a scream poised on her lips.

I lunged and smothered her mouth. "Hush."

She writhed and bucked, and thumped my arm.

"I'm not here to hurt you." I breathed hard, fast. My chest burned, body struggling to hold itself together. I trembled too. And my hand on her mouth was stained with blood; my clothes, the little I wore, hung askew. To her, I was a madman, breaking into her room to hurt her.

"Hush, please, listen... I'm not here to hurt you... I promise."

Please listen, please don't scream.

How could I make her see?

I let go and lurched back but held out a hand—my bloody, mutilated hand, but it was too late to hide it. All I could do was hope she saw me, not as a madman, but as someone who needed help.

She froze too, gasped and gulped air. But she wasn't screaming. "Who... are... you?"

I'd tell her, but first. "Are you with Justice?" The blue overcoat slung over the nearby chair suggested she was. But I had to be sure. If anyone else knew the truth, it might get back to Razak and we'd both be dead.

She nodded. Her eyes were blue too, but not cold, like ice. More of a summer blue, of warm skies.

"I do not have long. I need your help. Please do not scream, or I'll lose another finger, and as you can see, I'm already short a few." I tried to smile, to alleviate some of the tension.

She didn't smile, just looked into my eyes. "Go on." She smoothed down her vest, trying to cover her panties.

My timing could have been better. "I am sorry for the interruption—"

"Are you all right?" she asked.

The question stunned a laugh out of me. Where to begin?

"Are you running from someone?" Her voice was soft, level, calm. No accusation, no fear. "Shall I call the guards?"

"No, no guards." I'd done the right thing, coming here. Whoever she was, she *cared*. "What I'm about to tell you, you did not hear from me. I was never here. Please, if it gets back to him—

"Well, balance is all, and whatever you say will surely be judged. So, you'd better speak. Shall we start with a name? Mine is Noemi, I'm Justice Ines's aide. I can get a message to Ines for you. I assume that's what you want?"

"Names? Yes, let's start there. Mine is Zayan." It seemed strange, saying it aloud. So few knew the truth and Razak had kept it that way. Any mention of it, and he'd promised to take my tongue and hang it around his neck. "I'm the bastard son of Umair, King of Pain. I'm Razak's half-brother, and the courtly fool who brought down Love's court." Her eyes widened again, forcing me to pause. Would she think me the enemy? Justice did not judge without a trial. At the very least, she'd have to listen.

"You're the traitor's son?" she asked.

"My mother was the traitor, yes. She attempted to kill Umair and was hung for her efforts. I'm the son she tried to protect."

The woman—Noemi—bowed her head. "Forgive me, but this is... a lot. You burst into my chamber in a state of undress. How do I know you're not insane?"

"You don't, but can you afford to ignore me? Razak will not stop at ruining Love. He'll come for War and Justice. But listen—" I stepped forward again and she tensed. I could go no closer. "Please, listen? Razak doesn't want the kingdoms, it's not about ruling anyone. He wants the crowns."

"'The crowns'?"

"Yes. He burned Love to the ground but took only King Albus's crown. Nothing else. I don't know why, but I've heard talk of crowns among his council, specifically the four crowns. And a key... But I admit, I don't understand its meaning." Much of it was a blur; I'd been hurting and lost, drifting far away, because it was easier there than here, in reality.

"Well, Zayan." She lifted her chin. "This makes little sense. What good are crowns without kingdoms?"

"I don't know. I wish I did, I wish I had more. But he doesn't tell me. And please, I prefer the name Lark."

"Lark, yes." She arched an eyebrow. "The Prince of Love's jester. You turned on him, betrayed him." There was the cold justice in her gaze now. The facts were brutal, and each one true.

"I was never loyal to Arin's court. I betrayed no one. Although, I suppose I am now..."

"You don't sound convinced, Lark."

She was astute, but Justice had to be. I raised my bloody right hand again, all scratched and raw, missing its fingers— the ugliest part of me. "I slipped Razak's restraints to come here. I've lost much of myself to my brother. Where do you think my loyalty really lies?"

She took in my disarray, heard my voice, saw *me*. "Likely with yourself."

Right again. "Nobody else will look out for me, Noemi. I am all I have in this world."

"If that's the case, then I am sorry for you." She still hadn't moved from the bed, likely afraid of me. "Nobody should be so alone in this world. When Ines returns from her meeting with the prince, I will make sure she is aware of this new information. Balance is all, thank you."

Was that it? Was it enough? I tried to think of anything else I could tell her, but nothing came. "Razak cannot be trusted. He will lie and won't abide by any word or promise. Justice has no power over him."

"Justice Ines is familiar with the Court of Pain's methods. She has dealt with our courts for longer than you or I have been alive. I'm sure she has the prince in hand." Noemi stood. Until now, her face had been the picture of stoic grace, besides the occasional look of alarm. But she saddened now and took a soft step forward.

I stepped back.

"Can I do anything for you, Lark?"

She was asking if I needed help. But I didn't deserve it. My heart gave a small hiccup. "I fear, after all I've done, I am beyond saving."

"That cannot be true. Justice is fair, balance is all, we will hear your experiences—"

"I don't need you to tell me what I already know." I turned away, but she called me to a halt.

"Lark, I will see to it your voice is heard."

The hiccup in my chest surged up my throat and a sudden swell of emotion choked me. I gave a nod, because my voice was gone.

That was all I'd ever wanted... for my voice to be heard.

I put my hand on the door handle. I didn't want to go back to that room, back to him. I'd done my part, told Justice what I knew, and perhaps it would help with whatever came next. If I went back, Razak would use me to hurt Arin at his joining ceremony. And it wouldn't stop there. He'd use me again and again, taking more and more pieces of me.

But there was one more thing I could do, one final act that might balance out my mistakes. An act that would end the cycle and rob Razak of power.

"Was there something else?" Noemi asked.

"Yes, do you own a dagger?"

CHAPTER 24

$\mathcal{L}$ark

I HURRIED BACK to Razak's bedchamber and my room without being seen. After locking the door, I slipped the key back underneath. Hopefully he'd think it had fallen free.

I kicked the twisted lampshade under the bed, laid Noemi's knife on the pillow, and paced. The cuff still hung from the bedpost, where I'd left it. For my escape to go unnoticed, I had to force my wrecked hand back through that metal cuff.

The window drew my eye, and the full, fat moon hanging low behind a neighboring tower. The rain must have eased for the moon to peek through. It wouldn't last. The storms always returned.

Why was I delaying?

Blood and pain, it was my fucking life.

I pulled off my clothes, re-folded them, tucked them away,

and returned, naked, to the bed. The bloody cuff lay on the pillow, mocking.

Noemi's knife lay close too, waiting for its time to shine.

Pain did not control me. *I* controlled it.

I grabbed the cuff and forced my bruised hand back through. Scabbed wounds tore afresh. Blood dribbled again. "Gods..." Nausea and heat rolled over me. I shuddered, panting. But it was done.

Razak would see the blood, he'd see my hand, and of course, he'd see the knife. But it wouldn't matter by then.

With the cuff now holding my right arm aloft, I knelt on the pillow and wrapped my left hand's fingers around the knife's handle.

Would Arin want this?

Did he wish me dead every night before closing his eyes and dreaming of us together on his moonlit beach or in his bed?

It would have been good to speak with him, one last time. The Prince Behind the Door, who had vexed and confused me. He'd probably never be able to juggle all that well. Was there a world out there that wasn't bitter and twisted, a world in which we maybe could have lived, he and I? Perhaps that was what came after life, perhaps death was a forever dream? Although I surely did not deserve to dream of a happy ending.

I pressed the tip of Noemi's blade to my wrist.

The half prince from the gutter, Umair had called me, while my mother looked on, the noose around her neck. And then she'd swung.

Perhaps I would meet her again in whatever happens after life... This was the right thing. The only thing. Arin would be safe, my first and last gift to him. And he'd never know.

"Zayan?"

My name on Razak's lips drew my gaze toward the door.

He stood there, blurred and misshapen through my tears.

"Do not..." He raised his hands. "Zayan, don't..."

Strange, he seemed... concerned. He hadn't been concerned in the Court of Love when Arin had threatened to kill me. But then, he'd known Arin wouldn't. Razak had no such guarantee now.

I blinked and loosed the tears. But I didn't sob, just stared at the tip of the blade indenting my wrist.

"Where did you get that knife?" He inched forward. I glanced up, and he stopped. He even tried to smile. "Never mind, it doesn't matter. Put it down?"

A question. I'd expected orders, rage, madness. Not this... softness. I hadn't known him capable.

"I have a surprise for you," he said. "Don't you want to know what it is?"

A bead of blood welled under the knife's tip. I shifted my grip on the handle, bringing it close to the inside of my arm, poised to slice up the vein. Vertical was better, would bleed faster.

He was moving closer again, but it didn't matter, it would be over soon.

"Zayan, you are the only thing in my life that has meaning."

I wanted to ask *what meaning*, but that was his game, to draw me into a conversation, to delay. No, the time for words and meaning was gone.

"Did you hear me? We are brothers, we are kin, the same blood. If you want me to tell the council who you are, I will allow it. You can be my brother to them too."

I looked up and found him at the bedside, almost close enough to reach for me.

"I'll tell them all," he said. "Just put down the knife."

233

He lied with his every breath. But he seemed so sincere.

No, every time I fell for his kindness, but it was an act, like my time in Arin's court had been an act. He wasn't capable of good, he didn't care; I was a tool, a toy, a plaything, and I'd never be anything else. But I could do one good thing in my life.

I could do this.

I flicked the blade upward, and dark blood flowed.

rin

THE DREAM CAME AGAIN, but this time the Court of Love had already burned, and all the flowers were scorched on their stems.

Lark stood on the cliff, staring out to sea. And I knew I was too late. He lifted his face to the moon, arms spread, and tipped over the edge.

Grief choked me awake and panic crushed my heart. I spilled from the bed, threw on a dressing gown, and ran from the room, down the hall, passing quiet servants and flickering torches. I hammered on Draven's door. "Draven... It's Arin, please open the door."

His room was silent. But I had nowhere else to go. I couldn't go back, not with the nightmare stalking me. "Draven, please... I need—"

He tugged open the door and stumbled aside as I pushed

ARIANA NASH

in. "I'm sorry," I blurted. "I just... A dream, it was a dream, but..."

"Arin," Draven croaked, shoving the door closed and yawning into his hand. "Calm yourself. What's happened?"

Calm myself, yes. That would be wise. But the dream still burned in my mind. "It's Lark."

He brightened at Lark's name. "You have a message?"

"No, a dream..."

He frowned. "A dream?"

"I know, it's..." By Dallin, what was I doing here, in his room, in the middle of the night, ranting about Lark in a dream? I spluttered at my own idiocy. "I'm sorry, this is... I shouldn't have woken you."

"Well, I'm up now," he grumbled. "Sit..." He wandered toward the dresser. "Wine? Tell me about this dream."

I couldn't sit while the hurt still throbbed in my chest. I paced instead and watched Draven pour himself a drink. "Is there any hour in a day when you will not drink wine?"

"No." He grinned and held the bottle aloft. "From that reaction, I'm assuming you don't want any."

"No... Maybe? Yes." My galloping heart had slowed to a trot and the dream's haunting images began to fade. All but one. That stark image of Lark on the clifftop, arms spread as though to embrace the moon, and then... I sat in the chair. "Something has happened to him. I know it."

"From this dream?" Draven said, approaching with two glasses in his hands. His black and red dressing gown swooped like a cloak, tied only at the waist. He wore shorts beneath, and... nothing else. I blinked away. What was I doing here?

In the morning, I'd probably regret racing to him because of a nightmare, like a child. I was *already* regretting it.

Draven handed me my glass. "It'll do you good."

I sipped it automatically, but my mind was back on that cliff's edge with Lark. "I fear I have not been wholly truthful with you."

"Oh?" He dropped into the large chair beside mine, unsurprised by my confession. "About Lark, by any chance?"

"It's difficult. Because of what he did. But I... We had a connection, I think." I laughed at my own nonsense and drank more wine. "I am the Prince of Love, you'd think I'd know my own feelings. But I don't know how I feel... about him." I pressed a fist to my chest, where it hurt the most. "Lark and I, it was fast, and violent... and maybe I am mad, but we had something, among all the lies and games. Beneath it all, there was a truth to us, a realism. We both knew the other was lying, and frankly, neither of us cared. At least, not about the things we were supposed to care about..." Was I making any sense? I downed a huge gulp of wine and wheezed, then pressed the back of my hand to my mouth. "Goodness, that's potent."

"You care for Lark. I'm not an idiot. I know. Although, I'd suggest you be very careful caring for someone like him—"

"You think I don't know that? He's a brilliant liar, and quite vicious. He threw me through a mirror."

Draven's eyebrows shot up. "He did?"

"I mean... I had just"—I waved a hand—"tried to stab him, so... You think I haven't told myself a thousand times how he's the worst possible person to... like? But that doesn't change my heart's desire. And the dream? Draven, the dream was so real. I fear he's hurting, and I can't get to him. I betrayed him."

"He betrayed you."

"No, he *didn't*. Everyone thinks he did, but... We had a few weeks together, and he never told Razak about me. He could have. He told the Prince of Pain a hundred other things, but

237

nothing about me. And to thank him, I almost cut his throat as though he meant nothing." Another gulp went down. The room blurred at the edges of my vision. "I'm a horrible person."

"You're not as horrible as you think. You were trying to save more people by killing one. It seems like a reasonable trade."

"You're a warlord, of course murder seems reasonable. I need to reach him, to get a note to him, something. Before it's too late."

"Too late *how?*"

The dream was clear. If Lark wasn't already falling, he was close to it. "Before he plays a game he cannot win."

Draven leaned forward, his gaze sincere. "Lark has a knack for surviving. He'll be the last man standing on a battlefield. I've seen the likes of him before. Wherever he is, he's scheming and plotting. He's survived the Court of Pain before, he'll survive it again."

"That's what everyone thinks. That's what *he* thinks." But I was willing to bet nobody had seen him waking from a nightmare, reaching out in fear. "Inside, he's not like that. Didn't you see and hear him playing the violin before Razak destroyed everything?"

"No, I was recovering from your attack." He slumped back, sipping his wine.

"Had you seen it, you'd have seen his soul. He's suffered much, and he's survived it all, yes, but... he's a fool who doesn't believe in heroes. He'll do something foolish, something dramatic, some kind of final act to teach us all, because that's who he is."

Draven smiled and shook his head. "You're more tragically romantic than he is. Tomorrow, at sunup, we'll see if we can get word of his whereabouts. Will that put your mind at ease?"

"Perhaps."

"Good." He rested his head back against the chair. A small frown pinched his brow. "Forgive me, but I'm not sure Lark deserves your heart, Arin."

I almost laughed. My heart was a troublesome thing. It did not know its wants. "My heart is not so precious."

"Lark's the kind to twist what he touches."

And how would Draven know that? "And my heart is not so fragile a thing, either." I chuckled.

His serious face broke out in a smile. "I see that." He swallowed his remaining wine in a single gulp and pushed to his feet. "Stay, if you like. But I'm asleep on my feet. Do you mind if I...?" He gestured at the bed through the doorway into his main bedchamber.

"No, please... And I'm sorry again for intruding like this." At least he hadn't laughed me off as mad. Tomorrow, we'd send for word on Lark, and hopefully learn he was fine. As fine as he could be.

"Arin?"

I looked up. Draven had stopped in the bedchamber doorway, his back to me. "You are welcome in my bed, should you need the company."

"I... er..." This was the first time he'd spoken of feelings I'd suspected for a while now. There had been a few lingering glances and the occasional unnecessary touch. "Thank you, but I'll rest here, I think." Our walks, consuming bottles of wine until one or both of us fell asleep or fell about in fits of laughter... We'd become familiar, even friends.

His offer of company was tempting, probably more due to the wine dulling my wits and the fact he was nearly naked beneath that robe. But unlike Lark, I wasn't so frivolous with my affections.

"Good night, Arin," he said, then closed the door.

"Good night, Draven."

We were of course about to wed, and any invite to his bed would likely gain teeth once that happened. I couldn't think about that now, with Lark's fate filling my head.

Hopefully Draven was right, and Lark would survive, like he always had. Because the alternative was a world without him in it, and that world was a cold, bleak place.

CHAPTER 26

$\mathcal{L}$ark

"THAT WAS A DANGEROUS THING YOU DID." Razak's thin voice resonated nearby.

A fire blazed in its grate and someone else shuffled about the warm, sumptuous room. This wasn't my room, neither was it Razak's. I attempted to lift my arm, to touch my throbbing head, but a thick wrap of bandages kept my arm from bending.

"When will he be fully awake?" Razak asked.

He was no longer talking to me, which was good, seeing as his every word threatened to shatter my skull.

"Give him time, my prince," an elderly woman said. "Tomorrow, at the earliest."

"I want him mobile tonight. We have a gathering, and Zayan is to be my honored guest."

"Well, that's... very soon. I am not sure he'll be well—"

"Drug him, if you have to. He will not want to miss this very special occasion."

My eyes closed, too heavy to hold open, and I drifted in warm, gentle seas, until the woman woke me with a soft shake. "I'm sorry, Zayan, but the prince wants you dressed and aware."

The prince... Did she mean Arin? No, he wasn't here. Where was here? I blinked at the room, trying to clear my vision. Swathes of dark purples bloomed, and reality reasserted itself, so pin-sharp it hurt my eyes, bringing the throb in my arm with it.

I'd survived. Razak had made sure of it.

I dug my fingers under the bandage.

"Please, don't fight it. And no strenuous movements or the stiches will open. We'll dress it again later."

The woman, a nurse, had kindly eyes. Razak had probably forced her to care for me by threatening her, or someone she cared for.

I nodded and stopped trying to yank off the bandage. "You er..." I croaked. "You called me Zayan?"

"Here you are." She brought a stack of clothes to my bed and laid them out: trousers, a waistcoat, and a smooth silk shirt made of the deepest purple. The silk was so fine it spilled over my fingers like cool water.

This was too much, this was wrong. "Are you sure these are for me?"

"Yes, the prince was very clear. You're to wear this. I wonder what the special occasion is? I'm sure it will be exciting."

Razak's idea of exciting involved spilled blood and screaming. "I have no idea."

"Would you like help with dressing?"

Again with the pleasantries. It was unnerving. "No, I can manage."

"All right, I'll be just outside."

I eyed her as she left, and when the door closed, I waited for the snick of the lock. But it didn't come. Something was wrong. *Nice* in the Court of Pain was a prelude to agony.

I fumbled with the clothes and dressed, although the limited movement in my right arm made every motion awkward. A wispy fog lingered in my head. I'd been drugged to dull the pain and my thoughts. Not my first time, and just as unpleasant as before.

My reflection wasn't as ghastly as I'd been expecting. A little pale, but I'd likely lost a large amount of blood before Razak's physicians had saved me. I wet my hands in the basin and smoothed my hair, then tied it back in a loose tail. The man in the mirror laughed, as though this was all some joke to him.

The nurse knocked. "Come in." I adjusted my sleeve cuffs, tugging them down over the savage bruises mottling my right wrist.

"You're looking well," Razak said.

Not the nurse then, and so much worse. He was dressed in matching purple and black, but without his usual crown. He looked like the man in the mirror, like me. *Brother*.

The room—or my place in it—shifted, trying to unbalance me. I gripped the washbasin. Heat throbbed up my bandaged arm and through my chest, followed by the sickly wash of nausea.

"Out of respect for you, we will never speak of your mistake." He stopped behind me, and in the mirror, his face loomed over my shoulder. Side by side, our clothes similar, the resemblance was unmistakable. "I promised you the truth." He tugged on my shoulders, straightening me. "And so I will give it." His head bowed, and his hot mouth skimmed my neck, his breath fluttering. "But first, a gift, dear brother."

He swept away so suddenly my head spun. With me cuffed to a bed, I knew who he was, who I was. But this niceness from him was so much worse than any torture. Every word was a potential plunge of a blade, every touch like acid. And I couldn't see them coming.

"Come along," he said, already at the door. "You're expected."

I walked two paces behind him, dressed almost like a prince. Nothing made sense, and the drug dulled all the edges. Perhaps I was still dreaming. Around us, the building was nearly empty. Any staff we encountered stopped and bowed their heads. Razak didn't acknowledge them. They were of no more interest to him than ants. Outside, a carriage waited in the rain. The same carriage that had collected us from the Court of Love. Black horses snorted and pawed at the wet cobblestones. Rain drummed on the carriage roof, and my shoulders, soaking into my hair.

Perhaps this was some new kind of punishment.

"Zayan," he snapped, holding the carriage door open. He flashed a smile. "You're getting wet."

I climbed inside, and the carriage jolted into motion. It clattered and bounced, churning my frayed thoughts.

Razak gazed from the windows, not interested in me. This was some kind of punishment; soon the pain would begin. Razak's punishments were as inevitable as a ticking clock. But taking a finger wouldn't suffice. Whatever came of this, I knew one thing: I'd survive, if he allowed it.

THE CARRIAGE ROCKED to a halt on a winding mud-soaked track, far outside the city. The guards that had traveled in a second carriage opened our doors. I stepped down into puddles and accepted an umbrella. Wherever we were, there were no houses nearby, no other people, just trees and the track, continuing up a hill.

Razak stomped through the mud, and with no other option, I followed.

As we passed under trees, large drops of water plinked onto our umbrellas. Rain washed mud from the track on the hill, revealing jagged stones underfoot. This was familiar. Not the place, but the feeling of dread settling in my gut. Up ahead, atop the hill, a large oak loomed, its branches spread.

I knew that tree. I *had* been here before.

A figure stood on a stool beneath the largest outstretched branch. I stumbled, and Razak caught my arm. "Come along now." He pulled.

Several guards stood around the hooded woman on the stool. In the dark and the rodlike rain, I couldn't see their faces. But I saw the noose looped around the woman's neck.

Thunder rolled.

Razak's pace bounced with glee. He left my side and hurried forward.

A guard shoved me in the back, jolting me into motion.

Years ago, I'd walked this same track, climbed the same hill. Umair, the King of Pain, had been beside me then, his thin fingers locked around my upper arm like a steel armlet.

Who was this? Who was Razak about to hang? I had nobody left who mattered. No one he could reach.

Sloshy mud sucked on my boots. Rain pattered against my umbrella. The woman wore a blue, hooded gown.

Noemi?

Oh no... He knew... I stumbled forward, but as the woman lifted her head, she wasn't Noemi. Her skin was dark and weathered with age. Razak drew to a stop in front of her, and tilting his umbrella, he spoke at the woman. "As promised, here is the man you demanded to meet. The man so important to you that he will cost you your life."

She blinked, lifted her chin. Old, wise eyes narrowed on me.

Razak watched her, admired her even, as though studying what would surely be her final moments. "You were adamant you must speak with Zayan, yet now you are silent."

I clutched my umbrella's handle tighter. Noemi had promised to tell Justice Ines everything. But instead of taking that information back to the Court of Justice, Ines had confronted Razak.

And now here she was, on the end of his noose.

"This man"—Razak half-laughed and flung a hand toward me—"is, indeed, my brother, as you claimed. He was also Prince Arin's fool, put there, by me, to undermine Love's court. And so, while you deign to judge me from high upon your stool, perhaps you are now wondering if you should not have trusted Zayan's revelation." Razak placed his right boot on the stool, threatening to tip it over. "Or perhaps his sudden appearance was all part of my design?" He tapped his chin. "Did you think I'd allow my brother to run amok within my court after having him leashed for so long? No? Or is it more likely I sent him to you with those truths upon his lips?"

He was claiming to have orchestrated my appearance in Noemi's room. I wasn't a man crying for help, I was Razak's accomplice. And when Ines met my gaze now, accusations lay heavy in her stare. I was Razak's secret brother, I'd destroyed the Court of Love, I'd condemned her. I wasn't a victim, I was the villain.

I stepped forward. "I didn't do this. He's lying..." My words sounded like lies though, and I didn't know how to make them sound true.

Razak's head tilted. He looked at me curiously, patiently. "You wanted the truth to be known, brother? For the world to see who you really are? Well, here you are. This is your fault."

"Brother? I'm a tool."

He shrugged. "Rest assured, Justice Ines here sent her aide away with the information. Soon all four courts will know you as Zayan, my beloved brother, redeemed of his mother's treacherous ways. A brother who now sits at my side."

He didn't care what the four courts knew, this was about breaking Arin's heart and making the world think Razak was capable of forgiving, making them think he cared. If Arin learned I was Razak's brother, he'd doubt every moment we'd shared. Before, I was a victim, a pawn. It was one thing to be Razak's tool, quite another to be his brother.

I had to get a message to Arin, somehow. But that could wait. Ines was in a far more precarious position. "Fine, you've won," I said, lifting my voice over the relentless rain. "This was all our plotting and scheming. So, what now? You can't kill her. Justice will come."

Razak glanced around us. "And who is going to stop me? You?" He laughed.

"You'll start a war."

He sighed. "The courts are fragmented and weak and so engrossed in their own affairs that by the time they've discussed how terrible I am and voted on action, it will be too late."

"Why?" Justice Ines asked. Her voice held all the grace and power of her court in a single word.

"Why?" Razak echoed. "Finally!" He laughed. "Someone asks why! Because I can, and because a crown is much more than its court. The crowns are the key. And that key will soon be mine."

He was mad. I knew it, but now I saw it. "The key to what? What can be worth the lives you've already taken and the war you'll ignite?"

"What else, brother? But power." He kicked Ines's stool out from under her.

The noose snapped tight. Ines bucked, thrashed, and for all her grace and poise, in death, she was the same as all the others the Court of Pain had killed, my mother included.

Razak leaned closer to me. "They writhe like worms on hooks."

Her twitching slowed. Her eyes swelled, and so did her face. To look away would have been an injustice. Because, like before, this was my fault. I'd thought I'd done the right thing, I'd believed I could do some good, but Razak had poisoned it.

The choking gulps stopped.

And the sound of rain pattered all around, on puddles and in mud, tapping on our umbrellas.

Razak approached Ines's swinging body. "Your Prince of Hearts will hate you more for this," he said to me. "Every move you make against me, I will twist and make mine."

Shivers shuddered through me. I might have shivered this whole time but felt it only now. Adrenaline, fear, and rage. They buzzed through my veins.

Razak turned to me. His sneer softened. He touched my chin, then tried to skim his fingers up my cheek. I snatched his wrist, holding him still.

"Know this, brother," he said. "You will love me, and only me."

He pitched in, and his soft lips pushed against mine. His tongue probed. If I bit it off, I'd swing beside Ines. So I opened, let him inside, tasted his poison and vowed to one day see him swinging from the hanging tree.

rin

IF IT WASN'T for the stifling heat and sandstone architecture, my white-and-gold clad reflection in the floor-length mirror almost convinced me I was back at home, staring at the same Prince of Love I'd been before my court had fallen.

A gold clasp held the milk-white shoulder cloak to my neck. Gold lace trimmed the snug-fitting doublet. White trousers tucked into white leather boots with gold buckles. Where Draven had found white leather in this desert land, I had no idea. I was grateful, of course. Draven had not only saved me, he'd made it so I could stand as the Prince of Love in the Court of War, and that was no small thing.

He was a good friend in a land in which I was very much alone.

A knock sounded at the door. I tugged at my sleeves, fighting off nerves. "Come in."

Draven took two steps into the room, then slowed. He

carried a letter, which seemed important, but he also wore the courtly attire of a warlord about to be wed. The red sash at his waist was adorned with dramatic swirls of black silk. The same black swirls had been painted down his neck. They ducked beneath his loose collar. Did they continue on? Ribbons of red silk wove through his dark hair and its side plait, and kohl lined his eyes. Ruby-encrusted jambiya daggers adorned his sides, one on each hip. The overall affect was of a man about to go into battle, not of one about to be wed. He was... breathtaking.

Two men had never been so ill-matched.

"I er... I did not realize you were dressing." He averted his gaze. "I can leave—"

"No," I blurted, then fussed with my cloak's neck clasp so I didn't have to look at the man I was about to commit to for the rest of my life. "I'm done."

What if this was a mistake?

Razak was attending—might already be inside the palace or certainly nearby. So our plan had achieved its main objective, getting him away from his stronghold. Now we just needed to lure him somewhere alone, and Draven would do the rest, likely with those curved daggers at his hips. Assassinating Razak was the only way this ended, even if it did feel underhanded. The wedding was... a ruse. A feint. Sleight of hand. A distraction. It didn't mean anything.

I glanced over and found Draven standing motionless and staring at me as though I'd committed a terrible social mistake. "What is it? Am I so hideous?"

He chuckled. "No, no... Definitely not... hideous. I've been so accustomed to seeing you less formal that I'd forgotten you're a prince."

"You and the rest of the shatterlands." I forced myself to

stop fiddling with the array of buttons and buckles and nodded toward the letter. "What's that?"

"Oh, yes... I received word from our contacts about Lark."

My treacherous heart flip-flopped. After my dream several nights ago, Draven had sent a request for any information. I'd wondered if we'd hear anything before the wedding, hoping we did. Not that news of Lark would change my commitment. This had to happen. It was the only way I'd regain power. Yet... if I knew Lark was alive, and not hurting, then it would make what had to be done all the easier.

"You may want to sit down," Draven said.

My heart dropped. "Is he dead?"

"No, nothing like that. He's alive. He's on his way here, in fact, with Razak."

I sighed, relieved beyond words. I'd suspected Razak would bring him. Razak would want to see my face when I noticed Lark beside him, thinking his presence would hurt me. But after the dream, I'd feared Lark had gone. It didn't matter who he stood next to, just that he was alive and my dream had been a lie.

But Draven's face was as grim as though he *had* died. So what news did that letter contain?

I sat in one of the armchairs. Lark was coming... What did he think of this union between War and Love? And what did he think of Draven, the man who he had had sexual affairs with? Goodness, Lark complicated everything, yet my heart raced with irrational hope. I wasn't sure I'd laughed the same since leaving the remains of my court, since leaving Lark.

I should have practiced my juggling. "All right, tell me."

Draven scanned the letter in his hand. "There's no easy or gentle way of saying this."

By Dallin, how bad could it be? "Just say it."

"Lark is... His real name is Zayan. He's Prince Razak's brother."

My smile twitched. "What?"

"His name is Zayan and—"

"No, I heard you, I just—" I looked away, at the wall, at the swirls in the wallpaper and the flickering oil lamps. "Razak doesn't have a brother."

Draven took a few steps closer, his face as troubled as mine. "That's what everyone thought. But it seems the traitor's son refers to a bastard son, born out of wedlock to Umair, Pain's missing king. The traitor was Lark's mother, and she had a son with Umair."

This couldn't be true. Lark couldn't be Razak's brother. The implications were too huge. "There must be a mistake. Who gave you this information, how do you know it's not rumor?"

"The news came from the Court of Justice." He raised the letter, showing me the blue seal. "There is no doubt."

Lark was Razak's brother?

I slumped to the side and covered my mouth with a hand, if only to hide my grimace and perhaps my shame. Had I been so duped? Was he truly my fool *and* a prince? Half a prince, I supposed, illegitimate, but he must have known all along.

He *had* played me like a fiddle.

Draven was beside me suddenly, on his knee, his hand on mine. "I'm sorry, Arin. This must be a shock. I know you thought you could trust him."

I laughed, hiding what could have been a sob. "You were right. All of you. I was wrong about all of it."

Draven's fingers tightened, clutching my hand to my leg. "This is what Pain does, they twist things. Nobody is blaming you for—"

"For caring for him?" I barked a laugh, and now a sob did escape. "Perhaps my heart is the weakest part of me, and that's why I've lost everything." Draven began to deny it but saw my glare and cut himself off before he could speak. "Was there anything else in that letter?"

"Yes, he er... Razak has legitimized Lark as his brother. Which means Lark is arriving alongside him as a nobleman, in a position of power."

Two brothers, two princes.

I fought to keep my grimace from turning into a sour laugh. "By Dallin, I should have killed him, just like Ogden said. I had Lark in my hands, on his knees. I should have cut his throat."

Draven's eyes widened. "Arin, listen... This isn't your fault."

Pieces of my heart were breaking off, turning jagged and sharp inside my chest. "You don't understand. We... were together. I thought that meant something. I'm such a fuckin' fool."

"I understand you're a good man, and you were trying to do the right thing."

It hurt. It hurt so much I wanted to rip out my own damned heart and crush it so it didn't hurt anymore. What use was I, what use was love, if it was so blind? "What use is a good man with countless dead and my lands gone? Because of me?!"

Draven's arm hooked around my shoulders and hauled me half off the chair and up against his chest. I shoved, tried to push away, but the more he embraced me, the more my strength crumbled. I gave one final, pathetic push, but the message got lost, and that final shove turned into closing my fist in his shirt. I clutched his shoulder, tucking myself close, and the pain spilled over. I'd lost it all, lost everything—my family, my home, my people, my heart. I should have done more, been better, smarter, stronger. I'd failed everyone. I was weak, I was the fool, and the whole of the shatterlands knew it.

To think I'd cared for him.

Draven said something, murmured in what may have been War's language, I wasn't sure, but it soothed my fractured mind. I stayed in his arms, perched awkwardly on the edge of the chair and half on his knee. It felt good to be held, just held; it felt as though the world outside, with all its pain, no longer existed.

"We're going to stop them." He clutched my face in his warm hands and peered into my eyes. "I will kill Razak for you."

I wanted that. I wanted it so much I couldn't speak. I nodded, too broken for words.

I had to get myself together. This wasn't me, I didn't fall apart. Not when my mother had taken her own life, not when I'd learned of my father's indiscretions, not even when I'd woken to learn Razak had burned my world to ash. I always stayed together.

Draven stroked tears from my face. "You will have vengeance, I promise you this, on our joining day."

He meant it, and I trusted his word. Trusted him. I'd thought our match was wrong, too jagged, too conflicting, but now I wondered if our differences were what could bring us together. The fury in his eyes softened—fury for what had been done to me, not because of me.

I placed my hand on his face, felt the burn of his whiskers under my palm, and I might have seen Draven for the first time.

"Arin..." His hand slipped from my cheek, into my hair. I leaned into the touch, into him, and then his lips skimmed mine, and like fire to the touchpaper, desperate need sparked alive. I kissed him hard, meeting his desperation with my own. It wasn't love, not that, just need and hate and vengeance. I needed this man's hands on me to erase the feeling of Lark's mouth on mine, his kisses on my neck, his grip on my hips. I needed to forget how Lark had branded his name into my heart.

There was no more Lark.

Just Zayan, the Prince of Pain's half brother, and he was a stranger.

CHAPTER 28

*L*ark

HUGE LUMBERING MACHINES blew sand from a brick road far enough ahead of our carriage so as not to spook the horses. Behind, the wind gusted the sand back in, covering any sign we'd passed by and swallowing the road again as though it had never existed.

The land of War was a hot, vivid place.

This was my first visit, but I'd heard about its strangeness from warlords and ladies at Arin's court. They said the land was as brutal and unforgiving as its people.

It was not the place I'd imagined Arin would find a new home.

Sand filtered through the closed carriage doors. Razak sneered and brushed it from his black boots. He saw my glance, arched an eyebrow, then smiled, so pleased I was here. I turned my face away, and the carriage trundled on. Maybe, if I was lucky, a great sand worm would tunnel up from beneath us and swallow our carriage whole. Although the brick road likely thwarted those notorious desert creatures.

Two thumps on the carriage roof signaled our arrival. I pulled the window down. Ahead of the sand-clearing machines, a pale sandstone wall stretched from dune to dune, so vast it was surely made to keep giants out. Or in. The wall's watchtowers climbed so high into the sky I couldn't see their tops.

Once behind that wall, there would be no escape. My gaze slid to my brother. He was taking a huge risk coming here.

"I almost forgot." He scooped up a folded garment that had rested beside him for the entire journey and offered it to me.

"What is it?"

"A gift, clearly. Take it."

I looked at the black silk as though it was a bundle of snakes. Were their razor blades in its seams?

Razak laughed. "So suspicious, brother. Can't I give you a gift without having some ulterior motive?"

I didn't reply. Voices sounded outside our carriage, and the door opened, letting in jarring sunlight and a blast of sand. Razak dropped the gift onto my lap and climbed from the carriage. I followed, then shook the garment loose. It was a coat—a very fine coat of black and purple silk, so light that after I'd shrugged it on, its weight vanished.

"Very nice." Razak beamed, flicking his doublet collars up. "Check the inner pocket."

His guards milled about, readying his traveling chests; nobody paid us any mind. Behind Razak, and still some distance away, an enormous wooden door barred our way through the wall. War had yet to invite us in.

Patting down my coat, I discovered multiple pockets, some smaller than others—perfect for magician's tricks—but one pocket hung low with a subtle weight. I eased my fingers inside, expecting something to bite. But instead, I retrieved a small vial of clear liquid.

Delight sparkled in Razak's eyes. "After the ceremony, a drop in each cup should suffice."

Poison.

I held the small vial up to the sand-filtered sun, turning the liquid red inside. "What does it do?"

"You'll see." He faced the enormous gate and tugged at this gloves. "Oh yes." After digging into his own pockets, he handed over a pair of purple gloves; the two fingers on the right hand had been stiffened with wood to hide my missing fingers. "Cover up, hm? And brother, walk beside me. You're here as my equal. Act as such."

Equal?

It was all for show, of course.

I dropped the vial back into the hidden pocket and tugged on the gloves in time to see the huge gate groan open and two bristling-with-weapons guards emerge.

"Let the dance begin," Razak muttered, then grinned and started forward.

"Greetings." The guards dipped their chins. "You are to be searched for concealed weapons. Do you comply?"

Razak spread his arms, like a showman greeting his audience. "Please, go ahead."

The second guard searched me, missing the pocket full of poison.

"Your belongings will be searched too, but not here."

"Of course. What fool would bring a weapon into War?" Razak laughed, enjoying himself. He'd smuggled a blade into the Court of Love, but in all likelihood, the guards there had permitted it. He didn't need a weapon here, not when I served that purpose.

Two aides joined us. They explained that our luggage would be brought along later and offered us a tour, which Razak declined, claiming the journey had been a long one and we'd prefer to rest up before the ceremony. Passing through the enormous wall into War's palace was like stepping from the wasteland into an oasis. The palace sprawled far and wide, like a whole city within its walls. Terraces and open archways connected multiple levels, with waterfalls flowing between them. Splashes of verdant green drew the eye like emerald gems in a gold crown.

The aides escorted us to our rooms. Mine was connected to Razak's by way of a private door that he immediately wedged open.

He joined me on the balcony, gazing out at the ocean of amber sand. "Why the sad face?" He smirked and leaned against the balcony rail, folding his arms. "This is a time of celebration. War and Love, united at last. A shame it won't survive the night."

Was the poison his only plan, or was there more to his visit he hadn't told me? He knew I'd told Court of Justice everything about who I was. He wouldn't trust me with vital information. He'd be plotting another play, another trick. One he'd keep from me.

"That coat looks good on you." He stepped closer and tucked a loose lock of my hair behind my ear, pretending to care when we both knew he wasn't capable. "You're here as my brother, as a representative of the Court of Pain. Be sure to act like it."

"You mean, I'm to bend whenever you get the urge to fuck someone over?"

He blinked, and I glared back, daring him to strike me. He wanted to. Violence burned in his eyes. But he laughed instead and moved away. I breathed a secret sigh as he plucked an apple from the fruit bowl on the sideboard and crunched into it. "We will rule these worlds, Zayan," he said around chewing. "Take everything and anything we please. These people are nothing, the courts are nothing. They will learn soon enough how it's easier not to defy us."

"'Us'?" I snorted. "Whatever you're doing, I don't want to play any part in it."

"Well then, it's a good thing what *you* want has never mattered."

"Why am I even here? Why are you here? What is any of this for, Razak?"

He strode over and muscled up against me, driving me backwards into the balcony rail. "You are here so I can fuck you when it's done. I am here to claim War's crown. And all of this?" His lips parted, and he tilted his head back, the lust in his eyes not for me but for power. "Dallin wasn't a god, he was just a man, trying to disrupt the natural order of things."

Yes, keep him talking... But where his body touched mine, it burned, making my skin crawl. "What natural order?"

"You'll see, when the crowns are mine."

"War will never let you get your hands on their crown, and if you think Justice is going to let you within ten lengths of their court, you're delusional. They know you killed Ines."

"No, they know she's missing, and they may suspect my involvement, but they don't *know* I've done anything. Justice won't make a move without evidence. By which time, it will be too late." He grabbed my jaw. "Have some faith, brother. You're about to witness the collapse of War. You should be fucking pleased, because after everything *you've* done—undermining Arin's pathetic court—the only thing stopping them from killing you is King Ogden's pride."

"I thought *you* brought down his court, not me." I sneered around his grip.

263

His laugh coiled around me and when he dropped his free hand, he grasped my balls and his wrist nudged my cock—half-hard from temptation. "Be angry, Zayan. I do like you more when you fight." He pressed in, chest to chest, cheek to cheek. "When it's done, I'm going to fuck you here, on this balcony." His lips brushed my ear, setting free a cascade of shivers. "While all of War is buried beneath their endless sands, I'm going to fuck you until you smell like me, until I'm in your head and burned into every inch of your skin. You'll forget all about your Prince of Love. There will be only me, your god among mortals. And you will fucking worship me, brother."

He leaned back, his hand now tight but unmoving around my hard dick. It was wrong to want this pain, wasn't it? Wrong to get hard from his threats?

"Ask me how I know this with certainty," he said.

"How...?" I whispered.

"Because if you don't poison the Court of War, then your little Prince of Hearts will be dead by morning."

I clutched his arm, intent on pushing him off, but he stroked my cock through my trousers, and for a few crucial seconds I froze, didn't push him away, didn't even demand he stop. Then he was gone, backing away and laughing that horrible luscious laughter, and I was so goddamned hard I trembled with it. I was wrong, wasn't I? Broken. Ruined. To *like* what he did to me. But it wasn't Razak I desired, it was... the pain.

"Victory is going to taste so fucking sweet." He crunched on his apple and sauntered out of sight through the chamber's connecting doorway.

I turned, gripped the balcony, and gulped air, trying to center myself and stop the trembling.

Sand churned and hissed below.

If I jumped, it would drown me.

I looked up, and through burned clouds, the sun was setting, giving way to a rising moon.

Arin.

He was the only hope I had left, the only one who could stand against Razak. I had to find him before the ceremony, before I killed a whole court... to save him. Again.

rin

AFTER DRAVEN HAD LEFT my chamber for the ceremony preparations, I dressed in white and gold royal finery for the second time, pinned up my hair, and fixed all the golden clasps back in place. In the mirror, my reflection was the same as before, the only difference being the tousled bed in the background, pillows askew, where Draven had tossed them aside in his fervor.

A warmth radiated low in my gut, and in other places, where the warlord's mouth had skimmed, and his stubble burned. It felt good, like nothing had felt good in weeks. Nothing since... Lark.

Nerves no longer rattled my veins. My hands and heart were steady.

This joining was happening, Razak was here. And everything Draven and I had planned would fall into place. Razak would die this night, without fanfare or flare. Slain by an anonymous assassin. How terrible.

I left my chamber and met Draven in the main hall, beside an enormous palm tree so large it had tried to grow outside the vast glass canopies protecting the hall from sand. He spoke with two men and a woman, smiling, gesturing, while War's palace staff bustled, setting the places at long feasting tables. Cloths of red and black draped over the chairs and hung in ribbons from large columns. I knew so little about this court, and Draven's life, his friends. To my shame, I'd been so consumed by grief and revenge, I hadn't asked. It was time that changed. The group spotted me approaching, and as Draven turned my way, his smile grew, setting my nerves fluttering.

Our joining had been planned to lure Razak, but in light of recent events, perhaps joining with Draven was the right thing to do regardless of revenge and political power.

"Arin." Draven reached for me, and for the first time in public, I folded my hand in his. "These are friends of mine. Jordan." Draven introduced a woman with more muscles than most of the Court of Love's guards combined. She dipped her chin. "Erik," Draven said, pointing out a burly blond man who grinned broadly. "And Laslo." The last man had hair as dark and long as Lark's when it wasn't tied up, but twice as much muscle as him—and I wasn't thinking about Lark.

Laslo clapped me on the back so hard I almost swallowed my tongue. "We'll make a warrior of you yet. Give Draven some meat to cling to, eh?"

"Er, yes." Heat touched my face.

Draven closed his eyes a beat too long. "Forgive Laslo, he was born with his foot in his mouth."

"It's all right." I laughed, a little nervously. Men rarely

married men in the Court of War, but Draven's friends seemed supportive, which was the best we could hope for.

Erik extended his hand and almost took my fingers off when he shook them. "Nice to finally meet you. We did wonder if you existed or if Draven had dreamed you up."

Jordan laughed and folded her thick arms over her muscular chest. "He almost looks like you, Erik."

"Yeah, if I were eighty pounds lighter," Erik grumbled, setting all their laughter off again.

Draven steered me away as they continued to joke, probably at my expense. "They're an acquired taste. I hope you're not offended. They don't mean anything by it. It's just how we are..." He rubbed at the back of his neck and frowned.

"It's fine, really. I like them. I'd like to get to know them..." The implication was out there before I'd considered what I was saying, that perhaps we had a future together

Draven shifted a little closer, and under the shade of the palm we were tucked away despite being in the center of the filling room. "I wasn't going to get all personal about this, considering our... motives for today, but honestly, I want the ceremony to mean something. And if you don't, that's fine, I won't push it, but I hope you do... want this... for more than, you know, a seat at Ogden's table." He winced. "I'm er... I'm not good with romantic words."

I fought my grin under control. "I appreciate your honesty. It's a rare thing. And I'd like us to mean something too."

"Then there's a chance that you and I, that this, could be... a good thing?"

"There's a chance." My father would have been horrified. His son, falling for a warlord.

Draven checked over his shoulder, as though our joining was still taboo among his peers, then tipped my chin up and kissed me on the lips. "But first, I'm going to kill a prince for you."

That threw ice water on the warm glow I'd been nurturing. Of course, I knew what we'd planned, but that didn't mean I was as comfortable with murder as Draven was.

Draven drew me back to his friends. "Heard you tried to take Draven's head?" Erik rumbled.

"That true?" Jordan asked, asking as though she'd take me out behind the cacti later and hang me from an arch.

Draven lifted his chin and touched the pale white line. "A little to the right and I wouldn't be here."

"Vicious." Laslo laughed. "I respect that."

"It was a misunderstanding," I tried to explain, but only seemed to muddle things.

"Don't tell them that." Draven grinned. "Violence is just the starter here."

As their many, many weapons confirmed. Every arriving guest appeared to be carrying some kind of blade, be it dagger, sword, or axe. Even the staff carried small sheathed daggers at their hips. I was beginning to feel somewhat lacking.

"When do I get a dagger?" I joked.

"At the ceremony," Draven said. And the others smirked, suggesting they knew more than I. "I'd best make yours blunt."

They laughed and chatted, and more lighthearted jesting flew around me and Draven, which was apparently the custom for joining ceremonies. Huge pitchers had appeared on the long tables, and the wine had already begun to flow. The celebration would get lively soon.

The ceremony would take place in the pyramid temple, a short distance along the arched bridge, spanning the tropical gardens. If nothing else, I was eager to get inside and perhaps get all this display over with. Draven put a cup in my hand, smiling like he knew how much I'd enjoy it, and I began to feel as though I could, one day, belong among his people and his palace.

"You may have noticed Draven isn't as well-endowed as the rest of us," Jordan said, raising thick eyebrows.

"Clarify that statement, Jordan, before I clarify it for you."

The group looked at Jordan, then at Draven, whom she could bend in two with one hand, and all fell about laughing. Perhaps it was the wine, but I'd rarely laughed so much as I did with them. Until a dark figure caught my eye, standing behind one of the grand sandstone pillars.

He was there and gone again in a blink.

Just a shadow... wearing a black silk frock coat.

I scanned the people nearby. Staff and guests mingled, laughing, enjoying themselves, but there was no flash of black or purple among them.

I'd imagined him.

That was all.

The wine was going to my head. I stared into the drink. Perhaps I should take it slow and not guzzle every glass Draven poured me.

"Arin?" Draven stood at my side, his hand out.

"Hm?"

"The joining-time has come. Are you ready?" He was handsome, standing there, dressed to kill and armed for it. And this was the right thing to do. The only thing.

"Yes, of course." I set my cup down, took Draven's hand, and cast one last glance back. Lark still wasn't there—because he hadn't been there to begin with. But he would be in the temple along with Razak, and the other guests. I'd have to look him in the eyes then, knowing who he was, what he'd done, and how I'd fallen for his act since the day we met.

"Are you well?" Draven muttered under his breath as he steered me toward the main doors.

"Yes, fine... I'm fine."

We left the hall and climbed brick-laid steps, passing between banner holders, their red and black flags flapping.

A joining in the Court of Love meant music and laughter, petals raining from the sky—not hot sand, endless grating wind, and stern-faced guards all armed and ready for battle. This was the court I was about to join. I had to accept their ways, and even come to love them, I supposed.

A pair of guards fell into step behind us, and behind them trailed a procession of guests from all across the shatterlands.

We approached the bridge. At either side the steps fell away, leaving a drop of several hundred feet, with no guardrail, and the path itself was a three-person width. The wind buffeted us, trying to whip my cloak around me and tear my hair from its pins. Perhaps this was some kind of trial? Survive the deadly bridge to the temple and I'd be permitted into War's court.

Behind us, a few voices simmered around a disturbance. I glanced back, beyond the guards, and there he was. There was no mistaking Lark breaking from the crowd.

He strode from the procession, devastatingly handsome in a black silk coat with its flash of purple lining. The wind tugged at the coat's tails and his hair, trying to sweep him aside, but he strode on—coming right for Draven and I, in full view of the entire court.

My heart leaped into my throat.

What was he doing? Was he armed? Did he mean to hurt us?

His glare fixed on me, and his smile tipped up at one side.

Zayan, the Prince of Pain's brother, and now I knew who he really was, it was a miracle I hadn't seen it before. He had the same dark, arresting eyes as Razak, a similar angular jaw, the same hair color, but so much longer. They were so alike we were all fools to have missed it.

"What's he doing?" Draven growled under his breath.

The guards crossed their polearms, bringing Lark's pace to an abrupt halt.

He smirked at them, at me. He knew everyone watched him, knew they'd all heard who he was, and they knew our past. He'd done this to demand attention, like always. Hate simmered around my heart, trying to get inside. Not long ago, I'd wanted him here, but that was before the truth of him had been exposed.

"Let him through," I said.

Draven's hand squeezed mine. I squeezed back, then let go and faced Lark.

The guards separated, opening the way, and Lark strode forth. His half-smirk grew, and then he stood in front of me, a stranger, but also a man I'd thought I'd known and understood, a man I'd desired, cared for, let molest me into spilling my seed. Twice.

"Well?" I snapped.

All eyes were on us, the prince and the fool. He'd made *me* the fool.

He blinked slowly and reached out.

"Touch Arin and I'll take what's left of your hand." Draven freed a dagger from his hip. He held it in a backward grip, ready to slash.

Lark's gaze flicked to Draven, then back to me. He'd be thinking of all the words he'd use to insult us. Words were his favorite weapons. Which made his silence... interesting. What was this display for, theatrics or something more?

I glanced over his shoulder, along the bridge and into the crowd. There, some distance away, Razak stood among the guests, his face carefully measured, his gaze flat. My gut said he hadn't sanctioned Lark's performance. This was all Lark.

Lark still held his hand out, waiting.

If I did nothing, we'd be on the bridge all night.

I offered my hand in return. He took it lightly, then knelt, bowed his head, and placed a featherlight kiss on the back of my hand. "A gift," he said. "For the Prince of Love."

My heart hiccupped, but then hate flared like a shield. "That's enough." I snatched my hand back. "I appreciate you and your *brother* attending. Perhaps we'll see you after the ceremony?"

He stood, took a step back, and bowed his head again. "I'm sure you will." He turned on his heel and rejoined the procession.

The wind howled, or perhaps the howling came from inside my head. I swallowed, trying to moisten my dry throat, and tasted sand. Draven took my hand again. He steered me back around, toward the pyramid temple. "Lark can't get to you here," he said as we walked on.

But he already had. In my hand, tucked against my palm and hidden from anyone but me, lay the King of Hearts playing card.

CHAPTER 30

*a*rin

Painted art adorned every smooth inch of the temple's tapering walls to the pyramid's central point high above us. At first glance, the colorful scenes seemed jubilant. But on closer study, it became clear the paintings celebrated battles and bloodshed. If there had ever been a better sign that Love and War were not meant to join, it was this temple and its tapestry of murder looming over us.

My heart thumped like the war drums depicted on the murals, and Lark's playing card burned against my palm, like a wound. I'd crushed it in a fist, but it was still there, still scorched into my mind. What did it mean? Everything and nothing. So dramatic, so Lark.

A white sandstone altar loomed in the center of the temple, and behind it a stone needle pointed toward the pyramid's apex. Everything was sharp and cold and hard. I fixed a smile to my face and tried to present the idea that I knew what I was doing and wanted to be here. But this place, these people, this temple, palace, the desert sands, and Draven, standing beside me...

How had I gotten here?

I'd been swept here by one wave after another, without realizing I'd been drowning the whole time.

Draven handed me a dagger. Rubies winked in its hilt and the blade itself shimmered with decorative red sand, as though dipped in blood.

My choices had brought me here. There was no other way.

I said the words, accepted the dagger, smiled as Draven wrapped our wrists together with a red ribbon, and let the wave carry me along.

It was done, over too fast. Draven raised our ribbon-bound hands, the guests roared, and we walked back under the suffocating art to jubilant applause.

King Ogden boomed his congratulations, then took the axe from his back and raised it with a roar. The whole congregation grabbed their weapons and waved them above their heads. I smiled, even as I felt the grin breaking on my lips.

I hadn't looked for Lark—couldn't look for him.

But as soon as we stepped from the temple, Razak was one of the first to greet us outside. He extended his hand, smiled, and offered his blessing, as though he hadn't stabbed me twice in the side not so long ago.

Draven grabbed the prince's hand, hauled him close, and clapped him on the back. The grin was the deadliest I'd seen on the warlord's lips. "We'll see you later, Prince."

Razak straightened and smiled back. "I look forward to it."

It was done. I was joined with War and needed to get past

it so we could focus on the next part of the evening's plan. The sickness and dizziness would pass.

The relentless wind buffeted us on the return journey over the bridge, helping to push away the celebratory roaring. With the ceremony over, the celebration would now begin. I'd been warned it would be an experience, and as we entered the feasting hall, the spread of food and wine laid out before us was fit for the king's own joining.

I sipped from my cup, laughed when I was expected to, and was as present as I could be, with Lark in the back of my mind and the wrinkled King of Hearts card in my pocket. The card was a message, of that I was certain, but what message? A threat? A reminder of how he'd tricked me before?

"Arin?" Concern shadowed Draven's face.

"I'm fine, I just... need some air, I think." I scooped up my cup and pushed from the table.

"I'll come." He moved to stand.

"No, stay." I gestured for him to sit. His friends were around him. He was happier among them. "I'll only be a moment." I didn't look back and carved a path through the guests. So many people, so many weapons. The Court of Justice was here too, draped in ice-blue. I'd heard one of them wanted to speak with me as a matter of urgency. Later, it all had to be later. I couldn't breathe...

My chest burned, my heart too.

I stumbled out of the main hall, into one of the arched side walkways, where the breeze flowed from arch to arch, making the flame-torches dance. I grabbed the top of a half-height wall and lifted my face to the wind. The desert air had cooled enough to be pleasant and the chaotic noise from the gathering faded to the back of my mind. Finally, some space, and now that I could breathe again the ache in my chest faded.

I pulled the creased King of Hearts card from my pocket.

I had to let Lark go, like I'd let go of my home. There was no use clinging to the memory of a man who hadn't existed. It had all been a lie.

I held the card over the wall.

On the other side, sand hissed and swirled. All I had to do was let go, and Lark would be gone from my mind.

Just open my trembling hand...

I laughed. Even now he had a hold of me. "Damn you." Bringing my hand back in, I opened my fingers and stared at the card's crinkled design.

"I wondered if you'd throw it away," Lark said, his voice as smooth as always.

Of course, he would be here, watching. He'd followed me outside, invisible when he wanted to be. Chuckling, I raised my cup and sipped my wine, needing it. "I cannot be seen with you. They'll think me a traitor."

He emerged from the shadows and propped a hip against the wall beside me. "Welcome to my world."

Even now, when every piece of reason demanded I hate him, my heart thawed at the sight of him. He was so fucking beautiful in black and purple silk, his hair bundled back and his eyes fiercely arresting. I hated him for that too. "I don't know who you are, *Zayan*."

"Neither do I. We have that in common."

"Go away." It sounded childish, and I didn't care. "Leave us alone."

"Well, I would, but you invited the Court of Pain, so here I am."

"Because you're a prince now?"

"Half of one, when it suits my brother."

I snorted. *Brother.* The man who had killed my family, my court, and almost me was Lark's *brother.* "I trusted you."

"Did you, though?"

"A little..." I admitted.

"I trusted you, thought I knew who you were, listened to your promises, until you held a blade at my throat."

Laughter bubbled from inside the hall behind us, but outside, it was just Lark and I, under a bloodred moon in a land neither of us belonged to. I raised the tattered card. "What's this for?"

His eyes glittered in the dark, and his smile vanished. "You need to leave, now. Take Draven if you must, but go now."

"And go where?"

"Anywhere. But you can't be here this night."

"Why?"

"Razak..." Lark leaned closer. "He has something planned."

"So do we." I smirked and eagerly drank more wine.

Lark's gaze narrowed. He studied my face, looking for some clue as to our plan. "Whatever it is, it won't work. He wouldn't have come if he considered War a threat."

I knew Razak. He thought he was untouchable. He was wrong. "His ego will be his undoing."

"What are you going to do?" Lark whispered, and he was closer now. Too close. Whether the scent was from his clothes or the man, the familiar smell of warm amber triggered memories of he and I tangled between the sheets.

"Do you think me that much of an idiot that I'd answer you?"

He tilted his head. "I need you to go."

"What you *need* is of no concern of mine."

"You don't understand—"

"I don't want to." I slammed the card against his chest, rocking him back a step, and when I let go, the card fluttered to the ground. "*You* need to leave."

"What are you going to do?" he asked again, closing in once more. "It'll be simple, because you don't have the influence at War's court to do any more... Draven then, your new husband, what has he promised you? Vengeance? Did you let him fuck you if he promised to kill Razak?"

I almost struck him, but the lust sparkling in his eyes suggested he'd want me to. "Why do you have to be like this?"

His dark chuckle did things to my body it had no right to do. "This joining is a farce. Anyone with eyes can see your heart's not in it."

I flung what was left of my wine into his face and bared my teeth. He staggered and laughed. "Draven is all I have left. You and your wretched brother have taken everything! Leave, now, or I will go to Ogden and tell him there's a plot against him and *you* are at its center."

He wiped wine from his face and flicked it from his fingers. "Regardless of what you think of me, there *is* a plot this night, and if you don't leave then I will be forced to act."

"Then *act*. You're so good at it. I'm not going anywhere. War is my home, and Draven my husband. You are—" I raked my glare over him."—nothing."

His smile fractured. He huffed a silent laugh and shrugged a shoulder. "Very well. Then I can only hope you know what you're doing, Arin." He bowed, with ironic flamboyance. "I wish you and your husband all the best fortune, should you survive the night." He left in a swirl of silk coat.

I hated him, hated him so much I wanted to turn my face to the wind and scream. I picked up the King of Hearts card and threw it over the wall. It fluttered and spun, whisked into the air, and then the endless winds stole it. The desert would destroy it.

I grasped the wall and squeezed, my fingers turning white. I just needed to hold myself together a little while longer. I could scream and rant later. Tonight was too important and Lark would not take my chance at vengeance too.

It was time to lure Razak away from the crowd.

"Arin? Prince Arin?"

A woman in blue swept along the walkway toward me, her hand raised in a wave. "That is you? Of course it is, dressed as you are..." Puffing, she stopped, grinned, and thrust out her hand. "My name is Noemi, I'm Justice Ines's aide, and I really need to speak with you."

I gave her hand a shake. "Can we walk and talk? I'm expected back at the table—"

"Yes, I..." We walked, but after a few steps, she stopped, drawing me to a halt. "Arin, actually, I believe this would be better discussed away from everyone else. Can you spare a few minutes?"

"Later, then?" I tried to smile politely, but whatever Noemi wanted could wait. "Tomorrow would be even better, as this is my wedding night."

"Tomorrow? It's just that..." She stepped closer and said in a hushed voice, "I'm not supposed to speak of these things without evidence, but frankly, as I was the one who spoke with Lark, I feel my witnessing his confession is evidence enough."

"Lark?" *A confession?* No, I wasn't being drawn into this. "Hm, then I truly do not want to hear what you have to say." I hurried on, leaving her standing alone. Lark wasn't ruining this. I wasn't thinking about him. He had no place in my head—

"He's not lying," Noemi said.

I laughed. "He's always lying."

"No, wait..." She caught my hand in a firm, steellike grip and whipped me around. "I'm sorry, I just—" She let go. "Please, listen... He came to me, during a visit to the Court of Pain. He told me all the things you now know, about who he is. But it wasn't a ruse, Prince Arin. I saw the truth in his eyes. He risked much to tell me."

The poor woman. I'd been in her shoes too, so enamored and bespelled by Lark's sweet lies that he could have told me the moon was made of cheese and I would have believed him. "Trust me, Noemi, he's very good at making lies seem true." I made for the hall once more.

"His hand was cut up!" she called.

I stopped.

"And he was missing two fingers, on that same hand. He'd clearly been tortured and... restrained. And there were bruises..." I turned, and Noemi touched her neck. "Here, as though, well..." Her lashes fluttered. "As though he'd been choked." She sighed and her face fell with sadness. "He might lie with his words, but not with his body, Arin. I know what I saw, and I know Razak twisted the truths to make it seem as though they'd been his plan all along, but I suspect Lark telling me the things he did forced Razak to tell the world who Lark really is. And I think... I think Justice Ines paid the price."

I couldn't ignore this, or her. She wasn't one of Lark's flings. There was truth in her words. And Lark's hand... I'd seen his gloves, but of course, the fingers were fake. I already knew he missed one finger, but the gloves he wore this night covered the missing digit. What else did they cover? And bruises at his neck? "What are you saying?" I returned to Noemi and kept my voice low. The feasting hall was close, and the raucous guests loud, but we might still be overheard.

"Justice Ines is missing," she explained. "She was due back a day after me, but she hasn't been seen. Of course, the Court of Pain claims she left there safe and well, but we only have their word."

"And their word is worthless," I muttered, as my thoughts shifted and realigned around Lark once more. Nothing was ever solid with him. He made information and the truth fluid.

"Yes," Noemi agreed. "Razak has done something to her."

"Was Ines the one who confronted Razak with Lark's truth?"

"Yes."

"A secret like that, the identity of the traitor's son as Razak's own brother, kept for over twenty years... Razak would have been furious." I knew what that fury felt like. The scars in my side were proof of that. "If he took it out on Ines, then she is likely dead."

"That is my fear. But there is no proof, and without proof, Justice cannot act."

"Justice cannot, but I can." I took her hand and gave it a reassuring squeeze. "Thank you for telling me this. Return to your table. I'll deal with it."

"Lark said more to me. Information that has been kept quiet by the Justice nobles. Things you don't know."

"Oh?"

"Lark told me Razak doesn't want the kingdoms, he wants the crowns. I was hoping you'd know what that means."

"'The crowns'?" That made little sense. A crown without a kingdom was pretty jewelry. But I'd seen Razak's face when he'd taken my father's crown. He'd looked at it as though it held all the riches in the world. He'd taken nothing else that night, just the crown.

Draven tore through a nearby doorway, saw me, and jogged over. "There you are. I was beginning to wonder if I'd scared you off," he joked, then noticed the somber ambience he'd stumbled into. His smile stuttered. "Is everything all right?"

"Draven, this is Noemi, from Court Justice. Noemi has some interesting things to say about Lark."

Draven failed to contain his sneer. "Another night, perhaps? Let's not ruin this one."

"I fear it is already ruined."

CHAPTER 31

$\mathcal{L}$ark

DRAVEN AND ARIN were missing from the celebration. Perhaps Arin had taken my advice and decided to leave, or perhaps they were under a palm tree somewhere, Arin's cock deep between Draven's lips.

I sighed and swirled the wine in my glass. I hadn't touched my drink, didn't have the appetite for it after delivering a few drops from Razak's vial into any unguarded cup. The unattended cups had been easy to deal with. Other cups had required a little misdirection and some sleight of hand. People looked at me strangely, intrigued and disgusted now they knew my name. They probably also knew Razak had paraded me around on the end of a leash and fucked me when he pleased. Whatever their reasons, they couldn't help but stare, leaving themselves mortally exposed.

Hearing my real name whispered on their lips was...

unsettling. I'd been a secret my whole life. Now everyone thought they knew me.

Arin was right. I didn't know who I was, but I'd preferred being Lark to Zayan, the half prince, the traitor's son, Razak's pet.

"Your sulking is tiresome."

I flashed my brother a sharp smile. "I'm bored, waiting for your poison to kick in."

"The evening is still young," he smirked. "Have you attended every cup?"

I plucked the empty vial from my pocket and turned it over between my finger and thumb. "Every last drop."

"Not Arin's, I presume?"

"He's not here." Draven's friends were proclaiming tales of how they'd fought off vicious desert tribes and sand worms during a trek through the desert. Draven and Arin hadn't been among them for some time now. I wasn't sure if Arin had returned at all, since our earlier tête-à-tête.

His hate had been... genuine. I'd suspected it, but knowing it and seeing it in his eyes was a different experience altogether. A painful one. That was, of course, Razak's plan when he'd allowed the truth of me to be known. Hurt Arin, hurt me, hurt anyone and everyone.

The doors boomed open and King Ogden stormed in, two hundred and forty pounds of muscle poured into leather and plate armor. The crown atop his head sparkled with bloodred rubies. I caught Razak's hungry glare. My brother smiled.

The guests all stood—except us. Ogden waved them back down and strode toward Draven's table, probably to address the happy couple. He barked something about the pair being missing from the celebration.

"Looks real, doesn't it?" Razak said.

"What does?"

"The crown." He leaned in, bumping my shoulder. "It has its worth as metal and gems, but it is not the real Crown of War. The real crown is hidden in the temple."

I hadn't seen any crown during the ceremony, but I hadn't seen much of anything outside of Arin's hand wrapped with Draven's. "Why wear a fake?"

"Did you not see the art, all over the temple walls? Or were you to occupied with staring at Arin, wishing he'd renounce Draven and join you, perhaps?"

I laughed, despite feeling every word he'd said like multiple stab wounds to the chest. "Love and Pain? Hardly a recipe for harmony." Although, when Arin and I had been together, there had been a connection, despite our respective courts. Arin liked a little pain, and maybe, if I was honest, a touch of love in my life wouldn't have been so terrible a thing. But all that was in the past, burned to ashes.

"No, it is not..." Razak agreed with a smile and sipped his wine. He'd had his hand craned over his cup all evening, and never once let it out of his sight. I wasn't sure if he didn't trust me not to poison him or just didn't trust anyone. "He wears the fake because the Crown of War is cursed."

"'Cursed'?" I laughed. "Which one of us is the entertainer, spinning fantastic tales for bored nobles?"

"Had you paid attention to War's murals, you'd have known it to be true. Anyone who wears War's crown is assuredly driven mad."

Oh well, we had that to look forward to when Razak got his hands on it, which he would, if his brilliant smile was any indication. "How does a crown make a man mad?"

"The crown alone doesn't. Curses aren't real, but magic is."

Magic... I'd told Arin magic existed in the wonderment of a trick, in the mystery and myth, in a magician's quick hands and the joy on the faces of those in his audience. "What magic?"

Razak's eyes sparkled with knowing. "War's crown has been contested for generations, as has the royal bloodline. The true crown is hidden away for fear it will be stolen and placed upon the head of a usurper. It's happened in the past—that's the story the art told, the story you and probably every guest in the temple missed. A war was fought over the rightful Desert King. Many died. The people here believe dusk's red skies are the spilled blood of their ancestors, still bleeding today."

Where was he going with this? "Put the crown out of sight in the temple, and nobody asks questions?"

"Exactly. Shut the crown away, and Ogden doesn't need to think about it every time he looks in the mirror." Razak smirked at his own genius. "He'd probably give it to me, if I asked."

"Frankly, I think he's more likely to shove a sword through your chest than give you his crown, but by all means, do ask him. I'll watch."

"Prince Razak—" Arin's sudden appearance jolted me almost out of my seat.

Razak spilled some of his wine. He grabbed a napkin and mopped at his hand.

"Prince Zayan," Arin said to me, so very calm and polite. He kept his fury under tight restraint, but I saw it in the press of his lips and the too-long glare.

"So many princes in this room," I drawled, then skipped my gaze to Draven simmering beside Arin. "Draven's been desperate for cock for so long, he must be relieved to finally have yours—"

Draven lunged, foolishly reaching over Razak to get to me. Razak grabbed him by the doublet and threw him back, into Arin, almost knocking the pair of them off their feet. All around the sound of metal on metal screeched from a hundred scabbards. A hush fell over the festivities, which was quite the achievement considering the ruckus moments before.

I grinned; this was all *splendid*.

"Forgive my brother," Razak suggested, or was it an order?

Draven growled like an animal, and Arin... Arin glared at me, his face a peculiar mixture of shock and regret. What was going through that golden head of his now? He'd despised me earlier, so why the sad eyes?

This wasn't going to end well. I picked up my cup, stood, and bowed low. "I apologize, Lord Draven, and Prince Arin. Perhaps I can make amends. A song to celebrate maybe?" The pair sneered but the drawn weapons among the crowd slid home once more. "No? If someone were to hand me a violin, I'm sure I could whip up a storm to celebrate this joyous fuckin' occasion."

Arin worked his jaw around words he couldn't speak. I'd had him work his jaw around my cock and preferred it there than whatever this prickly dance was. It shouldn't matter that he was Draven's now. In the scheme of things, the fact they were probably having sex was the least of all the trials vying for attention inside my head. But it *did* matter, because Arin was my hope, my light, the break in storm clouds, and I'd assumed I was still his anchor. Even after the wounds we'd inflicted on each other.

Plus, I knew Arin. He didn't fuck for fun, or even because he was bored. He fucked because he cared, because he'd made a connection, and that special someone was no longer me.

I had no right to be jealous. But it burned in my veins like fury burned in his.

"You can make amends," Arin finally said. "Will you both walk with us?"

"Why?" I blurted. Getting Razak alone was a terrible idea. If they believed they could attack him, they were about to be surprised. Was *that* their plan? Have Draven assassinate Razak? By Dallin, it was a terrible plan. Clearly Draven's idea. A drunk eight-year-old could have thought of a better one.

"A pleasure," Razak agreed, already leaving his chair. "Perhaps Draven can give us a tour of the marvelous temple? We did only see its splendor for a short time during the ceremony, and it's so rarely open to guests."

I opened my mouth to try and stop the trio, but they'd turned away, and as they were all in agreement that being alone together was a fabulous idea, then what was I going to say that would prevent it? Did they know the crown was stowed in the temple? Did they even know Razak was here for that crown? And why did I care?

I lingered, standing alone at the table, cup in hand... I could go to Ogden, tell him all I knew, but my recent experience with Justice had taught me such things did not end well. The big man was bellowing about something near Draven's table, his axe glinting. Ogden would kill me the first chance he had.

A scuffle broke out at one of the tables, and the others cheered. Ogden chortled, loaded his plate with more food, and had his aide pour his wine from the pitcher... I watched him drink that cup down and demand another, then I scanned the rest of the crowd. My vial was empty; Razak's plan was already in play and had been since we'd arrived.

The noisy celebrations fell to the back of my mind.

Razak would walk out of this palace with a new crown on his head and a swathe of bodies behind him, just as he had the Court of Love.

Nobody could stop him, because nobody saw it coming.

Except me.

≈

ONE GUARD LEANED against the temple door, sleepy-eyed and bored.

I'd snuck ahead of Arin, Razak, and Draven, and in the dark, cloaked in shadows, I sprinted across the bridge. The guard didn't see me launch from the shadows. I stole his blade from its hip-sheath, spun, avoiding his lumbering grab, and thrust the shortsword up, beneath his armor. My hand stifled his cry, and he slumped in my arms, gasping in my ear.

"You'll live, assuming you keep your blade clean," I told him, shuffling him back behind a pillar and then propping him on his ass out of sight from the doors. "Just sit here a while. I'll send someone for you."

He glared, unconvinced and about to yell for help the moment I removed my hand.

"Fine." I tore a strip of silk off my coat with my teeth and stuffed it in his mouth, then tied it off. Leaving him behind the pillar, I scooted through the temple door. The pyramid had dwarfed us all earlier in the evening, but now empty, the yawning space defied words. The art Razak mentioned painted giants in red and black all over the walls—battles and bloody weapons, weeping people, rivers of blood. No wonder Razak had admired it.

A central spire rose up behind the white sandstone altar where Arin had pledged himself to Draven. The crown wasn't in the spire, and there were no other structures inside. The altar might hide it. It was large enough, and a significant focal point. I set my wine cup down, plucked off my gloves, and ran my hands along the altar's smooth sandstone surface. With no obvious handle or levers, perhaps there was a hidden switch. If the crown wasn't here, then I was all out of options—

My finger slipped into a dip in the stone. I stroked over it, eyed it up close, and pushed. A click released the button, and then the hiss of falling sand accompanied grinding stone. The altar top fell away, and there she was, an obsidian crown encrusted with rubies, each frond a vicious point, like the sharpest of the desert plants. It was nothing like the simple crown Ogden wore, and nothing like the soft gold and pearl crown of Love. I reached in, hooked my fingers under the crown, and eased it off its bed of red silk.

Razak had called it cursed. It *looked* cursed. Only Umair's crown had sharper points and a razor's edge.

The temple door heaved open.

Voices rose. I'd planned to hide *with* the crown, taking it out of Razak's reach long before he got here. But that was no longer an option.

With nowhere to hide, I did the only thing I could.

I placed the crown on my head.

CHAPTER 32

rin

HOW LARK HAD GOTTEN into the temple before us, or how he'd found the crown, I couldn't even begin to imagine. But there Lark was, propped on the altar, War's crown sitting lopsided on his head, legs crossed, and a cup of wine—I assumed it was wine—in his hand, as though he didn't have a care.

Draven stumbled to a halt. "What the fuck?"

Razak laughed then clapped and ambled toward the altar. "Oh brother, you always know how to entertain."

I had no words. What was this? A trick? Had they planned this together? Noemi had told me Lark had meant to do good with his words, that he'd been tortured and was suffering, and I'd begun to believe her. So what was this, a fresh betrayal? Too startled and confused to be angry, I focused on the one real fact here:

The Prince of Pain couldn't leave this temple alive. And if Lark had been a part of this, neither could he.

I glanced at Draven. He caught my eye, nodded, and slipped both daggers from their sheaths.

Lark circled his free hand in the air. "Any treasure so poorly guarded deserves to be stolen."

"How does it feel, Brother?" Razak asked, breezing toward him. "A crown of blood atop your head?"

Draven started forward, stalking Razak from behind. I watched Lark's face for any indication he'd alert his brother. Lark tilted his head, dislodging the crown some. He adjusted it while still holding his cup, continuing his performance. "I fear it does not fit me as well as it would you." Lark plucked the crown off his head and turned it over in his hand. "I do believe you're right, however. It is cursed."

Draven was close to Razak now; just a few more strides and he'd be close enough to stab him in the back. I moved too, drawn forward, enthralled, hungry for blood. These would be Razak's final moments. No man had ever deserved a dagger in the back more. Assassination wasn't the way of War, and certainly not of Love, but it was a fitting an end for the Prince of Pain.

Razak stopped. He thrust his hand out behind him and without looking back said, "Land those daggers, Warlord, and everyone in your court dies." He turned his head and smiled over his shoulder. "Was this really the best you could muster, Arin? Your dull blade of a husband to murder for you?"

"Do it, Draven," I snarled.

Draven took a step forward.

Razak pointed a finger. "There's enough poison in every cup inside the feasting hall to kill a man ten times over. Kill me, and your every wedding guest, and the king, will die before morning."

"Liar," Draven growled. He lowered his daggers. "We'd have seen you."

"Me?" Razak laughed. And touched his chest, as if offended. "I'm a prince, I don't blatantly poison people. How crude. But my brother here, he's something else entirely... Aren't you, Zayan."

No. Lark wouldn't have.

Lark popped the crown back on his head and hopped off the altar, spilling a little wine from the cup in his left hand. He reached inside his coat with his gloved right hand and withdrew a small glass vial. He held it up to the torchlight and gave it a shake, confirming it was empty. "Alas, 'tis true."

The fiend! "Justice came to me." I started forward, heading straight for Lark. "Noemi, you know her, she's Ines's aide—"

Lark smirked some more. "We've met."

"I thought you'd worked your magic on her, I thought you'd manipulated her, but she convinced me you were good, that you were—" I stopped, almost toe to toe with Lark. "— an unwilling victim."

"That is generally the definition of a victim? They're rather unwilling."

"Fuck, I hate you, all of you, every word that comes out of your sugar-coated mouth."

He arched an eyebrow, lifting his smirk with it. "Yes, but do I look good in a crown?"

I pointed at him, wanted to wrap my hands around his slim throat and choke him. The only person I hated more stood next to him, the pair of them so alike in their black and purple silk they could be twins. The hate boiled, and it was all I could do to step back.

"The crown." Razak beckoned Lark. "Hand it over."

Lark cocked a hip and began to circle me, sloshing more

wine from that wretched cup. The urge to knock it out of his hand surged within me. Why was he even carrying it? Everything about him was some kind of lie, some kind of performance. I knew that. I'd always known it. So who was he performing for now? Who were his lies directed at? Me... Draven? Or Lark's own brother?

Razak still held his hand out. "Zayan, the crown. Now."

Lark sighed theatrically, sauntered toward his brother, and offered him the cup, balancing it between his fingers. "Hold this for me, will you?"

Razak frowned at the cup, then Lark's face. "No more jests. Give me the crown."

Lark smiled, but a flicker of fear skittered behind his eyes, a flicker so brief, I may have imagined it. "Let me wear it a while longer? I'll certainly never get another chance. I'm sure, when we return home, I'll be back on your leash, bent over your bed, no?"

I knew, didn't I? I'd heard... what Razak did to him. But having it confirmed tore the breath from my lungs and squeezed my heart.

Razak's eyes narrowed as he considered Lark's request, then took the cup. "Fine, then. Have your moment. You certainly deserve it."

Lark beamed and raised his hands. "We should celebrate the victory, brother!"

This act wasn't meant for me. But it was a game. Everything I knew about Lark slipped into place in my mind. I drew closer to Draven's side, watching Lark's performance unfold.

"Neither of you will leave this court with that crown," I said. "There are a hundred warriors in that feasting hall, each one eager to run you through."

"And all those warriors have refilled their cups from the

poisoned pitchers countless times," Razak said. "They will all be dead very soon, unless I safely walk away."

"You have an antidote?" I asked.

"I do. And it will be yours, as soon as I go free."

He'd ensured his escape, but how could we trust him? "If you're free with the crown, why would you give us the antidote, why not let all of War die like you did *my* court?"

He folded his arms, resting Lark's cup against his sleeve. "I suppose you'll have to trust me."

"Trust?" I snorted. I stepped forward. "Only a fool trusts the Court of Pain."

"What's done is done," Lark said, abruptly drawing all our gazes back to him. "We have the crown, and we have yours too, Arin. With Pain's crown, that's three. One more to go. We should definitely celebrate." He turned to his brother. "A toast, to my brother, soon to be the king of all the shatterlands."

Razak smiled, soaking in Lark's appreciation. "I don't want to be king. Kings are so easily overthrown. I'll be a god." He raised the cup, tilted his head, and licked his lips, then paused, the cup poised at his mouth. A glimpse of some complicated expression, and a flicker of darkness, crossed his face. He wet his lips again, huffed a soft laugh, and lowered the cup. "Oh Zayan, you were so close..."

Lark's thin grin fell away, taking all his bluster and confidence with it.

Razak laughed harder and held the cup back out. "Take it."

I glanced at Draven, but his face was as puzzled as mine must have been. What was this?

"Take it!" Razak yelled.

Lark took the cap, spilling scarlet wine over his fingers.

"Drink it," Razak said. Lark sighed and eyed the cup.

297

Razak bared his teeth. "Drink. It. Brother."

Oh no. Lark had poisoned the wine. That was why he'd brought the cup with him to the temple. He'd planned to give it to Razak this whole time. Perhaps not here, but at the celebration.

"You don't have to drink it," I said. Razak couldn't force him to. He wasn't holding a blade to his throat. "Lark—"

Razak flung a hand out at me. "*You* need to be quiet. You still need the antidote. You still need me to cure your soon-to-be very sick people. So you will stand there, Arin, and you will watch as my treacherous brother drinks the fucking wine!"

"Lark, don't."

"His name is Zayan!" Razak flew at Lark, tore the crown from his head, and kicked Lark's legs out, dropping Lark to his knees. "Drink it, or I will *make* you drink it in front of your precious Prince of Hearts. Is that the last memory you want him to have of you?"

Lark shuddered a sob. "No," he whispered.

"What?" Razak demanded.

"No," he said, louder.

"Stop." I moved in. Draven's arm crossed in front of me, barring the way. Then his fingers closed on my arm, holding me back. "Lark, don't drink it, please... You don't have to obey him."

"He must drink, or hundreds die," Razak said. "Or is that what you want, Arin? A repeat of your own court? More dead because of *your* mistakes?"

"You vicious prick!" I snapped. "You have the crown, just give us the antidote and go!"

"No," Razak snapped, but his gaze softened as he looked down at his brother. "I want him to drink it, and die a slow, agonizing death, like all the rest of you courtly fools. Princes and kings, it means nothing. These crowns aren't even crowns. And you're all so tangled in your own lives you don't see the truth, the potential!"

Razak grabbed Lark's chin.

Lark hadn't lied, he'd told Noemi the truth in the bruises on his body—on his neck, his hand, the scars. The body didn't lie.

"Do something," I growled at Draven.

Draven shook his head. "I can't... I need that antidote. Laslo, me, you, we all drank the wine."

Lark tore his chin from his brother's grip, but instead of begging or pleading, he lifted his head, still on his knees, and he smiled into the storm of his brother's fury. "Draven, you don't need an antidote," he said, staring at Razak. "I switched your poison, Brother, for water." His smile twitched. "The only poison in the entire Court of War is the poison in *this* cup. All of it, in fact."

By Dallin, Lark had played his brother.

Razak backhanded Lark so fast, Lark almost fell. Then Razak had him by the jaw again, and he tipped the cup against Lark's mouth, forcing the wine between Lark's lips. Red spilled down Lark's chin. He spluttered, choked.

I freed my dagger and tore from Draven's hold. "Unhand him!"

But Razak only had eyes for Lark.

I sprinted forward, slashed the dagger toward Razak's neck, but he saw my attack, shoved Lark toward me, and danced away. The cup clattered to the temple floor, spilling the remains of its poisonous contents. I stumbled into Lark. He collapsed, spluttering, onto his hands and knees. The poison was in him...

Razak bolted—Draven chased him—but Lark was down,

choking. I went to my knees and reached for him. He coughed up wine and clawed at his throat.

"Lark, I'm sorry..." I said, helpless. "I didn't know—I don't know what's real around you. I should have seen it—"

"*Stop,*" he wheezed, head bowed and shoulders heaving.

I held his back, saw his gloved hands, a lie to cover up his pain. *His body did not lie.* He'd been tortured, put through agony, and I'd ignored it, because I'd thought him like his brother. But none of that mattered now. He was sick, the poison in the wine was already inside his veins. "Where is the antidote? If there is one. Was that true?"

"Don't know," he rasped. His tremors rippled up my arm. "In... his room?"

"How much did you drink?"

"Too much..." He slumped against me, trembling. *Oh Lark.* I'd thought him the enemy, but he'd been trying to save us all along. I scooped him onto my lap and swept his hair behind his ear, exposing his clammy cheek, already so cold. I couldn't stay. I had to get the antidote, if there was one. "I have to leave you."

"Stop-p R-Razak." His teeth chattered around his words.

"Yes, Draven will get him, but I have to save *you*... like I..." My voice cracked. "Like I promised I would."

His hand locked around mine.

"Lark, I have to go... I'm sorry... But I'll come back. I'll find it and come back..." I laid him down gently. His head lolled, and he blinked. His eyes shimmered with unshed tears.

"All the cards were the s-same," he whispered.

"What cards?" Was he delirious? "I'm sorry." I kissed him on the forehead as my heart tried to break into pieces. Leaving him felt so wrong. What if he died here, all alone? "I'm going to save you. Just... hold on—"

"The trick," he mumbled. "The cards were all the same."

The card trick he'd teased me with before my whole world had burned to ash? *That* card trick. I'd forgotten all about it. I'd demanded to know how he'd tricked me, but he'd refused to reveal his secret, claiming it would ruin the magic. "They were all the King of Hearts?"

"Yes, you... wanted to know...h-how."

"Yes, I did." I skimmed my knuckles down his cheek, then leaned over him and peered into his soft eyes. Tears escaped them now, sliding into his hair. "You're not dying here. I won't allow it. I've made mistakes, I've been wrong, but you will not pay for them."

His lashes fluttered. He fought to keep his eyes open, but the poison pulled him down. "Magic..." he whispered. His eyes closed. His chest shuddered, rising and falling. He lived, his heart still beat. But for how long?

I bolted through the temple door and sprinted across the bridge in the dark. He wasn't dying here, like this, for the rest of us. Damn him. Lark would be the last man standing, he had to be, he was my anchor. I needed him. The alternative, a world without his true smile, his wicked laugh, and his beautiful music, was unthinkable. Of all of us, he deserved something good.

Run.

I had to find the guest chambers, and Razak's room, but I didn't know the palace, didn't know where to start.

The celebrations continued in the feasting hall. Wine flowed, music played, people danced and laughed, and it was like a whole different world to the one I'd left. Draven wasn't here, but his friends were. But I didn't know them. What if they turned on Lark, turned on me for trying to help someone they'd think a traitor?

A figure in blue caught my eye, marching toward me. "Noemi."

"Is everything all right?"

"The guest chambers, where you're accommodated, can you take me?"

"Yes, certainly."

"Quickly, it's Lark... He's been poisoned." I told her all I could as we raced down the walkways, how Lark had lied to his brother, made it seem as though he was obeying his orders, only to reveal he'd been working against Razak the entire time. And how Razak had choked him on poisoned wine. The Prince of Pain now had his hands on a second stolen crown.

"We should tell the king." Noemi slowed and shoved open a door into a long corridor with open arches, lit by torches.

"Not yet... War will use violence. They'll kill Lark." He needed to be protected. He'd *always* needed protection, and I'd pushed him away, used him. He'd been alone this whole time. Dallin, I was a fool.

"These are the rooms we're staying in." She showed me a corridor of doors. "But I don't know which one is Razak's."

"We search them all."

"That could take—"

"Do it, please. Look for Pain's colors, purple and black."

We flung open door after door, disturbing any guests inside. I didn't care. I had to find Razak's rooms, find his traveling case and the antidote. I had to save Lark.

"Hey, you there?" A guard rounded the end of the corridor and started toward me. "Prince Arin?"

"Razak's chambers, which one belongs to him?" I demanded.

"That's not your business."

"It is, as a Prince of... War. Tell me. I'll explain later."

"Please." Noemi appeared, calm and in her Justice blues. "This is important."

The guard frowned at her, then at me. He didn't trust me, but any representative of Justice was always trustworthy. "This way."

This was too slow. How long had it been? What if Lark was already dead and I'd left him there, alone, in his final moments?

We jogged down the corridor, a small flight of steps, and then through a door the guard opened. "Razak and his brother are staying here."

I swept in, spotted the purple and black clothes strewn from a traveling case flung open on the bed, and dashed over. "Search those," I told Noemi, pointing at the smaller bags on the floor.

I couldn't tell if the case was Lark's or Razak's. Didn't matter. No time.

A door between an adjacent room had been wedged open. "The other room," I snapped at the guard. "We're looking for a vial of liquid. Search everywhere. Hurry." He did as I told.

I flipped the case, shook out its contents onto the bed, and tore through the shirts, and gloves, and trousers, and... Mixed in with all the clothes lay a thick leather collar, but Razak had not brought an animal with him. I picked it up. The leather was soft, creased, well-worn. Noemi had mentioned bruises on Lark's neck, as though he'd been choked. I flung the collar away and stumbled against the bedpost. "By Dallin." My head spun, the room twirling with it. The collar was Lark's, Razak forced him to wear it. The thought was so awful I used my hands to squeeze it from my head.

Lark, I had to save him.

But the traveling case was empty. I hadn't found anything.

The antidote wasn't here, and even if it was, Razak had likely hidden it. He wouldn't leave something so vital to his escape where anyone might discover it. We weren't going to find it.

"Lark's going to die."

Noemi reached for me. "No, he's not."

"No, the antidote is not here... It was never here." Grief tried to bubble up my throat and choke me. Just like my dream, Lark had stopped playing, he stood on the cliff's edge. And all I could do was watch him fall. "Razak has it." But Razak was gone. And Lark was out of time.

"Then we find him," Noemi said, her tone turning hard. "We tell the king. Now, Arin, we have to tell Ogden everything."

"They'll kill him."

"If what you're saying is true, he's already dead."

"My Lark... My beautiful lie." I looked at my hands. Why did everything I touch fall apart? "This is my fault."

I couldn't breathe. Dallin, I'd left him, and there was no antidote, and the one thing I'd promised, the one thing I'd vowed to do for him, I'd failed in.

"Arin?"

I clung to the bedpost.

"Arin, you need to act." Noemi cupped my face. Her hands were soft and warm. "Look at me. You are the Prince of Love. Ogden will listen. It's not over yet. You must act now. Lark hasn't given up, and neither can you."

"Yes..." The shutters came down inside, slamming around my heart. I could do this, I could be that prince again, the cold, hard man I'd made myself into. He was useful now, when feelings weren't required.

The guard hurried back into the room. "There's nothing—"

"Alert the king!" I growled, my voice unlike me. "Prince

Razak has committed treachery against our court! He must be found. Hurry."

"Yes, Prince Arin." The guard ran from the room, and moments later, a drum sounded. The drums of War.

I pushed from the bedpost. "The temple, I have to go to him."

"Arin, if he's dead, there's nothing you can do, and if he's alive, then you need that antidote."

But I wanted to be with Lark. I wanted him to know that hate hadn't been all I'd felt for him. I'd hated him so much because... it hurt, and it hurt like it did because that was love, wasn't it?

Noemi probably saw the brief flicker of pain cross my face. "I'll go," she said. "You do what needs to be done and find Razak. Lark won't be alone."

I nodded. And pushed through the pain.

CHAPTER 33

$\mathscr{L}$ark

SOMETIMES, a wisp of sand dusted the temple floor, deposited by a puff of desert wind that had found its way through the half-open door.

Fire devoured me from inside. I couldn't move, couldn't fight, my body was ablaze with Razak's poison. I lay on my back, tears leaking from my eyes, and I watched the murals of art shift like desert sands across the temple walls. Vicious battles played out, until the sand was stained red with blood, as Razak had said. But they didn't fight for the King of War, they fought for its crown.

That was what everyone had missed, what nobody wanted to see.

It was never about the kingdoms, just the crowns.

Dallin, the God of Order, had gifted four crowns to the four regions of the shatterlands. Love, War, Pain, and Justice. Together, they'd bring harmony. But when Dallin vanished, the four courts descended into discord, where we'd been ever since. Or so the story went. But it was just that, a story told to children, generation after generation. I knew stories. And I knew, in the end, most were made from lies. Some good lies, some bad, some *mixed* with the truth, to sell the tale. But lies, nonetheless. Somewhere, in the tapestry of war playing out above me, a kernel of truth lay hidden among War's lies.

Or maybe I was dreaming and dying, and all of this was madness. I'd have laughed if I'd had the energy.

Boots crunched on sand. Someone approached, slowly. Not Arin, so I wasn't to be saved. Such a shame, I had so many more songs to sing.

"Oh, my poor, sweet, bastard prince." Razak's shadow fell over me, turning my blood cold. He smiled, cocked his head, and showed me a new vial between his fingers. Its contents sloshed back and forth.

The antidote.

He'd had it on him this whole time.

Of course he would. So that if I'd poisoned him—as he'd suspected I would—he'd have the cure on hand.

He knelt and swept my sweat-soaked hair from my cheek. "You keep trying to die. It's really rather inconvenient."

I couldn't move, couldn't crawl away, couldn't even tell him how much I hated him with my last breath.

Where was Draven? The man was a cumbersome tool, but he'd chased after Razak. Had Razak killed him? Arin would be sad. They made a strange pair, but Arin would have tried to make it work because of that big heart of his. The heart he'd locked in a box to keep away from the world.

"When I learned I had a brother..." Razak stroked my cheek. "My first thought was how to kill you. I was father's son, his only son, and you weren't going to get in my way. But then I saw you, when they dragged your mother in. You were so quiet, clinging to her skirts. So afraid of everyone but her. I knew then, you were mine." He paused, briefly looking up, perhaps at the door. Some drums sounded, so far off they may have been my heartbeat stuttering out of rhythm.

"Father planned to kill you too. Bastard sprats like you were a threat, he said. If it wasn't for me, you'd have swung in a noose alongside your mother. I own you, Zayan. Your body, your mind. Every part of you belongs to me. You die when I allow it, and that day is not today."

He dug his fingers into my cheeks, forcing open my jaw. After using his teeth to pull off the vial top, he poured the silklike liquid between my lips and slammed my jaw shut, clamping it closed.

The antidote swam around my tongue, bitter and cold.

He tossed the vial and pinched my nose. "Swallow."

If I died, I'd win.

It would be easier to die. I'd tried to fight him, but he was always one step ahead in our dance.

His top lip curled. "Swallow, dear brother. There is much still to do."

My chest and head throbbed, my lungs now ablaze. I didn't want to die, even if it meant he won. I wanted to live, although I wasn't sure what for. Razak was right. He did own me.

But not all of me. Not my heart. Another owned that. A prince made of honey and sunshine.

I swallowed.

"Good!" He let go.

I spluttered, gasping for another chance at life.

"Get away from him!"

Razak's head jerked up. "Justice? Really?" He sighed, rolled his eyes, and stood. "You just don't know when to quit."

I twisted onto my side and blinked hot tears away.

Noemi stood halfway between us and the door, looking fierce in her blue robes and red hair. He'd kill her, like he'd killed Ines. "Run," I croaked. The wind gusted through the door behind her, flapping her gown and sweeping sand around her boots.

I'd witnessed Ines's death, I couldn't watch Noemi's too.

"Feisty thing, aren't you?" Razak was saying, swaggering toward her. I didn't see a blade on him, but he'd kill her with his bare hands if he got close enough.

"Leave Lark alone, you've hurt him enough!"

"Noemi..." I rasped. What was she doing?

"What happens in my court is of no business of Justice," Razak said.

"Justice oversees all!"

"No, it doesn't. You're just another puppet, desperately trying to hold the shatterlands together when all around, it falls apart. You think Dallin will one day return and tell us all how good we've been? Dallin doesn't exist, and if he did, he was just a man. Justice, War, Love, it's all insignificant. Only Pain matters."

"W-what do you mean?" Noemi stuttered.

"Ask your queen, she knows. Justice has always known our courts are pointless. They hid the truth. Zayan told you it's about the crowns, and Justice did nothing with that knowledge. Because they know, Queen Justice Soliel *knows*! And she knows I'm coming for her crown next."

Drums.

I heard drums. Loud and... coming closer.

They needed to get here quicker.

Razak would have a way out of this. He always had a way out. He wasn't behaving like a man about to face the wrath of War. He acted as though he'd already won.

"Stop right there," Noemi demanded. "I may not be

Justice Ines, but I have authority. You, Prince Razak, Court of Pain, shall be judged and all evidence weighed against—"

Razak's sharp laugh cut her off. "I do not recognize your justice, and I do not abide by your laws."

Closer, just a few strides between them. If I reached out, from my position on the floor, I could cup them both in my upturned palm.

Noemi blinked too quickly, her nerves showing. She was an aide, not a noblewoman. She didn't swing swords, or carry poison. She had no authority, despite her words. Razak was going to kill her.

"Where is the crown?" she asked, conceding a step, showing weakness.

The crown?

He'd had it with him when he'd fled, but not now.

I struggled to get my hands under me and lever myself off the sandy floor.

Razak tutted and tick-tocked a finger. "You are not equipped to play the game of gods, little girl."

The drums grew so loud that the sand all around jumped with their every beat. War's warriors were almost here.

Where was Razak's escape plan? I'd ruined his plan to poison everyone. But he'd have a failsafe, a way to wriggle out of being caught. Yet he stalked Noemi as though he had all the time in the shatterlands. Did he not hear the drums coming for him?

"Razak," I spluttered. "It's over!"

He stopped, straightened his shoulders, and looked back at me. A smile slowly lifted his lips. "Did I not say there is much still to do?"

"Not for you!" Noemi lunged.

Razak swung and backhanded her so hard she fell. The resounding crack echoed throughout the temple, taking

311

flight. Along with the clatter of a shortsword—the same sword I'd taken from the temple guard. She'd found it, and used it...

Razak touched the spreading patch of blood on his hip. "What...?" His hand, when he lifted it away, glistened red. The most beautiful blood I'd ever seen.

"You bitch!" Razak lunged for the sword.

"Stop!" Arin swept through the doors, his bejeweled dagger glinting in his hand. My prince of sunshine and honey in his gold and white. A wave of black and red poured through the doors behind him; every single warrior bristled with axes and swords, and they just kept coming, man after woman after man... More and more, ready to fight, ready to stop Razak.

"Razak, do not move." Arin's righteous glare burned. There was the Prince of Love, the man who had slapped me, lied to me, seduced me. I laughed, quietly losing my mind.

Razak staggered back a step. He chuckled, but his laugh was armor, nothing more. He still clutched his hand to his side, and when he stumbled back a second time, he went down to one knee.

Yes, fall, Brother.

Arin's glare skipped to me. His lips parted, his face so open and honest, it was surely a mistake to reveal his emotions. "Arrest Prince Razak!"

"You cannot arrest me." Razak snorted. "Your laws mean nothing."

Three enormous warriors crowded Razak, and even then, I was sure he'd spring his trap and somehow bring the entire court down around us all. But the warriors grabbed my brother's arms, pinned them behind his back, and hauled him to his feet.

"Unhand me! You have no justification for this. No evidence!" he barked.

Any moment now, he'd reveal whatever knowledge he'd use to bribe himself from their grasp, but the warriors marched him forward. And Razak struggled in their grip.

I shifted onto my ass, one arm braced at my side, propping me upright. Two warriors broke from their line and came toward me. I had no chance of fighting them off. If I was to be arrested alongside my brother, so be it.

"Leave him," Arin barked, his voice ringing through the temple. The warriors stopped and glanced back. Arin held them under his control, but not for much longer. He'd need the king soon, or Draven, someone of War's own colors to rule them.

Arin helped Noemi to her feet. She brushed sand from her gown and said something to Arin, something I missed.

They both looked at me. *Everyone* looked at me.

Well then, this was the moment I'd be condemned alongside my brother. Always a traitor, never the hero. Wasn't that the destiny of fools?

I smiled, expecting the worst. Punishment was inevitable.

Razak's backward glance shot through me like a spear. He put up a show of struggling, but when his gaze met mine, he smiled, and it was the same smile I'd feared for most of my life, the smile that followed me into my nightmares. The smile that said he'd won.

CHAPTER 34

rin

LARK WAS ALIVE.

Pale, trembling, but propped up on his arm. Every muscle in my body, every beat of my heart, every thought in my head screamed to go to him. He needed me, and I needed him. But it wasn't that simple. It could never be that simple. My control of War's warriors hung by a single thread. Violence simmered, close to boiling over. Any sign of weakness, and I'd lose my hold.

Lark was a traitor to my court, to his own, and the brother to a man I'd just accused of trying to poison the entire court of War. I couldn't go to him, not like I wanted to.

He slid his gaze away, and it must have landed on Razak, because his eyes widened in fear.

"Get Razak out of here," I ordered.

The warriors parted, and Ogden swaggered in with Draven beside him. Relief fluttered my heart. Draven was all right. Since he'd chased after Razak, I'd feared they'd fought, and Razak had somehow beaten him. But Draven was fine. Although, his expression had rarely appeared more severe.

Ogden being here meant I could step down—should step down. I bowed my head. "My king, there was no time to find you. Razak had poisoned the wine—"

Ogden raised a hand and silence fell. The wind hissed sand across the floor. The King of War studied his warriors, then moved forward, toward Lark. Lark lifted his chin, even as he swayed. Ogden might demand his execution, and there would be nothing I could do. He might free the axe from his back and take Lark's head in front of me...

I took a step, but Noemi caught my hand, holding me back.

"What justice is this?" I whispered. But in the quiet, my whisper became loud.

"'Justice'?" Ogden echoed.

Lark bowed his head. "I am at War's mercy."

His contrition may have saved his life.

Ogden dwarfed Lark's prone, shivering body. Any moment now, Ogden would reach for his axe and take Lark's head.

Ogden stiffened. "There is no honor in killing a beaten enemy." *Oh by Dallin, spare Lark... please, just spare him.* "Yet, vermin should be eradicated, lest it spreads."

Vermin?! How dare he...! This was not my court, not my place. But I couldn't stay silent. Lark didn't deserve this. Draven caught my eye and shook his head in warning.

"He saved you," I declared, then regarded the crowd. "All of you."

"Arin—" Draven moved, as though to stop me speaking.

"No." I pulled from Noemi's light grip. "He was sent here to kill you all, it's true—"

Growls rumbled. No gasps here. They all wanted blood, preferably Razak's, but Lark's would suffice.

"But he had no choice." I approached the king, and Lark —who sat with his head bowed and his shoulders heaving. "He's never had a choice." My heart broke for him, the traitor's son. Cast out, then imprisoned. If just a small amount of what I'd been told was true, then he'd known nothing but pain and agony. But I knew him now. I saw him, I'd seen him when he played his music before my court fell to his brother's scheming. His music was the truest part of him. Like his scars, it did not lie. To know Lark, you had to hear him play.

"Draven, rein in your *husband*," the king growled.

I stepped around Ogden, placing myself neatly between his bulk and Lark.

Draven approached. I could be restrained. I had the ceremonial dagger, our wedding gift, but I wasn't going to use it on Draven and they knew it. "I do not care what you think of me," I said. "I'll not stand by and let anyone, even a king, lay a hand on Lark."

A small sob fell from Lark. I heard his every ragged breath. He was hurting, but he was alive, and every second I stopped Ogden from swinging his axe was another second Lark would use to get stronger.

"You have Razak," I said. "If you want to take heads, take his. He orchestrated all this. Lark is... just his tool."

Ogden sneered. "I knew you'd be trouble in my court, Arin."

"Do you praise the sword for the kill, or the warrior?" My shattered heart thumped. I had to get through to Ogden, to make him see Lark was a victim.

Ogden relented and stepped back. "That man is no sword, and Razak no warrior." He turned his back and stomped away.

"I want Zayan out of my court by dawn! Razak shall be shackled and dealt with accordingly."

Noemi's voice lifted. "Razak must face Justice."

"Oh, he will," Ogden grumbled.

I stared after the king. His warriors stood down, sneering about the lack of bloodshed. Hopefully, they'd return to the feasting hall and drink and feast themselves into a coma. I couldn't have cared less what they did, so long as they left Lark alone.

Noemi hurried to my side. "Razak still has the crown."

"Go with him to the dungeon. Find out what you can, where he went after he ran from here, who he saw... anything. He hasn't left the palace, so the crown is here, we just need to find it."

She squeezed my shoulder and smiled. "Razak's in Justice's hands now. We'll ensure he can't hurt anyone else. It's over, Arin."

I should have been reassured, but the missing crown was a loose end, even if Razak was behind bars.

Noemi hurried after the warrior procession. She was, at least, on our side as much as Justice was on anyone's side. Draven remained, standing some distance from us, daggers back in his hip sheaths and the same severe expression as before.

Whatever he did next was his choice.

I'd made mine.

I knelt beside Lark. "Hold on to me, I'm taking you to my chamber." He turned his head, and the tracks of dried tears shimmered like ghostly scars. "You're safe," I told him.

He blinked, sighed, and closed his eyes, just for a few beats. "I will never be safe as long as Razak lives."

Draven appeared at my side, the sneer all gone, and offered Lark his hand. "We'll work on that."

rin

SCORCHING DESERT SUN burned away dawn's first light, bleeding the sand and sky red. The horizon was a blur this morning, obscured by a distant, tumultuous sandstorm. I'd have given anything to feel the sea breeze on my face again, or to stand barefoot on cool pebbles and taste the salt in the air.

Lark murmured, drawing my gaze from the desert into the room, and my bed, where he lay asleep, tangled in damp sheets. He'd thrashed so much in the night he'd almost kicked the sheets away. I'd tucked him back in at intervals while Draven had paced.

The physicians had claimed that without knowing the source of the poison, there was nothing we could do but wait and hope he woke.

Draven had left a little while ago in search of an update on Razak's whereabouts, and perhaps to interrogate the

Prince of Pain. He hadn't asked why I'd chosen to defy Ogden for a traitor and a liar, but the questions would come. He'd understand. He'd liked Lark, they'd been *involved*, and now we knew the absolute truth. Lark wasn't our enemy.

"Arin..." Lark's hand lifted.

I shot from the chair. "I'm here." His fingers were cold. I squeezed his hand and sat on the bed's edge. He blinked, trying to focus, then jerked his head, searching the room. "Easy." I pressed on his shoulder. "Take it slowly, you've been out for hours."

His dark eyes focused on me, desperate and fearful. But when he blinked down at his naked chest and saw the sheet pooled in his lap, his fear gave way to intrigue. "If this was a dream, you'd be naked. What you do next determines whether I'm experiencing a nightmare."

I chuckled and let him sit up. If he was jesting, then he'd be fine.

He fumbled with the pillows and the sheet, trying to keep himself covered. Sunlight made every tiny scar gleam. He'd become leaner during his time with Razak, sharpening his edges some more.

The sheet slipped below his hip. He reached for it.

"It's a little late for modesty."

"It's for your benefit, not mine," he said. "I can let it all hang loose, if you'd prefer, but I've seen your husband's blades."

My laughter thickened, but I moved from the bed, needing space to think around his quick words—why my heart had swelled, why I was so relieved Draven wasn't here, and what that meant. "You're clearly feeling better."

"I am. Thank you." He leaned against the stack of pillows and held my gaze. "I mean it, thank you, Arin. For everything."

I waved away his thanks. "I should have done more."

"Well, for what you did, I am in your debt." He fiddled with his sheet again, trying to lift it to cover his chest, then tucking it around his waist instead.

"No debt, Lark. You don't owe me anything." I slumped back into the chair. Now I had some distance, and my mind had stopped reeling, I could see him without emotions tying me up in knots. He wasn't thin, but close. His right forearm had a new vertical scar. I turned my head from that and sighed. As Noemi had said, Razak had taken another of his fingers. "There's no excuse for the way I treated you after I learned your true name. I made yet another mistake, in thinking you're like... him. I seem to make a great many mistakes around you."

"You assumed the worst, which was Razak's intention." He dropped his head back and blinked at the ceiling. "Countless miles away, but he'll still fuck you over."

"Not anymore."

He swallowed. "Where is he?"

"Being watched by War's armed guards."

"We'd better hope War's guards are better than yours. I escaped your dungeons within a few hours."

I laughed. "Yes, well, we clearly weren't equipped to deal with the likes of you."

His gaze skirted away. I'd hurt him... Something I'd said, probably. A painful memory, a triggering phrase. "I'm sorry."

"Stop. I don't want your pity." He huffed and folded his arms. "I would like my clothes though. Unless you plan to tie me to this bed and take advantage of the opportunity?" One of his dark eyebrows arched. He joked, but I knew there was too much truth in his words now.

I collected some spare clothes Draven had brought for

him and placed them at the foot of the bed. "I will never hurt you, Lark."

No more smiles, no more jokes. Perhaps it was too much to hope for no more lies, but we'd get there.

The humor drained from his face, leaving him so achingly vulnerable I almost wrapped my arms around him.

His grin flew back to his lips. "Unless I ask you to?"

"What?"

He shrugged a lean, pale shoulder, his smirk wicked.

I threw my hands up. "Must everything be innuendo? I'm trying to be forthright."

"Well, I'm just attempting to get the measure of what's happening here. I don't recall you ever being this nice. It's unsettling."

"I was nice, once, before you... happened. I've been working on returning to being myself, before I turned into someone less nice."

"Draven's cock that good?"

"I... That's not... We aren't... It's not like that." Oh, he *wanted* to fight. It was there in his eyes, the little sparkle of mischief. "I know what you're doing."

"And what is that?"

"You're more comfortable when fighting or distracting. Like this, being honest? You hate the truth. So you use that barbed tongue to trigger people. You want them to react and lash out or fight back."

He worked his jaw and considered my words. "My tongue is not barbed, as you well know." He beckoned, and I tossed him the shirt. "Then you aren't sleeping with him?"

"I er... I don't see why that's relevant. And even if I was, it's no different to... what happened with us." I danced my gaze away. "*That* certainly didn't mean anything." The lie tripped and fell off my tongue. I wasn't even sure why I'd said it. To see his face, to see if it hurt, and if it did, then did he genuinely care?

He flashed a smile. "No. We—us—meant nothing. Why would it, when we'd both lied about who we were? You're right, it's irrelevant." He writhed into the shirt, tugging it down over his speckled chest, hiding the scars. "You're staring."

But it felt relevant. It felt *very* relevant. Lark and I, what we'd had, it had been fierce, and barbed with lies, and so confusing, yet... it had felt more real than anything that had happened since, including Draven.

And now he was agreeing it was nothing?

"Draven and I, it happened once, and we didn't... It was just... fooling around." I blurted, and winced at my own idiocy. Draven and I were joined, and Lark had been the enemy at the time we'd taken pleasure in each other, my wedding day, no less. Surely, it was to be expected? I hadn't known then what I knew now, and even if I had, Lark had only bedded me because he could, because that was one of the weapons he used to manipulate people. He'd screwed everyone in my court in one way or another. His screwing me was no different, except, perhaps, I'd made it different, because I'd wanted it to be real, even knowing it couldn't be. I cared for him then, and I cared for him now. I hadn't stopped, which was why I'd hated him so much too.

"Oh, just once?" Lark teased, almost laughing. "Not so good then."

He just had to do that, had to get a dig in, like poking a knife into a wound.

I leaned against the bedpost, folded my arms, and dropped my gaze to the floor, ignoring his smirk. Lark was... complicated. So were my feelings for him, and us, and what we did or didn't have. When we had been together, everything had been different. I'd been different then. And so had he.

With everything happening, it really was irrelevant. "You haven't denied you prefer to argue," I said, diverting his attention from what may or may not have done with Draven. He huffed, lifting my smile.

"I may enjoy poking your ire," he admitted.

I'd almost lost him and the more that thought returned to me, the more its fear chilled my blood. "What you did... pouring all the poison into your own cup. You took a huge risk."

"I know. Trousers?"

I tossed them in his general direction without looking. The bed rocked, creaked, and then he was up and striding toward the balcony doors, the desert wind in his tangled hair and billowing through his loose shirt.

He grasped the balcony rail, tipped his head, and closed his eyes.

Like this, he was the rawest version of himself, the pure truth. Stripped of his fancy coats and silk gloves, his perfect hair and theatrical face paint... Here, now, he wasn't trying to entertain, or distract me. He was just Lark—or Zayan, I supposed. This was the man I'd vowed to save, the man nobody saw, including me. "Zayan?"

His lashes fluttered open. "Not that name. Not from you. Only Lark."

"All right." I propped a hip against the balcony rail. "Lark, I see you."

He smiled but his brow furrowed at the same time, muddying his expression. "Of course you do."

"No, I see *you*. The *real* you—the man you try to hide."

"I rather wish you didn't. I'm nothing special beneath the lies." He stared at the hazy sun.

He didn't see how unique he was, how brilliant and infuriating. Maybe he couldn't. Perhaps nobody had ever told him that he didn't need to fight to be loved, that he already was.

"You're staring. Again. If this is going to become a regular occurrence, people may talk."

I laughed and pushed off the rail, stepping closer. "You love it when people talk. Just so long as they're talking about you." His messy hair stuck out at all angles, encrusted with sand. I flicked a few stiff locks from his shoulder and found his eyes widening. I wanted to say something about keeping him safe, even though I'd already told him I would. He hadn't believed me then and probably wouldn't now. But I *would* protect him. I wanted to tell him about my dream of the meadow and his music, but it seemed silly, and too much. He'd think me mad.

The corner of his lips twitched and a little of that real smile appeared, like a ray of sunshine through storm clouds. Fleeting, but so very bright and full of possibility.

"My Prince of Storms," I said softly.

A slight blush colored his face. I'd never seen him blush before. I hadn't known him capable. "My Prince of Flowers?" he whispered, his words lifting in query.

"If I'm interrupting, I can return with news later?" Draven strolled through the bedchamber.

I hadn't heard him enter. Not that it should matter. Although, how much had he just heard? I stepped away from Lark and almost missed how Lark's smile vanished again.

"But you're going to want to hear this," Draven added, folding his arms and arching an eyebrow, judging and questioning in one gesture.

As Lark turned, his whole personality changed, subtle but loud now I knew to look for it. His act was sliding into place. He folded his arms, the motion smoother than before, as though he was aware how every gesture meant something. Did he know how easily he slipped his mask back into place? I'd tried to be someone else for a few years, and it had been a challenge. He'd been someone else for much of his life, always entertaining, always acting, always lying.

It was a shame my court was gone. Had I saved it, I could have kept him safe there too.

"Arin?" Draven said, perhaps having repeated it several times.

I'd been staring again. "Yes?"

"I said, Justice has demanded War release Razak into their care. They've sent a prison wagon to collect him."

"So soon?" I asked.

"No," Lark said. He shoved from the balcony. "That can't happen—"

Draven grabbed Lark's arm, pulling him to a halt, his rough handling almost enough for me to step in. But Lark scowled at the grip and yanked his arm free, scolding all he needed with a glare.

Draven swallowed. "You cannot leave."

"Am I a prisoner? Yours perhaps? What do you want to let me go? My mouth on your cock, Warlord?"

"Lark," I began, anticipating this spiraling out of control.

But Draven raised his hands and backed off. "Easy, Lark. I'm not your enemy. If you leave, looking like you do, the guards will stop you. Razak isn't going anywhere yet. Get cleaned up. You need it, you're a mess. I'll find you an outfit to help you blend in, and then I'll take you and Arin to see Justice. We do this the proper way. Anything else will likely get you executed and Arin and I exiled." He still had his hands raised and looked to me for help in handling the wild card in the room.

Lark might lash out, baiting Draven some more, or he

might see the sense in Draven's words. Speaking with Lark was sometimes like juggling those balls, and I hadn't yet learned how to juggle very well.

"All right," Lark conceded, propping a hand on his hip. "But must I wear red and black?"

Draven's face softened and he lowered his hands. "Through the door behind me, there's a private washroom. Use it. I'll be back with some clothes that won't get you arrested."

"It's infuriating when he's right," Lark said after Draven had left. He ventured into the washroom—a small room, fully tiled, with pipes that fed heated water into a perforated metal head that let the water fall like rain.

I leaned against the doorframe and watched Lark study the faucets and pipes. "War like their contraptions. Try it, it's good." I leaned past him, twisted the faucets, and scooted out of the way of the rainlike water falling from above.

Lark's gaze turned sly, and without waiting for me to leave, he removed the shirt he'd moments ago tugged on.

Of course he'd strip with me in the room, hoping to spark a reaction.

I left the washroom but stayed nearby, holding the door open a crack. He would be weak from his ordeal; I needed to stay close.

"How is it?" I called.

"Hm, good..."

I'd used it, it was good. We didn't have shower rooms at my court, just bathing houses, but if I ever returned home and built something from its rubble, I'd make sure to have them installed.

Water splashed, drawing my gaze through the gap in the door. Steam rolled, but I saw Lark through the mist, one arm braced against the wall, his head bowed. Water cascaded through his hair, painting it against his pale shoulders and down his naked back. I looked to check he wasn't in any way wounded or about to collapse. No other reason.

His body was a marvel, somehow lithe but strong with it. He'd definitely lost weight, and his leanness defined his muscles. He was made for dancing. I knew, because I'd had my hands on that body, stroking up his back. I'd felt him quiver under my touch, and I'd moaned for more.

It was wrong to watch him while he thought he was alone, especially as he was recovering.

But even knowing it was wrong, I couldn't turn my gaze away for long. Water spilled over the curves of his ass and ran in rivulets down his legs. The steam obscured much, but I caught glimpses, and my memory filled in enough to want to join him. I'd sweep his wet hair back from his neck and kiss him there. Softly, so he knew he was safe. I'd make the hurt go away and erase everything done to him. I'd erase all those scars, if I could.

Sighing hard, I shoved from the wall and crossed the room to the balcony. Watching him was self-inflicted torture. Nothing could come of it. I still didn't know if he cared at all for me, or if it had been one of his performances. And now was not the time to have my heart get in the way.

We had a crown to find and Justice to stop from taking Razak away. I couldn't shake the feeling that we were still playing Razak's game, even now. And if he was removed from War, the crown's whereabouts might never be discovered.

CHAPTER 36

ark

I WAS out of my depth, with no cards left up my sleeves to play.

And now Justice was trying to move Razak. That couldn't happen, not until we knew where he'd hidden War's crown.

But despite Draven's most charming smile, and Arin's sickening politeness, the representative of Justice, a woman named Justice Sonya, refused to change their plans.

Razak was due to be wagoned out by sundown.

"We need to talk with Razak," Arin said.

We'd gathered in a shadowy corner of the palace, where the heat didn't reach. Palms swayed in a nearby garden. Small waterfalls trickled into larger pools. I ground my teeth, tasting sand.

None of this felt right.

I'd woken in a dream... Because in the real world, Razak didn't ever get caught, and Arin wasn't nice, and Draven...

well, Draven was typically Draven, so there was that. But none of it *felt* right. I was missing something, something obvious.

The crown...

We had to find the crown.

"He hasn't left with it. It's here somewhere," I thought aloud.

"Not in his room," Draven said. "I had it searched."

I snorted. "As though he's just going to toss a crown in his traveling case where anyone can find it."

"Do you have any better ideas?" Draven groused.

I didn't. And that was a problem. I always had ideas. But not this time.

I was out of my depth.

Adrift.

"Should he even be out of bed?" Draven whispered, not quietly enough.

"You try keeping him there," Arin replied.

I looked down at my folded arms to where my borrowed shirt rode up my scarred wrist. "It's really quite simple. A single cuff will suffice."

They both fell silent.

I wasn't angry at them, but they were so easy to hurt. Pain was familiar, my only friend. I huffed and turned to face them both. "I'm sorry... for being an asshole."

"But you're so good at it." Draven grinned.

"I see you got all your voice back. How wonderful."

He laughed, and it felt good, seeing him smile, and Arin too. Were we friends? Were friends something I had now? No, friends were dangerous liabilities, weaknesses Razak could use to get to me. Better not to have friends, and not have them hurt.

I started down the corridor. "I need to talk to Razak." They'd chase, and argue, but they wouldn't stop me.

"What? No." Arin jogged alongside, trying to keep up. "Lark, no. He'll get inside your head."

"He's always in my head."

"Lark—"

"What choice do we have?" I stopped, making Arin stop and Draven saunter over. "He won't talk to Draven. He'll take any opportunity to bait you, Arin. But me? He'll want me to know he's won. He might make a mistake, say something he shouldn't. I have to go to him."

"Then I'm coming in with you," Arin said. I rather liked this protective side to him. He'd always had it, but now he let it show.

It didn't change my mind though. "No. You can't. I go alone or he won't talk."

He glanced at Draven. The warlord shrugged.

We had no more time to waste. I left the pair of them in the corridor and hurried toward the detainment area. The first pair of guards barred my way, refusing to let me though, until Draven appeared. I thanked him with a nod and he followed me, smoothing the way with each set of guards, until the final door.

The cell they kept Razak in consisted of an iron cage inside a stone room. He sat cross-legged in the middle, hands on his knees, too calm. He didn't look like a man about to face trial for countless murders and Justice Ines's disappearance.

I gripped the bars.

We were alone. No guards. They remained outside with Draven. It was just my brother and I.

"Where's the crown?" I asked.

Razak sighed and raised an eyebrow. "You should leave.

You're not welcome here. Ogden will have you killed if you stay."

"And that would piss on your plans, as you're the only one who is permitted to kill me."

"Indeed."

I couldn't get to him behind these bars. But there had to be a way to make him slip up, something I could say that would anger him into revealing too much. "You know what I thought when they dragged my mother and me into your court, and I saw you?"

He listened, staring into my eyes.

"I thought it must be difficult, being the king's son. Not a person, but a thing, a tool, something to hang a crown on."

His brow furrowed. "You didn't know our father. He fucked your mother. You were never anything more than an ejaculation to him."

"I didn't need to know him. Mother told me enough. He was cold, heartless, more stone than man. I don't blame you for being what you are. You were made this way, made to be his tool."

Razak shook his head and grimaced. "You don't know anything."

"You're as much a victim as you've made me."

He shot to his feet and lunged, thrusting his arms through the bars. I danced back, out of reach, and grinned. "Under all that..." I raked my gaze over him. "You're nothing. Just the same as me. We're so fucking alike, it's almost poetry."

"I'm not like you. You're mine. *My* tool!"

"And you were his. I see that now. I see you. You're worthless." I tossed him a dismissive laugh. "Justice will hang you, and nobody will care. Not a god yet, are you?"

He grasped the bars, thrust his face against them, and hissed. "When I come for you, I will kill Arin first, cut him to pieces in front of you, make him scream as he chokes on his own fingers—"

I rolled my eyes and sighed. "Goodbye, Brother."

I had my hand on the iron door loop when his laugh bubbled up. That laugh was so rich, so confident. He'd won, it said. But I'd caught him. I just needed to reel him in.

"You think you're special?" he asked. "You think I'm defeated?"

Keep on talking, Brother, spill your little secrets for me. "What are you going to do in there, behind bars?"

"You forget, dear brother, nothing happens by chance. I'm right where I need to be."

Wait. He'd *wanted* to be captured?

I didn't need to look back to know he was smiling. I couldn't look back, couldn't let him see how I cared. "I hope that Justice's noose is made too long, and you swing for days, *dear brother*."

I left his cell and walked so fast down the corridors Draven struggled to keep up.

"Well?" he asked, once we were outside and back in the relentless heat.

"Razak said..." *He was right where he needed to be...*

"What, what did he say?"

I glanced at dusk's sky, so red with the setting sun and swirling winds that it appeared to be ablaze. "We have to stop Justice."

CHAPTER 37

$\mathcal{L}$ark

"I DON'T UNDERSTAND, he planned to be arrested?" Arin asked, face pinched in confusion.

I paced his chamber while Draven glowered nearby. "Razak wants Justice to take him. Justice has the last crown." It made sense now. Razak had no plan to escape. He'd expected to get caught. Once in Justice's hands, we wouldn't be able to get to him. "He was never going to walk out of War a free man. We have to stop Justice."

"What about Noemi?" Arin shot to his feet. "If we go to her, explain how Razak cannot be taken... she'll listen. She'll make the others listen too."

"No," Draven's tone rumbled. "If you try and stop them taking him, they'll think you're working with Razak." He wasn't as dimwitted as he made himself out to be. And he was right.

"Doesn't matter..." Outside every window, the red sands

howled. The heat of the day had vanished under a furious storm. We were out of time. "If he leaves, he's won." I strode for the door. Justice had to be stopped, by any means. "Let's try Noemi."

"Wait," Arin said, jogging after me. "She's more likely to listen to the both of us." But as we neared the door, his steps slowed, and he turned back to Draven. "We need your help."

Draven sighed and gave his braided head a shake. "If I do this, I'm done here. We're both done here. Ogden will never allow us in his court." Arin took a step back toward the warlord, and a tender knowing passed between them. Draven responded immediately and came forward. He skimmed his fingers down Arin's cheek, and some fragile piece of me cracked open, making my heart ache.

I was on the outside. I'd known, hadn't I? For all his flowery words, Arin's heart belonged to another. He'd said we were nothing, he'd said the moments we'd shared in his bed had been nothing. But somehow, in all this madness, I'd mistaken his touch, his words, for more.

Had he always been in love with Draven?

It didn't matter. It was good, in fact. He'd live, they both would. They even looked like the perfect couple. Draven, the large, dark-haired, grumbly, slightly dimwitted one. And Arin, all bright smiles, glowing hair, and fierce righteousness. They were destined to be heroes. Heroes didn't die in the best stories. Only villains did.

"All right, let's go," Draven said.

I didn't see Arin's face. I couldn't stand the pity there. Since he'd learned who I was, he'd looked at me differently. Softer. Perhaps assuming I was weaker for all I'd been through, when he should have known the opposite was true.

We hurried toward Justice's guest chambers, but when we

arrived, the rooms were empty, their traveling chests gone. Noemi had gone too.

"We're too late," Arin mumbled.

"Not yet..." I spun and raced down the corridor. There was one place left, one gap in the battlements everyone had to pass through. The main gate.

We hurried outside and down onto the main entrance plaza. The giant gates hung open, and a small crowd had gathered to watch War's machines clear sand from the road.

"Quickly..." Arin jogged down the steps.

Members of Justice climbed into their carriages. And there was the blue-painted prison wagon. Every side was boarded and barred, with just one slit of a window in the back door. I couldn't see Razak inside, but he'd be there.

"Wait!" Arin fought through the crowd, but the carriages were already in motion, trailing out of the gates. Outside, the huge sand-moving machines growled at a wall of swirling sand. The sandstorm was here. That wind and its churning sands would burn everything it touched.

Strange, how Noemi traveled atop an open carriage, open to the elements.

The wind whipped her red hair and blue gown around her. Arin called for Justice to stop, and she looked back, wide-eyed.

A strip of blue cloth gagged her.

She was their prisoner? No, that couldn't be right...

"Noemi?" I ran down the steps through the crowd, but slowed, thoughts whirring like that storm. She'd been silenced. She'd been accused too. Why? It didn't make any sense. Unless she'd been accused of helping Razak, helping me... and Arin.

I skidded to a halt near the front of the crowd. Red sand

sloshed like water around my boots, pushed in by the winds through the open gates.

Arin still marched ahead like a prince in command of his court. He didn't see War's warriors emerge from behind the huge palms behind us, didn't see the crowd withdraw and the warriors close. This wasn't a leaving party, it was an ambush. And we'd walked straight into it.

Draven backed up alongside me and freed his daggers. "Fuck," he growled.

Indeed, we were about to be.

I raised my hands, and turned, to show the warriors I was no threat. "Arin?" I called, searching over my shoulder for him.

The wind tore through the gates, blasting us with sand. Arin hadn't heard me, and he pushed on, gaining on Justice's caravan. They had to be mad, leaving in this storm, or perhaps they thought they could get ahead of the worst of the winds. It was true, Razak was too much of a risk to be left in War's hands.

"Stop!" Arin called. He passed through the gated archway. "Just stop, he can't leave!" He slowed, then yelled, *"Razak!"*

My brother's face appeared at the prison wagon's small window. The sand roared now, the storm barreling around Justice's carriages. I couldn't see Razak's smile on his lips, but it was in his eyes, wicked and full of satisfaction.

He'd won this game, just like he'd won the Court of Love too. Somehow, he had War's crown. Somehow... But there was no way he could have removed the crown from the palace. He didn't have it with him now. Regardless, he knew it was safe, knew it was his, and that was enough.

"Arrest them," Ogden ordered, arriving now to see his own plan to ambush us slam into place. The king pointed his axe, directing a wave of warriors toward us.

I turned my back on War and its warriors.

The enormous gates began to rumble closed. Once they were sealed shut, there would be no escape. Razak had known that.

He'd told me to leave.

Arin turned, shielding his eyes from the buffeting sand. His golden hair lashed his face. The closing gates towered over him, making him small—making us all small and insect-like.

I side-eyed Draven. He couldn't fight them all. He'd take down two or three. They'd arrest him. Me, they'd kill. Arin would be exiled, cast into the desert and left there.

Arin whipped his head around, looking back into the storm. The carriages, and all of Justice, were gone now, swallowed by the wave of red sand. When he faced me again, he stared unblinking. His blue eyes shone with fierce knowing and determination. He nodded.

I caught Draven's gaze. He breathed hard through gritted teeth, flicked his gaze to Arin, and back to me. He nodded too.

All right then.

There was only one way out of this. One way we all survived, for a while.

We'd made our choice. At least if we died, we did so together.

"Go!" I bolted toward Arin, toward the storm. Draven ran too. We ran together, side by side, legs pumping, my heart ablaze. Sand blasted my face, but Arin was there, gold and white, a ray of sunshine in the storm.

The gate rumbled, closing more with every one of my ragged breaths. A roar sounded around us, either from the king or his many warriors. Or perhaps the roar was the storm's.

Sand reared up in a great wall.

I flew into Arin, pulled him with me, and we sprinted into the maelstrom. We didn't look back. It was too late for that. His hand clutched mine, fingers crushing tight. Sand burned my face, my eyes. We staggered, and sand shifted underfoot. Running blind was madness, but madness was all we had left. I pulled Arin against my chest, tucked his head under my chin. The roaring wind pummeled our every side.

Draven's arms clamped around me, dragging us to our knees. "Stay down!" he yelled. Sand crashed over us, scorched my eyes, burned my mouth. Arin shuddered and panted, flinching. I wished I'd told him the lies didn't matter, that I didn't care how he'd hurt me. I wished I'd told him he was beautiful and fierce. I wished I'd told him... I loved him, and I had since the moment we'd met.

War's giant doors slammed closed, booming like its battle drums.

No way back, the drums said.

We belonged to the desert now and were at its mercy.

Lark and Arin's story continues in Fool Me Twice, Court of Pain #2.

ABOUT THE AUTHOR

Born to wolves, Ariana Nash only ventures from the Cornish moors when the moon is fat and the night alive with myths and legends. She captures those myths in glass jars and returning home, weaves them into stories filled with forbidden desires, fantasy realms, and wicked delights.

Sign up to her newsletter at: www.ariananashbooks.com

Printed in Great Britain
by Amazon